'Well?' Seren

'What are you ga[...]
your intention to finish w[...]
Blackwell began?'

Unperturbed by her anger, Kit laughed. 'If you believe that, I can only assume that the fiery colour of your hair has baked your brain.'

'Do you think that because I was unwilling to succumb to his vile attentions I might be more amenable towards yourself? I have a care for my virtue and am particularly choosy who I surrender it to!'

Kit chuckled. 'I don't doubt it!'

Helen Dickson was born and still lives in South Yorkshire with her husband on a busy arable farm where she combines writing with keeping a chaotic farmhouse. An incurable romantic, she writes for pleasure, owing much of her inspiration to the beauty of the surrounding countryside. She enjoys reading and music. History has always captivated her, and she likes travel and visiting ancient buildings.

Recent titles by the same author:

AN INNOCENT PROPOSAL

CONSPIRACY OF HEARTS

Helen Dickson

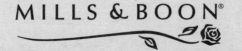

MILLS & BOON®

First published in Great Britain 2000
Harlequin Mills & Boon Limited,
Eton House, 18-24 Paradise Road, Richmond, Surrey TW9 1SR

© Helen Dickson 2000

ISBN 0 263 82305 9

Set in Times Roman 10½ on 11¼ pt.
04-0006-88218

Printed and bound in Spain
by Litografia Rosés S.A., Barcelona

Chapter One

1605

Riding beside her brother Andrew—a Jesuit priest in his late twenties, who had been home to Dunedin Hall in Warwickshire for three weeks and was returning to his priestly duties at the Vatican in Rome—Serena Carberry sighed with deep regret at their parting. It had been so good having him home again.

Pride stirred her heart at the sight of him. Never had she seen a man who looked less like a priest. Officially all priests were classed as criminals by the Government, and so it was necessary for them to disguise themselves in order to avoid detection, which was why Andrew was garbed in the fine apparel of a gentleman, consisting of a deep purple velvet doublet, puffed trunk hose of the same hue, and a short matching cloak lavishly embroidered with gold thread around a high stiff collar.

His features were tanned by the hot Mediterranean sun, and his auburn hair fell to his shoulders from beneath a purple toque. With all this, together with his humorous mouth and laughing green eyes, he possessed all the charm and sophistication of a gallant one would expect to see at the court of King James.

Andrew looked at his sister with a deep and abiding affection. 'I'm glad you accompanied me so far, Serena. I could not have wished for a prettier escort.'

'I wish you didn't have to go, Andrew, but I know you must. It's far too dangerous for you to remain in England. But I miss you and James dreadfully,' Serena said sadly.

James was their younger brother who was a pupil at the Jesuit school at St Omer, near Calais, a school which attracted the children of wealthy Catholic families in England. For a young Catholic man to be educated with the possibility of obtaining a university degree in England, it would compromise his faith, as it would involve taking the Oath of Supremacy—an oath acknowledging the supreme spiritual authority of the Crown instead of the Pope, one that no Catholic could swear, which was why any kind of education was sought abroad.

'I'm glad you are to see him before going on to Rome,' Serena went on. 'You have my letter to him safe, don't you?'

Andrew patted a pocket in his doublet. 'I have it next to my heart. I intend spending several days with James before travelling on to Rome.'

Andrew studied his sister, struck by her beauty, by the vibrant colour of her auburn hair and the burning luminosity of her eyes. In the two years he had been in Rome, she had changed in a way that delighted him, and also filled him with misgivings, for she had bloomed into an extremely lovely and exotic creature who would be sure to draw the attention of every hot-blooded male.

At nineteen she was still headstrong, with an uncurbed wildness to her spirit. The bones of the adolescent girl had fleshed out, becoming rounded and supple. Her heart-shaped face, with its angular cheekbones, the dark wings of her eyebrows and twin orbs of her vivid green eyes were both captivating and bewitching. When she smiled her soft lips curved upwards, betraying the sensuality of the woman she had become.

'You will take care, won't you, Andrew?'

'I will. But Father worries me. He follows the dictates of his religion and his conscience too rigorously for my peace of mind. He's never slow to voice his opinion— which may lead to trouble. In this time of renewed persecution against the Catholics in England—since King James has not the slightest intention of tolerating the old faith— he must be diligent.'

'I know. But ever since the king ordered all priests to be put to death, and imposing severe fines for recusancy once more, there is little wonder Father is angry. Nowhere in England can the Mass be celebrated. If a priest is caught saying Mass, his punishment is death by the most gruesome means. Small wonder priests live under aliases, not only to protect themselves but also their families.'

'Which is why I am returning to Rome. There are many priests in England being forced to live in a twilight world, but their presence does enable you to maintain those rituals which are important to the faith.'

'With great danger to all involved,' Serena replied. Like many other Catholics who attended Church of England services as required by the state, she secretly went to Mass in one or another of their recusant friends' houses. 'The mood of optimism that prevailed when King James came to the English throne is not what we hoped,' she said bitterly. 'Indeed, he is proving to be as harsh a monarch as Queen Elizabeth was before him.'

Coming to the fork in the road where her brother would leave her, Serena halted her mount and looked at him, her lovely eyes troubled. 'But why speak of it now, Andrew?'

'Because I'm going away and I worry about you both alone at Dunedin Hall.'

Serena cocked her head sideways, giving him a suspicious look. 'And do you know something that gives you cause to worry?'

'Nothing for certain, only rumours that have been bandied about in Rome. But ever since the king introduced the bill in April classing all Catholics as outlaws—and the signing of the Anglo-Spanish Treaty in August, dashing all hopes of Spanish intervention to aid the Catholic cause— it has caused a great deal of unrest.'

'Are you saying there are those among us who would conspire against the king?' Serena asked in a shocked voice.

'If so, it will not be for the first time. I suspect that something ugly is about to manifest itself, but I must stress that that is all it is—suspicion. I will not reveal the source of my information. The less you know, the safer you will be.'

'I respect your concern for my well-being, Andrew, but if something is afoot I'd rather know about it. I suspect your information comes from a reliable source, otherwise you would not have come all this way to warn Father. That is your reason for coming to England, isn't it?'

Looking into her questioning eyes, Andrew began to regret speaking of so grave a matter which would only trouble her. 'I came because I wanted to see you and Father. I miss you both greatly. The information I have is not all that reliable. Indeed, what is these days?'

'But how did you learn that something is afoot in England when you live in Rome?' Serena asked, determined to glean as much information from her brother as she could before he left her.

'The king's chief minister, the Earl of Salisbury, has an energetic network of spies everywhere—not only in Flanders and Spain but also in Italy—so we do hear of the occasional conspiracy being hatched in England. The treacherous intriguers abroad provide a rich source of information for Salisbury in exchange for pardons and their own advancements. There are Catholics in England who hold on to the hope of liberalisation in the wake of the treaty with Spain, but there are those who are impatient and will not be quiet and will do whatever they can to bring about change.'

'And would you have them be quiet?'

'Yes. England and Spain were at war for many years and now we have peace. The diplomatic solution must be allowed to prevail over the Catholic situation in England. I believe we should trust in God to bring about toleration in His own good time. Be vigilant, Serena. Should you hear of any conspiracies being hatched, I beg you to persuade father to distance himself. If not, then I fear that he and any conspirator will be crushed and not escape with their lives.'

After bidding him a fond farewell, Serena, deeply troubled, watched her brother go on his way. There had been a deep concern in his eyes, a warning when he had told her to be vigilant.

Eliza Nugent, the housekeeper at Dunedin Hall, which was a rambling rose-coloured brick house situated on the outskirts of the village of Ripley, between Stratford-on-Avon and Warwick, threw her arms up in despair when she caught Serena sneaking out of the house when it was almost time for Sir Henry's guest to arrive.

In the five years since her mother's death, Serena had changed in a way that worried Eliza. Her wilfulness would lead her into trouble one day if Sir Henry didn't set about finding her a husband soon. Perhaps if he'd spent as much time guiding her along the path of goodness and beating the waywardness out of her, as he did on religious matters and travelling across to Flanders to see young James, then perhaps she would have turned out as her dear departed mother would have wished.

'Upon my soul,' Eliza scolded, 'where do you think

you're off to? Your father wants you here when the marquess of Thurlow arrives.'

Serena threw Eliza a cross look, which relaxed into a sweet, disarming smile as she set about trying to placate her. Eliza would be outraged if she knew the reason that drew her towards the village. The ageing housekeeper would go directly to her father with the information, who would be equally outraged and order Serena to her room immediately.

'Don't fret so, Eliza—and please don't lecture me,' Serena complained with a toss of her lovely head. 'The marquess should have arrived hours ago and I will not sit about waiting for him any longer. I won't be gone very long, I promise.'

'But it's almost dark.'

'I'm going to the stables. I want John to saddle Polly first thing in the morning. It's hoped that the marquess will buy two of our horses, and I suspect that he and Father will be in the saddle early to try them out before leaving for Woodfield Grange. Lord Payne has invited them to take part in the hunt, and it's expected that a large party from nearby Coughton Court—which Sir Everard Digby has rented for a few weeks—will attend.'

Horses, after his religion, were her father's abiding passion. Possessing some prime horseflesh, he was immensely proud of his large stable, which was envied and praised by many in the surrounding counties. He was also an expert horseman, who adored his gun dogs and his falcons.

Sir Henry was also a devout Catholic who had led an eventful and troubled life, having frequently wielded his sword during the reign of Queen Elizabeth in the hope of improving the Catholic lot. This and being a leading recusant—a man among many others of his faith who refused to submit to the authority of, or comply with, the Protestant religion—had resulted in hefty fines and frequent spells of imprisonment; on one occasion when he was confined in the Tower, torture was applied.

However, his spirit remained undimmed, and his crusade for toleration and liberty for Catholics to be allowed to practice their religion openly in England went on. Serena wished he would take Andrew's advice and be more acquiescing, trusting in God to bring about the conversion in His own good time.

An additional worry was the apprehension she felt each time he went to Flanders. Ostensibly he went to visit James and some of his friends, who chose to live there in order to practice their religion freely, but Serena was uncomfortably aware of his close association with a widow, a Mrs Davis, whose husband had left her a wealthy woman with two children.

According to Andrew, who had met Mrs Davis on the occasions he had passed through Flanders, she was hankering after a proposal of marriage from their father. But he was as reluctant to leave England and his horses as Mrs Davis was to leave Flanders and her freedom to practise her Catholic religion unhindered. Unless a compromise was reached, this was how things would remain between them; secretly Serena, not wanting to see another woman take her mother's place, hoped it would stay that way.

After leaving John, foolishly and heedless of any dangers, Serena took the darkening lane to the village, all thoughts of her father's guest, the marquess of Thurlow, banished from her mind. The man was a stranger to her, definable only by his name; the only interest he aroused in her was because he might want to buy two of her father's magnificent horses.

The name of the man Serena wanted so much to set eyes on blazed through her like a comet. Her mind had been in a whirl ever since Eliza had let slip earlier that Thomas Blackwell had returned from fighting in the Low Countries.

Prolonged and boisterous celebrations to welcome his return were taking place in the White Swan in the village, and would no doubt go on well into the night.

Thomas Blackwell lived at Ashcombe Manor on the outskirts of Ripley. It had been a year since Serena had last seen him, when she and her father had been invited to his home and she had looked into his eyes. They hadn't exchanged more than a few words in all the years of their living in close proximity to each other, and yet that one look, that stirring of pleasure, had spoken volumes. From that moment her life had changed. She had become aware of her womanhood for the first time.

On reaching the village green Serena paused, hoping Thomas would still be at the White Swan. Sounds of laughter coming from the inn across the green beckoned her and she ran towards it, cautiously entering a passageway at the side of the building from where she would be able to observe the occupants in the rooms without being observed herself. The stale odour of ale pervaded every corner of the crowded inn, and light from a guttering lamp inside the taproom was dim as Serena took her place in the shadows out of sight. The air was hot and fetid and she scanned the faces of the men inside the room, recognising some, others strangers to her.

But she only had eyes for one man, whose mere presence commanded the attention of all present. Charismatic Thomas Blackwell exercised an extraordinary influence on his contemporaries. He possessed the kind of qualities that captured the hearts of men and women alike. Almost six foot tall and well proportioned, his deep brown eyes and persuasiveness and charm drew the eyes of the village girls and set their hearts aflame. But he was also wild and hot-headed, swaggering and boorish in his arrogance and opinionated ways, and Serena, dazzled by his masculinity, could not imagine the ferocity of his violence if provoked.

Having looked her fill and eager to return home before

her father discovered she was missing, Serena slipped out into the darkening light. The opening and closing of the door caused a draught and the lamp inside the taproom to flicker. Several in the room glanced absently towards the door, and Thomas was just in time to see a woman's skirts disappear round the jamb.

Having drunk heavily with his friends and in dire need of another kind of entertainment, suspecting the woman who had been looking in to be one of the village wenches and arrogantly aware of the fever his presence never failed to arouse in them, he followed, just in time to see Serena disappearing along the lane in the direction of Dunedin Hall. Through the liquor fumes that fogged his mind, Thomas recognised her. More important, he recalled that her brother was a Jesuit priest—no doubt hiding at this very minute in a dank and miserable hole behind a chimney in one of the many spacious recusant houses that were thick across the Midlands, offering sanctuary to these criminals.

Thomas was implacable and inordinately cruel in his hatred of Catholics, which went way beyond the call of duty. He had killed many in the battles in the Low Countries; now that he was home and the estate his to administer as he wished since his father was dead, he would be ardent in the pursuit of priests and recusants.

He recalled the last time he had seen Serena, when she had accompanied Sir Henry to dine at Ashcombe Manor. Thomas's father had offered to buy a large chunk of Sir Henry's neglected land, which he had coveted for years, but Sir Henry had surprised and angered his father by firmly declining the offer.

A grim, calculating smile spread across his full lips. His eyes narrowed with mingled lust and menace when he pondered on the fun to be had with this deluded Papist wench. Clearly she wanted to see him so much that she had come looking for him. It would be a mortal sin to disappoint her now, he thought, and deny himself the pleasure of enjoying her delectable anatomy.

Darkness shrouded the countryside as Serena hurried along the narrow lane. Having left Ripley behind, she did not look back, and yet every nerve tingled when she sensed she was being followed. Breathlessly she paused and turned to find that Thomas was right behind her.

'Oh!' she gasped, amazed and overjoyed that he must have seen her at the inn and followed her. Her heart began to beat unevenly in her chest and an embarrassed flush rose to her cheeks at being caught out.

With a smouldering light in his eyes and a smile beginning at the corners of his mouth, spreading slowly into a grin of pure lechery, Thomas's gaze moved hungrily over her delicate features, pausing at length on her softly parted lips. 'Did you think I wouldn't follow you when I saw you flee from the inn?' he whispered huskily. 'How could I possibly resist such a blatant invitation? It was me you came to see, wasn't it?'

Serena stared at him in confusion. Thomas laughed softly. His strong fingers closed around her wrist and he drew her, unprotesting, away from the lane into the shelter of some bushes, his touch almost destroying her will power. 'Come now,' he murmured, pulling her into his arms, clumsily and without tenderness, 'don't deny what is in your heart, my sweet. You want me—admit it. Let's enjoy a kiss before we get down to more serious matters, shall we?'

Without ceremony Thomas's mouth clamped down on to Serena's and she quivered, the heat of his lips searing her own. Fighting to retain her sanity, to quell the emotions that threatened to overwhelm her, with chilling reason and her body rigid, Serena told herself this was wrong. Thomas should not be doing this to her. Hovering above her face, his eyes were heavy with desire, his mouth slack and insistent. His breathing became ragged as his embrace tightened around her, his breath fanning foul liquor fumes over her face. Suddenly it was an ugly face she saw, one that disgusted her.

Sensing her withdrawal, Thomas raised his bewildered gaze. 'Don't tease, Serena—don't be coy,' he said with mounting impatience when he sensed her lack of response. 'There's nothing to fear, my pretty. No one will see. You're quite safe.' Once again his mouth clamped over her moist lips, his hands moving greedily over her body, and Serena was shocked to feel them fumbling at the intimate parts no other hands had touched but her own.

Although she was inexperienced, she could tell Thomas's words were glibly spoken, coming from the lips of a practised seducer. Immediately she pulled back, her sanity, which had momentarily left her in the heat and excitement of the moment, returning, triggering her anger. Pushing against his chest when his fingers boldly began to fumble with the laces of her dress, cupping and squeezing her breasts, she stepped back as though he had struck her.

'Stop it. Let me go.'

Thomas's face twisted angrily, the handsome mouth which Serena had so recently yearned to feel on hers becoming a savage leer of pure evil. 'Damn you for being a temptress. You want me, I know it, and I shall have you.'

'No,' she cried but, as his mouth ground down on to hers once more, her cries of outrage were smothered. His strength overpowered her. Feeling his arousal pressed hard against her thigh, she was overwhelmed with horror and disgust at the violation he intended, without decency or tenderness. She retaliated by jerking away from him and swinging her arm with a cry of unleashed fury.

Thomas lifted his head at the same moment that she hurled her clenched fist into his belly, finding it hard to believe such a hard punch could have been thrown by such a winsome and fragile young woman.

'How dare you?' Serena shrieked accusingly. 'If you

think I'm game for a quick tumble in the grass, then you've lost your wits, Thomas Blackwell.'

Intent on having his pleasure and determined not to be cheated out of it, Thomas grabbed her wrist and pulled her against him once more.

'So you want to play it rough, do you?' he hissed, his features contorted with cruelty. 'I can be as rough as you want me to be, you little hellcat,' and he lunged for her again, his face ugly now and twisted with lust, filling Serena's vision so that she could see nothing else.

Dreadful visions of what her possible fate might be flew through her mind. What a fool she'd been. How could she have imagined for one minute that she was in love with this crazed beast, intent only on his own pleasure? The passion, which had been so intense that she had been unable to think of little else, withered and died. Her year-long infatuation with Thomas Blackwell was over. Now she felt only loathing and disgust—and anger directed against herself for foolishly wasting her time dreaming of him.

Undaunted and determined to free herself, driven by self-preservation, she reacted violently, struggling and twisting in a frenzied effort to escape as her rage peaked. Hearing the rending of the silk ruching that trimmed the neck of her bodice, she felt the cold air on her exposed body. One glimpse of the creamy flesh that swelled out of her bodice seemed to incite Thomas even more. Driven by some kind of demon inside her Serena lashed out, kicking his shins like a wild thing, clawing and raking her fingernails down his cheek which drew streaks of blood.

With cold sweat drenching her body, Serena managed to thrust herself away from him as, with a grunt of pain, Thomas raised a hand to his injured cheek. Unable to conceal her loathing, Serena glared at him with a challenging gaze, daring him to attack her again, her fists clenched and ready to strike if he made a move towards her.

'Don't you dare touch me again, you vile wretch,' she

fumed with unladylike vehemence, in the grip of an ice-cold, venomous rage, unable to still the shaking in her limbs. 'Find someone more pliant to lust after. You disgust me, you clumsy oaf, with your clawing hands and foul breath.'

'Disgust! Ha!' Thomas roared with a savage snarl, his face having turned a mottled red. Tiny droplets of blood gleamed and trickled down his lacerated cheek to the small white ruff circling his neck. 'It wasn't disgust that brought you to the village in search of me like a bitch on heat, was it? Your behaviour is hardly in keeping with the pious little virgin you profess to be.'

'Better to remain a virgin and die an old spinster than to acquaint myself with the likes of you,' Serena flared in outrage.

Seeing red, Thomas advanced menacingly towards her once more. 'Shut your mouth, you hellcat—you dirty little high-minded Papist bitch,' he snarled in a flying rage, raising his hand to cuff her.

Surprised by what he was witnessing, Kit, the marquess of Thurlow, Lord Christopher Brodie—just two of his many titles—who was on his way to Dunedin Hall accompanied by his servant Robin, quickly dismounted. Having seen a flurry of hair, petticoats and creamy flesh, and heard much of what was taking place between these two, he had formed his own conclusion as to what was happening.

Kit had not intervened sooner because he thought the young lady seemed well able to take care of herself, but when he saw the man raise his fist to strike her he was impelled to act. If there was one thing he had been taught from an early age it was to respect the opposite gender, and this show of brutality against such a dainty wench was too much to ignore. Drawing his sword, he was diverted when his eyes settled momentarily on the face of the woman—a face of unforgettable beauty.

It was white, as white as alabaster in the gathering

gloom, with eyes glittering like darting chips of ice, and her utter contempt for the man who intended to violate her was manifest in their translucent depths. Her lips were clamped together in a savage line, her small chin set in forceful determination, and the assertive and compelling steeliness in her expression told Kit that had she been in possession of a dagger, she would have had no qualms about thrusting it into the pulsating centre of her aggressor's heart.

'I wouldn't do that if I were you,' Kit said, his tone deadly calm. 'It would be a pity to mar a face of such exquisite beauty—and if you do, it will cost you your life.'

Unprepared for the interruption, Thomas gave an enraged curse and spun around in his fury, but then he felt the cold and hungry tongue of a rapier pressed threateningly against the soft flesh of his neck. He stared askance at the black garbed figure at the other end of the steel blade, seeing the wicked pale blue light that danced along its length, and he felt his skin prickle and the hairs at the back of his neck stand up on recognition of the intruder, who commanded both his own and Serena's attention with his awesome presence.

'So, you remember me, Blackwell—even though we are a long way from the Netherlands?' The tone was sardonic, the faint smile sneering.

Beginning to sweat profusely, his face darkening to an apoplectic crimson, Thomas continued to gape as his sluggish mind fought to grasp more clearly what was happening. Respectful of the threatening blade, he felt its point already penetrating his flesh and a slow trickle of warm blood begin to run down his neck and mingle with that from his torn cheek. He stood stock-still, eyeing warily the man who was taller than himself, whose eyes bore into his like dagger thrusts.

'You seem surprised,' Kit remarked, speaking lightly, but his mildly amused smile and cold dark stare did not waver from the face of the man opposite, who was eyeing him with a profound hatred. 'What's the matter? Have I sprouted horns? I've never seen you sweat so much, Blackwell. It does not surprise me to find you up to your old tricks. Violating maids appears to be your favourite pastime—but it seems to me that you annoy this particular lady…that your attentions are unwelcome.'

'And your interference in a matter that is none of your concern *I* find most unwelcome. Although it's hardly surprising you come to the maid's defence, considering the comradeship that exists between yourself and certain members of the Catholic hierarchy,' Thomas sneered with derision, angered at finding himself at a disadvantage, and knowing he faced an experienced soldier who did not flinch under adversity.

To begin with, Brodie set Thomas on edge. He was taller than Thomas, with shoulders as broad. The man was also extremely wealthy and a smooth sort, being close to the king and his courtiers, although the fact that he could count many Catholic noblemen as his close friends—among them Sir Everard Digby and that other Catholic magnate, Sir Thomas Tresham—suggested to Thomas that Kit had Catholic sympathies himself.

To make matters worse, Brodie's equestrian skills had attracted the eye of many a commander in the Low Countries, and he had proved his military prowess in combat many times. His reputation with both sword and pistol was an enviable and well-known fact, and Thomas had neither the means nor the clarity of mind to test it just then. But most chilling of all was the fact that Kit Brodie was also the man responsible for having Thomas and his regiment recalled from the Netherlands in disgrace—which was a score he had yet to settle.

'And you believe that because the lady does not share your faith that it gives you the right to violate her?' Kit's lips curled with contempt. 'I think it must have slipped your mind that you are no longer fighting the Spanish in the Netherlands,' he said with heavy sarcasm. 'The lady is right, Blackwell. You are even more of a lecherous swine than I took you for. It is my opinion that you should have been hanged for your violation and massacre of those unfortunate women at the convent near Ghent.'

'You remember too much, Brodie,' growled Thomas.

'Some things are unable to be forgotten, Blackwell. That is one of them. However,' Kit said with a savage taunt and a look to indicate the still bleeding scratches on his face, 'I think enough bloodletting has been done for one day, so you have a reprieve. At least the lady has left you a momento to remember her by—which is more than can be said of the unfortunate women you so brutally murdered.'

Kit moved back and held his weapon aloft as Thomas tried to shake the cobwebs from his brain. Feeling the blade relinquish its position on his flesh, Thomas took a desperate, threatening step forward, at which Kit quickly wielded his sword once more, the dark wings of his eyebrows snapping together, the hard gleam in his eyes becoming brittle and his mouth tightening into a line of aggravation.

'Have a care, Blackwell. Do not force my hand.' Kit's voice was like steel, his expression the same, and Thomas checked himself, knowing that Brodie was a man who brooked no argument from anyone.

'You find me at a disadvantage, Brodie,' growled Thomas, breathing heavily and holding his arms out from his sides to indicate he did not carry a sword. 'As you see, I am without my weapon so I cannot defend myself. But the next time we meet you will not be so fortunate. You will discover I am as skilled with the sword as you purportedly are.'

Kit's cold gaze travelled over Thomas with contempt before settling on the side of his face that was dark with blood. 'I shall look forward to it. Now—be on your way and have your face tended before you bleed to death before my eyes.'

Thomas's face was set in lines of violent, menacing rage, his gaze going beyond Kit to Serena, whose eyes were smouldering with unsuppressed hostility. With her colouring and snapping eyes she resembled a wild vixen, and did nothing to conceal her newfound hatred and revulsion for him. Drawing his upper lip into a snarl, his eyes settled on her pale features with cruel contempt.

'I'll make the Papist bitch sorry she ever drew breath. I swear I'll find her.'

'Then take care, Blackwell, lest she finds you first,' scoffed Kit, his chiding laughter mocking the other. 'After what my eyes have just witnessed between the two of you, you may not fare so well the next time either. The lady has clearly taken her measure of you and appears to have quite a temper.'

'I'll not give the spitting she-cat another chance to sink her claws into me.' Thomas's eyes settled once more on Kit, the cords of his neck standing out quivering and tense. 'I have a score to settle with you both. I shall have my revenge for what you have done to me this day—and before that, Brodie. Our paths are destined to cross again, so prepare yourself for when they do. I will give you no quarter.'

As he strode away, hatred nestled like a tiger in Thomas Blackwell's heart. Time would tell if Brodie was all his compatriots extolled him to be, when he had reaped his revenge and crushed Kit beneath his heel.

Thomas was determined to prove ruthless in his ambition to destroy both Lord Brodie and Serena Carberry, and to gain that end he would slander and scheme without the least regard for the truth. Unbeknown to him just then, an event was about to occur that would rock England with its infamy and would assist him greatly in his efforts. His grievance against them would not be assuaged until they were dead.

Chapter Two

Serena looked at her rescuer's visage, seeing that this was no lust-crazed beast but a strikingly handsome man with aristocratic features, hair and eyes as black as jet and the lean, hungry look of a hawk. The elegance of his attire and accompanying servant told her he was a gentleman.

However, the brutish treatment she had just undergone ignited all the fires of rage which she unfairly directed at this stranger. He appeared to find the whole incident highly entertaining and to take an infuriating delight in her sorry plight yet, if Serena had paused to consider, he had just saved her from an ordeal so terrible she could never have imagined it.

The disquieting, contemplative smile gave her no assurance that her treatment at this stranger's hands would be any better, and all she could think of at that moment was that he had borne witness to her humiliation. It was this that penetrated her paralysed thoughts and she hated him for it. It was to form a tempestuous foundation to their future acquaintance—one that might have been so very different had they met in more conventional circumstances.

Her pride seared, with elbows akimbo and her fingers drumming impatiently on her waist, Serena flung her hair back from her face, sending it spilling down her back, and glared into the black, humour-filled eyes sweeping over her with a rakish gleam.

'Well?' she snapped irritably, treating Kit as if he was somehow responsible for what had happened. 'What are you gawping and grinning at? Is it your intention to finish what Thomas Blackwell began?'

Unperturbed by her anger, Kit laughed. 'If you believe that, I can only assume that the fiery colour of your hair has baked your brain.'

'I would have sent him on his way without your inter-vention—and you can expect much of the same if you dare come any closer. I have a care for my virtue and am par-ticularly choosy who I surrender it to.'

Kit chuckled. The fire-spitting green eyes seared right through him as he raked her with a brazen gaze, amazed by her spirit. At first sight he had thought her too slender and fragile for such a furious onslaught but, after seeing her in action, it was clear there was nothing timid or docile about this young woman. Kit was convinced that she would have defended her virtue until her last breath was drawn.

'I don't doubt it, and you are right, you were doing splen-didly without my intervention. Blackwell's face will smart for a month and he will bear the marks of his encounter with you for a good deal longer.'

'For ever, I hope,' Serena said heatedly, dabbing at a nasty scratch on her wrist with a handkerchief.

Kit's lips twitched with ill-suppressed amusement, his gaze lightly caressing her face. 'The poor man must be in torment at being cheated out of what he intended. The glare you gave him would have shrivelled the pride and the pas-sion of any man.'

'And you would do well to remember it,' she snapped, fired up with ire, her eyes flying to his brazen and over-confident smile.

'You are much too fragile to get the better of a man of Blackwell's size and strength,' Kit chided. 'I doubt you would have the stamina to oppose him for long. Had I not come along when I did, you would have been ravished most cruelly.'

Serena ignored the fact that his words held some element of truth. 'Fragile! Sir, I am more resourceful than you give me credit for, not some meek, simpering milksop. What I lack in strength I make up for in agility—so, if you value your looks, I advise you to keep your distance.'

Kit could only marvel at her tenacity. His eyes glowed as he gave her a lazy smile, realising that both her dignity and pride had been mightily bruised. 'You, dear lady, are a veritable tigress. But you have judged me before I can voice a plea—and unfairly, too. Rest assured that I am not in the habit of taking that which is not freely given,' he said, his voice soft and deeply resonant, grinning leisurely as his perusal swept slowly over her delectable form, liking what he saw.

Her figure was slender, her features fine and soft, and yet he had borne witness to the fact that she wasn't nearly as fragile and delicate as suggested. There was also a proud courage in the way she had leapt to defend her honour. She was a firebrand, and he could easily understand how she had captured the salacious attention of Thomas Blackwell, who had been left with more than a little wounded pride.

This young woman was in possession of a tempestuous will, and Kit could be forgiven for taking her for a gypsy wench—with her tumbling auburn hair and flashing eyes. Looking at her with heightened interest, he noted that her attire proclaimed her to be the daughter of a gentleman. If so, he was curious as to the circumstances that had brought her to this place alone to be set upon by Thomas Blackwell. Had she enticed him, and how well did she know her tormentor?

Serena smarted beneath the closely perusing eye of the stranger. His gaze seemed to touch her everywhere, stripping her body bare as he made no attempt to hide his interest. Becoming aware of the object of his gaze as it dipped, she followed it, realising the twin peaks of her breasts were taut and pointing high above the ripped fabric of her gown. Feeling her cheeks burn hot with embarrassment, she was immediately prompted to check her appearance and gather the torn bodice of her dress together, dropping her handkerchief into the road.

'You, sir, are the most despicable man I have met in a long time.'

'Come now. Not since half an hour ago at least,' Kit laughed. 'Do you mean to tell me you prefer Blackwell's company to mine?'

'I cannot say that because I do not know you. I can only hope you are enough of a gentleman not to gossip about what has just occurred.'

'My lips are sealed.' Highly amused by her angry confusion, Kit swept an arm across his chest and bowed low in a courtly manner, the quirk in his lips deepening into an amused, lopsided grin. 'I am happy to have been of service, and would wish to hear your gratitude rather than your anger. Your eyes are more lethal than a set of duelling pistols.' Bending to retrieve her handkerchief, he made no move to return it.

Relaxing a little, Serena deliberately softened her manner, thinking that if she appeared to relent a little she could escape his odious presence and be on her way. 'Very well. I suppose I must thank you for arriving when you did. Perhaps you did help save me from a terrible fate,' she conceded reluctantly whilst remaining aloof. 'I am indebted to you, sir.'

Kit's look became serious suddenly. 'Did Blackwell hurt you?'

'I told you. I can fend for myself. Now, if you will allow me to go on my way, I will bid you goodnight.' Unfortunately it was not as easy as she hoped to be rid of him, for he briskly ignored her request.

'You may still have need of my services. I insist on offering my protection and escorting you to your home. Who knows—your tormentor may come back.'

'I don't think so. It's my guess that he will have returned to the White Swan where he will consume more liquor before the night is out and he seeks his bed—or someone else's.'

'Nevertheless, I do insist.'

His insistence was beginning to stretch Serena's nerves. 'You are extremely gallant, sir, but that will not be necessary. I can see myself home. It is not far,' she replied tersely.

'And where is that?'

The softness of a moment before left Serena's eyes, turning then to flint. Her mouth hardened to an unsmiling resentment as her temper rose once more. Feeling less than proud of herself for the way she had acted, the mere thought that this arrogant and impertinent man had heard and witnessed the scene between herself and Thomas Blackwell was too embarrassing to contemplate. 'What has that to do with you?'

Kit suppressed a smile with amused patience as he sheathed his rapier. 'Absolutely nothing. Tell me, do your parents often let you out alone like this—to make assignations with men of Blackwell's ilk?'

Icy fire smouldered in Serena's eyes as she faced him with chilled contempt. 'My encounter with Thomas Blackwell was not an assignation—and, no, my father does not even know I have left the house. But I am a gentlewoman, if that is what you mean.'

Kit's bold eyes sparkled with merriment in the face of her anger, and his strong, animal white teeth gleamed in the gathering gloom. 'No gentlewoman remains a gentlewoman after doing and saying what I have just overheard,' he answered airily.

'Then I would be grateful if you would forget what you

have overheard, sir, and forget your encounter with me. Good evening.'

Spinning on her heels, Serena stalked ahead with an indignant swing of her hips. Grinning broadly and, with a soft chuckle, grasping the reins of his horse, Kit tucked the young lady's handkerchief into a pocket inside his doublet. Quickening his stride he followed, indicating for Robin to do likewise, who was watching his master with an amused expression on his boyish face.

'Wait,' Kit said, having no mind to let her go lightly.

Serena turned and waited for him to approach, taking stock of him for the first time. Attired in the manner of a wealthy lord, he was a magnificent man—as handsome in physique as he was of face. Her eyes wandered over his strong shoulders encased in a black velvet doublet, tapering to a narrow waist, and long, lean, muscular thighs—so unnervingly masculine.

Her anger began to drain from her and a small frown of perplexity creased her brow when he came close and stood looking down at her. His mere presence touched her senses with an acute sensual awareness that left her weak. She flushed, angered by her wayward thoughts. No proper lady would think such things and allow such imaginings to take root in her mind—but then, no proper lady would have done what she had done and gone searching for a man she had foolishly become infatuated with.

'Well?' she said, her tone brittle.

'Since we seem to be going in the same direction, perhaps we might walk a little way together? Being a stranger to these parts, I would be glad of the company.'

Serena stared into his eyes, which still sparkled with unbridled humour. After a lengthy pause she slowly released her breath, relenting a little, if reluctantly; the sooner she was rid of this disconcerting man, the better she would feel. They were going in the same direction and she would only have to suffer his company for a little while.

'Very well,' she conceded, beginning to walk on. 'My home is not far. Are you just passing through Ripley, or visiting friends?'

'I am here on business—although Sir Henry Carberry, who I am visiting, is also my friend.'

Thunderstruck, Serena froze, and with an expression of stunned horror she stopped dead in her tracks and looked up into his dark eyes, realising who he was. 'You are visiting Dunedin Hall?'

'I am. Do you know it?'

'Yes—I—I should,' she stammered hesitantly, suddenly wishing the ground would open and mercifully swallow her up. For the first time since meeting him she was almost at a loss for words. 'I—I am Serena Carberry. Sir Henry is my father.'

Seeing the horror and dismay on her face, Kit smiled slowly, his gaze sparkling and taunting. Cocking a handsome eyebrow, he gave her a lengthy inspection, his teeth gleaming behind a lopsided grin. 'Well, well,' he murmured, letting his breath out slowly. 'I see.'

Serena was unable to prevent the onslaught of shame that engulfed her. Of all the people in the world to visit her father, it had to be this terrible person who had witnessed that awful scene between herself and Thomas Blackwell that would haunt her for ever.

'You—you must be the marquess of Thurlow?'

'Yes—and I can quite understand why you would rather I weren't.' Kit chuckled, seeming to enjoy her discomfiture. 'I realise how uncomfortable it will be for you having me under your father's roof for a whole night—knowing what I do,' he said quietly, meaningfully. Looking up at him, Serena saw something in his look that challenged her spirit and brought back her strength and a surge of dislike.

'I would appreciate it if you did not mention any of this to my father. He would be extremely angry, you understand.'

'I consider he would be better off knowing in order to deal with his wayward daughter so she does not repeat her misdemeanour.'

'I will remind you, sir, that this is none of your affair. You are here to see my father's horses and to ride to Woodfield Grange tomorrow for the hunt. I am reluctant to lend myself to my father's anger should my encounter with Thomas Blackwell become known, and I would be more than grateful if you did not tell him. If he should hear of it, his tirade will challenge the loudest broadside and my reputation will be in ruins.'

Kit gave her a wolfish grin. 'Then let me set your mind at rest. You can rest assured, dear lady, that your guilty secret is quite safe with me.'

'Thank you, sir,' she said as graciously as she was able under the circumstances, walking briskly on her way.

Kit fell into step beside her. 'I am Lord Brodie by the way—Christopher Brodie—Kit to my friends.'

'Because I do not know you, sir,' Serena replied testily without looking at him, her nose in the air, 'I shall address you as Lord Brodie. To be more familiar would be inappropriate.'

Kit grinned. 'As you wish.'

With Robin following at a discreet distance, they walked side by side. Serena felt herself enveloped in Kit's perusal which brought a flush to her cheeks; if she had turned and glanced at him and noted the attention he was paying to her gently swaying body—his gaze passing with leisured interest over her hair and slender hips swinging provocatively in unison—her flush would have deepened to poppy red.

Kit's thoughts turned to his sweet-natured betrothed, Dorothea Carberry—this young lady's cousin—with relief. His betrothal to Dorothea was recent, and he would call on her and Lord Carberry after the hunting at Woodfield Grange. The gentle nature of Dorothea was far more favourable than the fiery nature of her cousin. Any man finding himself attached to this particular firebrand would know no peace. Kit felt heartily sorry for anyone this wench unleashed her tongue on. And yet, he was beginning to understand how a man could so easily succumb to a woman's charms that he would forget the troth so soon made to another.

Serena slipped into the house ahead of Lord Brodie. Not until she reached her chamber did she allow her mind to conjure up an image of Thomas Blackwell's face—the man she had foolishly allowed to dominate her every waking hour since she had last laid eyes on him. The image she had of him now was distorted and ugly beyond recognition.

Unbidden, the humour-filled black eyes of her rescuer took its place, and she realised he posed as much a danger and threat to her emotions and senses as Thomas Blackwell had before. Collecting her scattered wits, she formed a firm resolve not to let the marquess of Thurlow intimidate her. Earlier he had stung her pride by playing humorously on her own confusion, and she was determined that tonight she would be more in control of her emotions and herself and set the marquess of Thurlow agog.

She chose to wear an extremely fetching ruby-coloured velvet gown, one Andrew had brought as a present for her from Italy. The full skirt draped luxuriantly over hoops, and the sleeves were puffed, the ruche-edged stomacher emphasising the slimness of her waist. The collar, elevated at the back, framed her delicate, heart-shaped face.

After her maid had quickly and deftly arranged her hair in soft, high curls and Serena felt confident that she looked her best, she went downstairs to the great hall with its vaulted, rib-caged roof, unable to think of a plausible excuse to remain in her room. A murmur of voices came from one of the chambers leading off from the hall. Serena advanced towards it, her footsteps on the tiles heralding her arrival. Her father and Lord Brodie were standing before the giant hearth where a fire burned bright, the lively flames sending dancing shadows over the richly tapestried walls.

At fifty-five, Sir Henry should have been a rich man. The fact that he was a relatively poor man was largely due to his own recklessness throughout his life—the large recusant fines, the funding of the Catholic cause and the amount of money he spent on his beloved horses. He was still a handsome man, jovial and of average height, with twinkling blue eyes and thinning dark hair liberally sprinkled with grey. Like that of King James, a small square-cut beard covered his chin.

Conversation between the two men ceased when Serena made her entrance. When she stepped into the range of Kit's vision, he could not believe the beautiful and well-groomed lady—who seemed the very spirit of virtue and moved with all the poise, grace and cool dignity of a queen—was the same bedraggled shrew he had encountered earlier.

Serena's gaze flicked over Lord Brodie before coming to rest on her father, sensing his displeasure that she had absented herself from his side on his guest's arrival.

'Ah, Serena! You have finally deigned to grace us with your presence,' Sir Henry rebuked. 'Kit, may I present my daughter, Serena, and apologise most profusely for her absence on your arrival. I would like to say she is not usually so absent-minded or so ill-mannered, but I am sorry to confess that when other matters of interest crop up to occupy her mind she is forgetful of all else.'

At nineteen, the frequent flashes of childlike ardour and deep affection in Serena's eyes whenever they settled on her father blinded him to her wilfulness and often reprehensible behaviour. Despite his gentle reproach there was a warm admiration in his eyes when they rested on her. It was no secret that he doted on his daughter unashamedly, and was in no hurry to marry her off. She was just one more reason why he had not yet succumbed to the quiet charms of Mrs Davis.

Kit watched Serena approach with interest. She came to stand close, tilting her head as she gazed into his handsome visage from beneath eyebrows delicately sweeping like a winged bird's. A bloom of rosy pink heightened her high cheekbones, and her eyes—emerald green orbs flecked with brown—were thickly fringed with silken black lashes tipped with gold. The firelight gave her hair a rich warm hue the colour of rosewood, and the heady fragrance of rosewater on her skin was intoxicating.

Kit felt his pulses leap and the blood go searing through his veins at her nearness and the coyness of her little smile as she demurely lowered her eyes. Drawing his dark eyebrows together in a frown he became cautious, strongly suspecting he was being beguiled and led into a trap. Serena lifted her gaze, the eyes beneath the thick fringe of lashes steady and disconcerting, shining with an intelligent brightness which proclaimed an agility of wit and a craving to taste all that life had to offer.

Her beauty fed Kit's gaze, rekindling the ache he had felt earlier. Never had he met a woman who intrigued him more, but because he had given his troth to another, the tantalising Mistress Serena Carberry was forbidden fruit—and he was beginning to thank God for it. She would bring him nothing but trouble.

'Mistress Carberry, I am honoured to meet you.' Kit's eyes met hers with amusement as he bowed with a grand, sweeping gesture.

'Lord Brodie,' she acknowledged.

'Don't be disheartened,' he murmured, taking her hand and raising it to his lips. His dark eyes, holding hers, sparkled with humour when he felt her fingers tremble involuntarily on coming into contact with his lips—which told him she was not altogether as in control of her senses as she would like him to think. 'You are forgiven.'

Snatching her fingers from his strong hold, Serena favoured him with a sweet smile and feigned a slight curtsy. 'Thank you, sir. I apologise for keeping you waiting.'

'You are forgiven,' Kit replied, his voice deeply resonant, his eyes, openly unabashed, displaying their appraisal of her attire as they travelled the full length of her body. 'The wait was well worth it,' he murmured.

Kit's perusing eye left no curve untouched, no article of clothing intact, until Serena felt completely naked. She felt a sudden impulse to retreat before his smouldering gaze, but held her ground admirably.

'We are waiting to eat, Serena,' said her father with impatience, unaware of the secret play that was taking place between the other two as he led the way into the dining room. 'The meal is getting cold.'

With reluctance Serena placed her slender fingers on Lord Brodie's gallantly proferred arm to be escorted into the dining room. Feeling his gaze on her face, she looked up at him inquiringly. 'Is something troubling you, my lord?'

'Forgive me. I do not mean to stare, but you seem familiar. I have a rather peculiar feeling that we have met somewhere before. But then, I ask myself, how can that be? I am not one to forget a face—especially not when one is as unforgettable as yours.'

Kit spoke casually, his words faintly teasing and meaningful. In alarm Serena's fingers tightened on his arm and she threw him a savage look, appalled that he might be about to betray her misdemeanour to her father when she had begged him not to. Earlier, her qualms had been eased by his promise not to speak of the incident, and she was incensed that he should continue to find so much humour in what, to her, had been the most brutal and embarrassing experience of her entire life.

'I can assure you we have not met before,' she answered firmly.

Kit smiled calmly into her glare, a corner of his lips lifting roguishly. 'No? Then I must take your word for it.'

'Perhaps it's the likeness my daughter bears to Dorothea,' said Sir Henry, with a low chuckle. 'They are very much alike.'

Bemused, Serena glanced from one to the other. 'Dorothea? Do you know my cousin, Lord Brodie?'

'Kit has recently become betrothed to Dorothea, Serena,' her father explained. 'No doubt she will tell you all about it when you visit Carberry Hall in a day or so.'

Serena stared at Kit in astonishment, and so amazed was she at this announcement that she almost overstepped the bounds of decorum and laughed out loud. It was impossible to believe that this overbearing man was to marry her gentle cousin. Her eyes were bright with humour as they met his with disbelief. 'You? You are to marry Dorothea?'

Kit's black eyebrows lowered in a frown. 'You find it amusing that I am to marry your cousin?'

'I find it strange and intriguing that someone as faint-hearted as Dorothea would agree to wed someone so— so—'

Kit raised a questioning eyebrow, watching her closely. 'So what?'

'So very different from the type of man I expected her to settle for.'

'And do you find it so incredible that she has settled for me?'

'Yes. I can only think that my cousin must have taken leave of her senses.'

A smile touched Kit's lips. 'I can assure you she has not.'

'Nevertheless, you cannot know each other well, otherwise she would have mentioned you to me.'

'And you see your cousin often, do you, Mistress Carberry?'

Serena had not seen Dorothea for several weeks. Dorothea's father, William Carberry, and Serena's own father were half-brothers, their father having married twice. William, the elder of the two, like his mother was staunchly Protestant and had a strong dislike for the Catholic religion. Over the years this had been the cause of much contention between the two brothers and was deeply felt by Serena, who resented her uncle's lack of tolerance. Serena and Dorothea were close, but of late, because of the volatile situation that existed between Uncle William and her father, and knowing that whenever she went to Carberry Hall her uncle tolerated her presence only out of family duty, Serena had not visited her cousin.

'Of late I have not seen Dorothea,' she replied quietly, on a more serious note. 'I wish you both every imaginable happiness. You are indeed fortunate in your choice of bride, sir.'

Kit looked at her thoughtfully, curious as to the sudden change in her. 'I couldn't agree with you more. In the short time I have known Dorothea, I find her to be an exceptional woman.'

'I know she is,' Serena agreed.

Kit held the heavy, high-backed chair as she slipped into it. As the meal progressed and Sir Henry conversed about political matters, Serena was aware of his guest's unrelenting stare. Meeting his gaze, she found in his black eyes a glowing intensity and a slow, brazen perusal that brought the colour mounting to her cheeks and ire to burn through her.

Having him so close was agonisingly distasteful to her. Bestowing on him a cool stare, she tried her best to ignore him, but it was difficult when he sat directly in her sights. The man bedevilled her. He was insufferable and doing his best to antagonise her. Clenching her teeth in irritation, she tried concentrating on her food until she was drawn into the conversation by her father.

'You know Kit is here to look over our horses, don't you, Serena?'

'Yes.' She smiled, glancing at her father at the end of the table.

'It's my intention to purchase three or four of your finest mares available to replenish my stable at Thurlow—if they are as magnificent as they are reputed to be,' Kit said.

'I don't think you will be disappointed,' Serena told him, 'although, had you come two weeks ago you would have had more to choose from.'

Kit glanced at her sharply. 'Oh?'

'Yes. Several are promised to Mr Grant and Sir Robert Catesby—isn't that so, Father?'

Sir Henry suddenly looked discomfited and coughed nervously, causing Kit's brow to become furrowed with a deep frown as he contemplated his host. No comment was made, but Serena had a peculiar feeling that her father would rather she had kept quiet about the matter. She also sensed that Lord Brodie had taken particular note of what had been said and that he would not forget it.

At the time she had been curious when Sir Robert and Mr Grant from Norbrook—Mr Grant's home at nearby Snitterfield—had come to look over the horses, purchasing twenty of a strong and heavy breed. When she had inquired of her father afterwards the reason for the purchase, he had told her that Catesby was to form a troop of horse to enter the service of the archdukes in the Spanish Netherlands.

Knowing this was legal since the peace with Spain the previous year, Serena's curiosity had been appeased. But, as she recalled Andrew's words of warning, a feeling of disquiet settled on her. She prayed her father had not become involved in something she knew nothing about.

'Are you acquainted with Robert Catesby?' Serena asked in an attempt to cover the awkward moment.

'I am. As your father may have told you, I have only recently come into my inheritance at Thurlow on the death of my cousin. It was necessary for me to spend some time in London to attend Parliament until it was prorogued until November. The lodgings I took in the Strand were adjacent to Catesby's.'

'And what was your opinion of him?'

Kit smiled and his eyes twinkled at Serena. 'He is certainly a popular gentleman.'

'And handsome, too,' chuckled Sir Henry. 'At least my daughter thought so when last she saw him.'

'Father!' gasped Serena, hot colour flooding her cheeks. Wasn't it enough Lord Brodie knowing she was involved with Thomas Blackwell without adding another to the list?

Kit laughed good-humouredly. 'I'm not surprised. Robert—or Robin as he is called among his friends—in spite of his rather headstrong disposition is an irresistible charmer and very much admired. He left London for Stratford with some associates at the same time as myself.'

Kit had spent many long hours in the company of Robert Catesby, an ardent Catholic, whilst in London. He was a likeable man with a dominant personality, and deeply involved with religious malcontents. Kit had been present at several of their gatherings when they had met at the Mermaid or the Mitre Inn on Bread Street. A silent, curious observer, he had supped with them whilst thinking it prudent not to become too involved. Their conversations had been discreet, but he sensed a strong agitation manifesting itself, and felt that something might occur during the next session of Parliament.

'You are to visit Dorothea, I understand,' Kit remarked to Serena. Turning the conversation to more pleasurable topics, he thrust unpleasant thoughts of conspiracies, which were forever being hatched against the king, from his mind.

'She is expecting me tomorrow afternoon. I am to stay at Carberry Hall for a few days. In the light of your betrothal we shall have lots to catch up on.'

'Then you will still be there when I call on Dorothea and

Sir William before I have to return to Thurlow,' Kit said, a smile touching his lips and his eyes taking on a new gleam as her bewitching beauty fed his gaze. The light of the tapers illuminated her to advantage, and he found himself dwelling with a good deal of pleasure on the tantalising vision she presented across the table.

Having hoped that when he left for Woodfield Grange she would not have to see him again, Serena was disappointed and extremely vexed that she might. 'Perhaps.' She met his dark eyes with resentment, thinking furiously that even though he was aware of her dislike he was amused by it. Shoving her chair back, she intended leaving the gentlemen to drink their port in peace, but her father halted her.

'Eliza informs me you that you intend riding early in the morning, Serena?'

Serena had decided to forgo her ride and have one of the servants go to the stables to tell John not to bother saddling her horse after all. Not even an early morning ride over her beloved heath could tempt her to ride in the company of Lord Brodie.

'That—that was my intention,' she said hesitantly, 'but I—'

'Then you can accompany Kit,' her father said quickly before she could finish what she was about to say. 'Forgive me if I don't accompany you,' he apologised to his guest, 'but you will find that not only is my daughter an excellent horsewoman, but she also knows as much about the horses as I do myself. John will also be on hand to assist you and tell you anything you wish to know.'

Serena looked at her father in alarm. Usually he wouldn't miss an opportunity to show off his horses. 'What is it, Father? You're not ill?'

'Nothing that a good night's sleep won't cure.' Sir Henry laughed lightly in an attempt to allay his daughter's concern—but the truth of the matter was that his joints pained him a great deal—especially now the weather had taken a turn for the worse. Unfortunately, his sufferings were a lasting legacy of the year he had spent in the Tower at Queen Elizabeth's pleasure.

'I fear that an early ride will put me out of sorts for the hunt later—and I have no wish to disappoint Lord Payne by not turning up. If you find a horse to your liking, Kit, try him out at the hunt—or you are more than welcome to take mine. He's a strong, spirited brute, but I'm sure the two of you will get along.'

'That's generous of you, Sir Henry,' Kit said, easing back in his chair, his heavy-lidded gaze speculative as his dark eyes leisurely watched the tension and emotion play across Serena's expressive face, sensing she had been about to cancel riding out early to avoid his company.

He reserved little hope of establishing any kind of peace between them, for she glared at him as if it would be pistols at dawn and she contemplated a duel to the death, instead of a gallop upon the heath. A mocking smile curved his lips and he found himself looking forward to his ride with this intriguing young woman, although he told himself there was a dire need for caution.

'I am honoured to have Mistress Carberry accompany me,' he murmured. 'It will be a privilege.'

The subtle way Lord Brodie's smile changed was not to Serena's liking. Irate sparks flared in her bright green eyes as she thought how easily she had been snared, and she lowered her eyes to hide her annoyance, standing up.

'Very well. I will see you in the morning, Lord Brodie.'

Beset by emotions quite new to her, Serena went to her room. She was seized by a biting, raging fear at the knowledge that the marquess of Thurlow, having been privy to her degradation earlier, was enjoying every moment of her misery and was determined to play it out to the bitter end.

Chapter Three

When the light of dawn was struggling to show itself, Serena rose and went to the stables. The weather was blustery, cold and wet, which suited her mood. The sharp air sent shivers along her flesh, but the stables were a cheery glow of lantern light against the dark, unwelcoming exterior.

As the familiar warm smell of hay assailed her nostrils, she found the stables were already a hive of industry. Under the watchful eye of John, the stablemaster, on Sir Henry's instructions the stable lads and grooms had been hard at it for over an hour to have the horses ready for the marquess's inspection at first light. John hurried over to Serena, his shirt open down the front to reveal his barrel chest.

Pulling on her kid gloves and with her crop tucked beneath her arm, Serena paused beside a mare which had been led out of its stall and was being held by one of the grooms. She was vaguely aware that someone was on the other side of it, but because he was hidden from view she paid scant attention. 'Good morning, John,' she greeted him. 'Such as it is. I've known better mornings for riding over the heath.'

'Aye, the rain looks set in for the day, miss—but I know it'll take more than that to put you off your ride.' John chuckled. Having known Serena since birth, ever since Sir

Henry had introduced her to the horses as a toddler, he was aware that riding had become her abiding passion.

'I shall be leaving just as soon as our guest stirs himself. Is Polly saddled?'

'She's all ready for you—but the marquess has been here for the past half hour looking over the horses.'

Serena stared at him in astonishment. 'He has?'

'Yes,' replied the marquess, rearing up from the other side of the mare, startling Serena almost out of her wits. 'I was impatient to see for myself your father's splendid horses. I couldn't sleep, anyway,' he said, almost as an afterthought, as he ran practised hands over the horse he was inspecting.

Disappointed that he had reached the stables ahead of her, Serena stood and calmly watched Lord Brodie examine the horse in silence. He stood back and looked at it from every angle, picking up a hoof and going on to examine its teeth with a thoroughness that did not surprise her. She sensed that everything the marquess did would be controlled, certain and sure. Distracted, she saw he had removed his doublet, and that his white silk shirt was open at the throat to reveal the strong muscles of his neck.

He had the supple body of an athlete, vigorous and arresting, and with his wicked smile and shoulder-length raven black hair—a rogue wave spilled over his brow and shone like glass in the lantern light—Serena thought he would have made the most handsome pirate. His tight hose detailed his narrow hips and tautly muscled buttocks, bringing a flush to her maidenly cheeks.

Satisfied, Kit slapped the horse's flank, nodding for the lad holding it to take it back to its stall, before giving Serena his full attention. Observing the soft flush on her cheeks, he raised a questioning eyebrow and studied her for a long, drawn-out moment. A slow smile curved his lips. The sparkle in his eyes gradually evolved into a rakish gleam, and Serena's flush deepened. She had no way of discerning the workings of Lord Brodie's mind or where his imagination wandered.

'I'm sorry to have dragged you from your bed at such an early hour,' Kit said, his gaze unyielding. There was a suave, almost teasing note in his voice.

Collecting her crumbling poise and wanting to shatter his cocksure arrogance, Serena gave him a steely flash from her green eyes. 'You didn't,' she replied curtly. Looking at him with a stilted coolness, she tried to overcome the resentment she felt, although why she should feel such antipathy towards him when he had rescued her from being brutally ravished by Thomas Blackwell confused her. 'I'm in the habit of rising early to ride before breakfast. I'm sorry you had difficulty sleeping. The bed was comfortable, I hope.'

'Perfect. It was the noise of the storm that kept me awake.'

'And the horses? What do you think of them?'

'Splendid,' Kit replied, casting an appraising eye down the length of the stable. 'Their reputation has not been exagerated. John has been helpful in showing me those which are available.'

'And? Are you interested in purchasing any?'

'There are three I have my eye on—good, strong mares. I have a stallion from a good strain, big and in his prime. I'm keen to breed off him, which is why I want only the finest mares. I'll have a word with Sir Henry over breakfast.' Retrieving his doublet which was draped over a stall, he thrust his arms into the sleeves. 'Having decided to reserve my own horse for the hunt, I have taken the liberty of having one of the lads saddle your father's horse—one he won't be riding in the hunt, I've been told. You are up to riding in weather such as this, I hope,' he said, throwing her a challenging look.

Serena bristled. 'I never allow weather to put me off my ride.'

'Shall I accompany you, Mistress Carberry?' John inquired.

Much as she hated the idea of riding out alone with the marquess, Serena could see John was much too busy to leave the stables. 'That won't be necessary, John. I'm sure I shall be perfectly safe with Lord Brodie,' she said, cracking the crop against her skirts and moving to the stall where her mare Polly was waiting.

On seeing her mistress, Polly responded by arching her neck and whickering gently. One of the lads led her out into the yard followed by another leading a huge stallion. It was Monarch, Sir Henry's horse, black and as smooth as silk, with a long flowing mane and tail. Kit ran his hands over its quivering flanks.

'He's a splendid horse,' he breathed admiringly.

'Yes—my father's. Andrew also rides him when…' Serena faltered, biting her lip to stem the flow or words. She was usually so careful not to speak of her brother to strangers.

Kit looked at her with a keen eye. 'Your brother! You can speak of him to me, Mistress Carberry. He is a priest, I believe.'

'Yes,' she replied crisply, looking away. 'He's in Italy at present.'

'I know. Out of harm's way.'

Stung by his remark even though it had been spoken lightly, and ever sensitive about her brother's profession, Serena swung her head to look at him, on the defensive. Sparks of indignation flashed in her eyes, sorely incensed by what she thought Lord Brodie might be implying. 'My brother is no coward, Lord Brodie.'

'I did not imply that he was, and I hold nothing against him. I am merely saying that he would be wise to stay where he is. It's no secret that Catholic priests are being hunted the length and breadth of the country and are dealt with most severely when caught.'

A deep pain entered Serena's eyes, her expression suddenly one of anguish. 'Do you think I don't know that? Do you think I don't know the fate that awaits my brother if he were to return to England? Which is why I hope and pray he remains in Rome. At least there I know he is safe.'

Towering over her, Kit's lean, hard face bore no hint of humour or mockery. 'I apologise if my words offended or distressed you. It was not intentional, I do assure you. Now—shall we go?'

Kit locked his hands together to accept Serena's small booted foot, and was not surprised at the agility she displayed when he raised her up to the side-saddle, where she sat arranging her skirts while he strode towards his own mount.

Serena threw him a look as he hoisted himself into the saddle, seeing Monarch bunch his muscles and flare his nostrils. She smiled, wondering if she was about to see the arrogant marquess of Thurlow stripped of his dignity and tossed into a puddle on his backside.

'Take care, my lord. Monarch is not usually pleased at having strangers ride him. He is swift and also temperamental. You have to show him who is master right from the start. He's thrown many a stranger who sits on his back.'

Serena might as well have saved her breath. Kit controlled Monarch superbly as the horse reared up and pawed the air, his hooves hitting the cobbles so hard when he brought them down that it would normally have unseated the most experienced rider. But Kit remained firmly in the saddle, his lips drawn across his gleaming white teeth in a devilish grin. He flashed a triumphant look at Serena.

'A horse after my own heart. We'll get along splendidly,' he laughed. The lean, hard muscles of his thighs gripped the horse, and he kept him on a tight rein to control his high-stepping prancing as they clattered out of the yard.

The landscape was stark and colourless against the grey

sky, the wind buffeting them, exciting the horses. Shrouded in long cloaks they rode in silence, the fine drizzle washing their faces and dampening their hair exposed beneath their hats. Serena couldn't resist sneaking a glance at her companion. The sight of him on the black horse with its high-flying tail drew her admiration. Horse and rider flowed along together. After a while she halted, waiting for Kit to do likewise.

'My compliments, Mistress Carberry. You ride well.'

'Praise indeed coming from you, my lord,' she answered, not without a hint of sarcasm. 'Have you ridden with Dorothea on your visits to Carberry Hall?'

'I have not yet had that pleasure. Does she ride well?'

Dorothea hated riding and did not sit a horse at all well, but Serena would not abuse her by saying so. 'She rides well enough but, as you will have observed, Dorothea and I are not alike. Apart from being cousins and extremely fond of each other, we have little in common. She is quiet whereas I talk a lot. She is sweet tempered and mild mannered, whereas I am often quite the opposite. Dorothea also has a high opinion of almost everyone she comes into contact with, whereas I—well,' Serena said, throwing her companion an intriguing smile, 'my judgement is often critical and harsh. So you see, Lord Brodie, faults I have in plenty.'

Secretly, Kit couldn't complain about that. Serena was too warm and vitally alive for him ever to reprimand her for faults such as these.

Buoyed up by the ride and feeling a little mischievous, Serena had no qualms about laying down a challenge. Under normal circumstances Polly was no match for Monarch, but these were not ordinary circumstances. Lord Brodie was not familiar with the stallion and nor was he familiar with the tricky terrain, so she was confident she would win.

'We'll ride towards the woods over there,' she said, pointing towards the trees in the distance. 'But before we do I'll make you a small wager, my lord.'

Kit's eyes danced at the idea. 'A wager? When I recall your actions of yesterday, it seems to me that you are hell-bent on self-destruction.'

Serena's eyes flashed with a feral gleam. 'Must you remind me of that?'

A leisurely smile moved across Kit's lean brown face as his perusal swept her. 'I apologise, but you seem to have a genius for getting yourself into impossible situations. I might even be so bold as to say that not only do you go looking for danger, but you actually seem to thrive on it. What kind of wager have you in mind?'

'If I reach the woods before you, if I win, you return my handkerchief—the one you took from me yesterday, if you recall. If you win, you can keep it.'

Kit laughed heartily. 'I've accepted some wagers in my time, but a lady's kerchief? Never. I must point out that I never wager on certainties.'

'That's an arrogant assumption. Are you saying I will lose?'

Kit bowed his head in mock deferential respect. 'My dear Mistress Carberry, I wouldn't dare. It would be more than my life is worth. All I am saying is that I intend to win. Would you like a start?'

'What? And put you at an unfair disadvantage?' Serena laughed, warming to the chase, her cheeks dimpling quite deliciously. 'Come, my fine lord, you're wasting time.' Like lightning she headed in the direction of the woods, her swift and agile mare galloping off ahead of the marquess.

The heath was undulating with many open ditches and brackish, swampy bogs, making the going dangerous and the riding hard, but Serena and her horse knew every inch of the terrain. In exhilaration she exerted all her skill as she snaked her way around bogs and avoided ominous patches of slate-coloured water, clearing open ditches boldly and

unheeded, urging Polly in a final burst of energy towards
the woods.

Within the dripping confines of the trees stood the sinister figure of Thomas Blackwell. There was a cold gleam
in his eyes as he watched Lord Brodie prancing along beside Serena Carberry, observing the apparent closeness between them.

It had come to his notice that Brodie had recently become betrothed to Dorothea Carberry, a young lady he himself had a fancy for. Dorothea had all the necessary requirements Thomas considered important in a wife. She might
bore him weary, but she wouldn't complain at being left
tucked away in the country while he sought his pleasures
in London. More important, Dorothea was of the same Protestant faith as himself. Lord Carberry was also extremely
wealthy and would drop a fortune at his feet as soon as
they were wed, which would not go amiss.

But it would seem he had been supplanted in Dorothea's
affections by Brodie, which was not acceptable. He would
succeed in making Lord Carberry loath the arrogant marquess of Thurlow almost as much as he did himself.
Thomas touched the livid wounds on his cheek where Serena's fingernails had raked the flesh raw. He was not done
with her, either. But he would reserve his punishment for
that hellcat until he had dealt with Brodie, and then he
would show her how futile it was to struggle against him.
He would call on Lord Carberry at the earliest opportunity,
but for the present his vanity prevented him from doing so.

Pounding hoofbeats sounded alongside Serena and she
turned to see Kit separated from her by several yards, his
cloak spread out behind him like the wings of a giant hawk.
Monarch's hooves sent up splatters of water in his wake,
and his tail whisked like a pennon in the wind. With a
triumphant yell Kit pulled ahead on the big stallion, out-

pacing Serena's mare and reaching the woods first. With a broad smile he whirled round to wait for her, his horse's ebony coat slippery and shining with rain and sweat. Serena reached the trees a few yards behind him, her face flushed and breathing hard, her heart pounding.

'Congratulations,' she gasped. 'The race is yours.'

'And you are a gracious loser, Mistress Carberry,' Kit laughed, his voice full of admiration, thinking how delightful she looked with damp curls clinging to her face, her cheeks as pink as pink could be and her green eyes sparkling like early-morning dew drops on summer grass. 'I must congratulate you, also. You are an excellent horsewoman.' His eyes twinkled. 'However, I am glad I get to keep your handkerchief,' he said, producing it from a pocket inside his doublet. After placing it to his lips and sniffing its delicate perfume, he returned it to his pocket.

'We'll give the horses a chance to breathe and take a steady ride back. With any luck the rain might hold off until we reach the stables.' He glanced across at Serena as her horse fell into step beside his own. 'Did you really believe your mare could win against the power of Monarch?'

'Why not? You and Monarch may be superior in both stamina and strength, but I am familiar with the terrain, which is an important advantage. You can't deny that it's a testing course for any horse and rider—it could prove disastrous to someone unfamiliar to it.'

'My experiences have taught me how to read every kind of terrain.'

'Of course. I forget you are a soldier.'

'Was,' Kit corrected. 'I did serve for a time in the Low Countries, which was where Blackwell and I became acquainted—but we were never friends.'

'What's he like?' Serena ventured to ask tentatively. 'Our homes are close, but I cannot say that I know him well—not even after what occurred between us yesterday. It would not have happened had he not been drunk.'

Kit lifted a dark, winged brow, knowing that drunk or sober made no difference to Blackwell's behaviour. He was often to be found frequenting brothels where there were women aplenty to gratify his sexual appetite. But Kit could not tell this young maid the full extent of Blackwell's bestiality, of his brutal methods when dealing with others.

Blackwell's reputation was sealed by the aftermath of a massacre of nine Catholic women—five of them nuns—at a convent a short distance over the border from the United Provinces in Flanders. By all accounts Blackwell had stood and watched his soldiers violate the women before butchering them, and afterwards had drunk a toast to their deaths.

But well before that his arrogant bullying style had made him feared by his enemies and hated by the soldiers beneath his command. Kit had not met Blackwell before the massacre; in his opinion Blackwell was one of the cruellest, most dissolute officers he had ever known. Coming upon the murdered women at the convent, Kit had considered Blackwell's behaviour so outrageous that he was moved to complain to a higher authority. Shortly afterwards Blackwell's regiment had been recalled, but his reputation was blackened forever.

'I shall not offend your senses by giving you an account of Blackwell's crimes in the Low Countries. Be satisfied when I tell you that they were committed with the utmost barbarity, and that he should have been hanged for them.'

'Then why wasn't he? Lesser mortals would have been.'

'True. But Blackwell has friends in high places—not least Salisbury, the king's chief minister. Blackwell is famed more for his valour in the boudoir than on the battlefield,' Kit told Serena with a cynical smile. 'He is not a particularly savoury character and made many enemies when he was in the Low Countries. Living his life on a short fuse, he has a penchant for excessive carousing and brawling. Wherever he is to be found wars are not always confined to the battlefield. In between fighting he has led a pretty dissolute life, both in London and abroad.'

Kit was still curious as to how Serena had come to be alone with the villain yesterday. Did Blackwell accost her or did she meet him of her own free will? He had a strong suspicion it was the latter. 'Take care, Mistress Carberry,' he said, his tone grave. 'You would do well to steer clear of Blackwell. He is not a man to be trifled with or made a fool of.'

'Which I have discovered to my cost,' Serena replied drily, yielding her gaze to Kit's unwavering regard. 'Do not underestimate him either, Lord Brodie,' she advised. 'You may have cause to regret stepping in to rescue me. Since his father's death, Thomas has become a man of importance and influence.'

'Blackwell is also a man of arrogance,' said Kit, a wry twist curling his lips. Grinning suddenly, his eyes gleamed across at her wickedly. 'Do I detect a note of concern for me in your voice, Mistress Carberry? If so, I am deeply touched.'

Serena's cheeks burned and she lifted her head imperiously. 'Oh! You insufferable beast. You are mistaken.'

Kit laughed softly at her confusion, enjoying watching the fluid motion of her body as she sat her horse. His gaze dwelt on the rain running down her hat and settling on her hair, fascinated by the mass of tiny curls that clung to her face. Droplets of moisture clung to her thick lashes and upper lip. Unconsciously she licked them off with the point of her tongue, and Kit found this small action provocative in the extreme and felt the heat flame in his belly.

He felt the urge to pull her on to his horse, to hold her, to have her body pressed close and have his own mouth kiss away the droplets of rain from her lips, to taste their velvety softness, sure they would taste as sweet as honey. He looked straight ahead, the rain swirling all around them, knowing it was madness to think like this when his thoughts should be directed towards his betrothed, to that gentle creature soon to be his wife in shared tenderness, faith and mutual respect.

Forcing his mind along a different path, Kit remembered there were things he wanted to ask Serena concerning her father that had troubled him before leaving London and which, since reaching Dunedin Hall, now troubled him more.

'I'm glad to have this opportunity of speaking to you alone. There's a serious matter I wish to speak with you about,' he said after a long interval, his voice grave and his expression serious. 'If you will permit me, that is.'

'What is it?' Serena asked, glancing across at him curiously.

'Last evening you mentioned that Robert Catesby came to see your father to purchase some horses.'

Serena stiffened. Although she didn't look at him, she felt Lord Brodie's scrutiny. The time her father had spent alone with Sir Robert and Mr Grant when they had come to Dunedin Hall concerned no one but them, and was not to be discussed with this Protestant stranger she had no particular liking for.

'Yes, he did, but if you don't mind, Lord Brodie, I—'

'Understand that I have no wish to pry or to meddle in your father's affairs,' Kit interrupted quickly. 'I do so on this one matter only out of deep concern, for I strongly suspect that the purchase of those horses will, in time, have a far-reaching and disastrous effect on a great many people.'

With a growing dread, Serena looked at him, a feeling of doom curling itself round her heart. 'What do you mean?'

'Tell me—how many horses did Catesby and John Grant purchase?'

'Twenty, in all,' Serena told him with reluctance. 'Why is it important for you to know?'

Kit shrugged easily, watching her reaction closely. 'I'm interested. I consider it a number far beyond domestic requirements. Come. Why the secrecy?' he demanded, his eyes narrowing in question.

'I wasn't aware that I was being secretive. But if you are to see Mr Grant at the hunt later, perhaps you should ask him why he purchased them.'

'But would I get the right answer?'

'Why ever not?' Serena bestowed a brittle smile upon him. 'Although he might surprise you and tell you to mind your own business.'

'I expect he would—and I would not blame him in the slightest.'

'Don't concern yourself, my lord,' Serena said lightly, trying to ease the sudden tension that had developed between them. 'Let me put your mind at rest. The reason for the purchase is quite simple and can easily be explained.'

'Then tell me.'

'Mr Catesby is hoping to obtain a military commission under the Archduke Albert in Flanders, which, as you will know, being a military man yourself, is a perfectly legal venture after the signing of the peace treaty with Spain last year. He needs horses to form a troop of horse and my father has horses to sell. Have you reason to doubt what I tell you?'

'Yes, I do. Who told you this?'

'My father,' Serena replied, trying to sound calm, but she was more troubled than she cared to show.

'And you believe him?'

'Of course I do,' she flared, indignant. 'My father does not lie.'

'I would not insult him by accusing him of such. But I suspect that if this is what Catesby told your father, then it's a useful piece of dissembling on his part.'

'Please explain why you raise this matter with me and not my father? I find it extremely alarming and fear your reason for doing so.'

'You are right to fear it, since I do myself. I raise the matter with you because I feel you should know—that you must be warned. It's only right that you should be prepared should something of a vicious nature occur that may prompt awkward questions to be asked of Sir Henry. What we are discussing is of an extremely serious nature—one I have not discussed with anyone else. If something should happen—and my instincts tell me it will—events have a nasty way of implicating the innocent. I have no wish to see my own head roll by making myself conspicuous.'

Serena stared at him in horror, swallowing against a restricting tightness in her throat. 'Is it as serious as all that?' she whispered.

'Yes. I'm afraid it is.'

'And do you trust your instincts?'

'As a soldier I had to—and they could usually be relied upon. Since the king's renewed persecution of the Catholics, I suspect there is something afoot, that a scheme is being devised to bring down the king and his government. I also fear your father may have unwittingly been drawn in to become a part of it.'

'And how do you know this?' Serena asked with a sinking heart.

'Whilst in London I often supped with Catesby and his friend Thomas Percy at various taverns and eating houses, where they and their associates would meet. Robert Catesby, as you know, is a man of powerful charm and a dominating personality, who cuts a wide swathe in most company. He also has the easy ability of a man who can talk anyone into doing anything. I believe he is a convert to Catholicism—and, indeed, he has a typical convert's passion for his faith—with an ill-conceived ardour which will make him as willing to kill for it as to die for it.

'It's no secret that he is deeply involved with religious malcontents like himself. I can name several—all opulent and obstinate followers of their religion, most of them living in the Midlands in their large mansions. Some you know well,' Kit said, speaking gravely, his dark eyes surveying Serena closely, 'whose houses you visit to conduct the rituals of your faith—where priests are condemned to secret refuges to hide from pursuivants.'

Serena met his gaze calmly. 'You are well informed, Lord Brodie. The rituals are conducted with some trepidation, but their importance overrides any disquiet we might feel at the possible consequences should we be discovered.'

Kit nodded slowly. He admired her words, which were repeated by many courageous Catholic women playing a crucial part in the survival of the Catholic faith in the face of ruthless persecution.

'Bravely spoken,' he commented quietly. 'It is no secret that Catesby has been involved in failed conspiracies in the past. When Queen Elizabeth was moved to save him from a premature death after his involvment in the Essex conspiracy in sixteen-oh-one, he was fortunate to leave the Tower with his head intact. On the surface there was nothing unusual in the meetings I was privy to, but I am no fool and strongly suspect some enterprise more serious than cards or dice to be their reason for meeting.'

'And they let you, a Protestant, listen in?' Serena commented with irony. 'I beg your pardon, Lord Brodie, but that I cannot believe.'

'There was nothing secretive in the gatherings, which were social, jovial affairs, where not everyone was of the Catholic faith.'

'Then tell me this. Are you saying that my father could be endangering his life by selling his horses to Robert Catesby?'

'That depends on his true reason for doing so.'

'You don't believe they are to go towards raising a troop of horse for the Spanish Netherlands?'

Kit shook his head in consternation. 'I don't know. I doubt it and believe it to be a smokescreen to conceal the true purpose of the purchase of so many horses. But I have not the slightest inkling of what is going on.'

'What other reason could there be?'

'Unfortunately I cannot answer that. I only know that since King James has crushed Catholic hopes for liberty of conscience and will not meet certain concessions, there are those of a violent, impatient nature who will not wait with passive endurance for change to come about.'

Serena was appalled at what he was implying. 'But any violent means to bring about tolerance can never be justified. The sentiments of honest Catholics would never support this. If there is a conspiracy, then those involved must desist from such wicked actions that can only result in weakening the cause. But why does it interest you? Why involve yourself—especially since you are not of the Catholic persuasion?'

'I don't take religion seriously, I confess. I worship God in my own way and believe others should be allowed to do the same. I concern myself because your father is my friend, and I value his friendship. All I know is that it has been hinted that something of a seditious sort will be attempted by Catholics when Parliament reconvenes next month.'

Serena paled. 'But that is treason.'

Kit looked at her steadily. 'Only if it fails will it be called treason.'

'There have been failed conspiracies before. How can this be any different?'

'Well may you ask. Who is to say at this stage what will happen? But I believe that the Catholic cause, the throne and succession itself, could hang on this.'

'If my father is in danger I should know about it. If you

have discovered a conspiracy against the king, which may include him, please tell me.'

'I wish I could tell you more, but what I have are suspicions, nothing more.'

'Aye!' Serena exclaimed irately, clutching the reins tighter as at a threat. 'My brother said much the same to me before he returned to Italy.'

Kit looked at her sharply. 'Your brother has been here recently? He gave you warning?'

'Yes. Andrew has heard rumblings as far away as Rome, which brought him to England to see Father—no doubt to warn him about a scheme he was already aware of,' she uttered bitterly. 'He said much the same as yourself—that something ugly is about to manifest itself.'

Kit's brows drew together as he contemplated this latest information. 'As early as that! Then it is worse than I thought. Any conspiracy will have been deep laid and well and truly thought out by now—and I suspect Catesby, who is capable of great ambitions and is multitalented in the subtle stratagems of devising a master plot, of being the clever mind behind it. However, I very much doubt that Sir Henry is part of any such scheme.'

Serena was both angry and hurt, strongly suspecting that Andrew had withheld information because he believed such things were not a woman's concern. But how could it not be when she was the one left alone with their father? If it was her father's concern, then it was hers also.

'Why not?' Serena flared bitterly. 'It wouldn't be the first time. I love my father dearly, Lord Brodie, but he has been playing the Catholic cause since he was old enough to understand. He is not likely to stop now—even if it means dragging me in, too.'

'I'm sure your father loves you too well to involve himself in anything that would cause you harm.'

'His past behaviour leads me to think otherwise, and if he is involved then so am I by association.' Serena looked at Kit beseechingly as they rode into the stable yard, her lovely eyes wide and deeply troubled, stirred despite her earlier animosity by what he had confided to her. 'Lord Brodie, will you speak to him—discover how deeply he is involved? Please tell him of your suspicions and warn him.'

Kit shook his head slowly, jumping down from his horse when a stable lad came to take it from him. 'If he is embroiled in any conspiracy, then I doubt he would disclose it to me. But after saying that, my instinct tells me most assuredly that he has no hand in any scheme.'

The sky loomed dark and impenetrable, and by the time they reached the house a heavy downpour was unleashed on them. Kit paused, taking Serena's arm and turning her to face him. Knowing full well what she was going through, he was genuinely reluctant to leave her, but he had been right to speak to her. She must be warned in order to prepare herself should his suspicions be realised.

Serena blinked droplets of rain from her lashes as she looked up at Kit in question, seeing his expression was grave but calm.

'I won't speak of this matter again,' he said, 'but if it will make you feel easier I will have a word with Sir Henry later.'

It was his tone that caught all Serena's attention and made her look long at the swarthy, rather saturnine face. As she searched those dark eyes which studied her closely, she realised that Lord Brodie had not spoken to her casually. He was deadly serious about what he had confided to her.

'Yes, thank you. I would appreciate that. But please don't involve yourself further on my father's behalf. It could prove dangerous to you. But what can I do?'

'There is nothing you can do except wait for events to unfold.'

'What? Wait for my father to be arrested?'

'Let us pray it doesn't come to that.'

Chapter Four

As soon as Serena's carriage drew up outside Carberry Hall, Dorothea hurried out of the house with a welcoming smile.

'Serena! I should scold you severely for staying away so long.'

'The same could be said of yourself, Dorothea,' Serena laughed, embracing her cousin affectionately. 'Your absence from Dunedin Hall has been noted, too.'

'I'm sure it has. Father will not hear of me visiting Dunedin Hall for fear of me being converted to your faith. He's terrified I'll become so involved that I'll take the vows of a nun and live out my life in a convent abroad. I tell him I'm much too sinful to do that,' she said on a slightly cynical note, 'but he won't have it.'

'You? Sinful? If ever there was a person without sin, Dorothea, it is you,' Serena told her, and was sure this was true. Yet there were times when her cousin puzzled her, times when she suspected Dorothea was not the quiet mouse she would have everyone believe. She submitted herself to her father's authority without complaint. But, despite her poise, which she always managed to maintain throughout his angry blusterings, Serena suspected that rebellion stirred within her breast.

Serena entered the high impressive hall of Carberry Hall, the house in which her own father had lived before his marriage to her mother, Lady Anne, who had brought with her Dunedin Hall. A welcoming fire blazed in the hearth of a small sitting room; pulling her down on to the sofa, Dorothea hugged her cousin again.

'I have missed our chats. I have so much to tell you. How long can you stay? A few days at least, I hope.'

'I have nothing to hurry home for. Father's days are so taken up with hunting that he won't miss me too much. You look wonderful, Dorothea—and I hear dramatic changes have been taking place in your life. You are to be married, I believe…to the marquess of Thurlow.'

A fleeting frown touched Dorothea's brow and she looked a little pensive. 'Yes, that is so. Have you heard of him?'

'He stayed at Dunedin Hall last night, as a matter of fact. Lord Brodie came to purchase some of Father's horses for his stable at Thurlow.' Sensing that Dorothea felt no joy in her betrothal, Serena's curiosity was kindled. 'You can't have known each other long, Dorothea. When I last came to stay there was no mention of Lord Brodie.'

'You are right, and I confess I don't know him very well. The match was hastily made three months ago. Father has a high regard for him, having come to know him through the old marquess before he died. Since then, when Lord Brodie returned from the Low Countries to take over his inheritance, they have become better acquainted and he has called here on occasion.'

'It is a good match,' said Serena. 'According to my father he is influential in government and court circles—and thought very highly of by the king, too, by all accounts.'

Dorothea's lips formed a tremulous smile. 'I know. Since titles and wealth are paramount to Father, he was determined to choose the man with the highest rank who offered for me. Since the marquess was the only one who did, there was no choice to make. Lord Brodie is a fine man and always polite and very charming. He is also extremely handsome—as you will have seen for yourself.'

Yes, Serena thought, Lord Bordie was that—but he was also the most arrogant, insufferable and confounding man she had ever met.

'And do you want to marry him?' Serena asked gently, concealing her own tumultuous thoughts where that gentleman was concerned. Sensitive and sympathetic to her cousin's concern, she sensed Dorothea was far from reconciled to becoming Lord Brodie's wife. Marriage to that particular gentleman would be enough to raise troubling disquiet in any woman. If their roles were reversed, Serena would consider it just cause for complaint and violently oppose it. 'Are you happy about it?'

'I am happy enough and contented,' Dorothea replied, without enthusiasm, Serena observed. She noted a fleeting, wistful look enter her cousin's eyes which puzzled her. Was it possible that someone else had won a place in Dorothea's heart?

'I have no sentimental illusions about my betrothal,' Dorothea continued, 'and there have been no courtly love games between Lord Brodie and I. We do not know each other well enough for that.'

'But you will.'

'I know, and I can think of worse men to be paired off with. I have to obey my father. Neither he nor Lord Brodie are men to be refused lightly. Whatever Lord Brodie says and every impression he makes are serious and permanent. He's so formidable—so frightening, in a way—that I can't help feeling he will exert so much influence on me that I will not fulfil his expectations as a wife.' Dorothea sighed deeply. 'How I wish Father had chosen someone with a quieter disposition for me to wed.'

Serena was deeply sympathetic. 'Dorothea, if you have

any doubts about this marriage you must make them known
to your father.'

'How can I? Father is not to be gainsaid.' She smiled
softly into Serena's eyes. 'I'm not like you, Serena. You
have more nerve than the devil himself. I would never dare
question my father's judgement or his wishes—but I feel
that he, too, is having doubts about the match.'

Serena's eyes opened wide in amazement. 'Oh?'

'Yes, it's true. At first he was keen for me to marry the
marquess, but it has come to his ears that Lord Brodie may
have Catholic sympathies. A large number of his friends
are not just of the Catholic faith, but are also well-known
recusants—and you know Father's views on that. He is
afraid that Lord Brodie will by persuaded to become a convert, and that I, too, will be drawn in when we marry.'

'And what is wrong with that? I am of that faith—and
so is my father,' Serena exclaimed in a rush of indignation.

'But you are blood kin. I suppose that's different.'

'No, it isn't, Dorothea. It's hypocritical of your father to
practise standards contrary to his beliefs. If he denies one
then he should deny them all. But I don't think he need
worry on Lord Brodie's account,' Serena said, recalling the
conversation she'd had with that gentleman on this very
subject. 'I think if he had any Catholic leanings at all he
would have been converted long before now.'

Lord Carberry chose that moment to enter the room, having been told of Serena's arrival. Immediately and simultaneously both Serena and Dorothea rose from the sofa. In
a calm and dignified silence they waited for him to speak.

Lord Carberry was a hard and dispassionate man. Tall
and gaunt with the profile of a hawk, he bore no resemblance to his brother. His grey eyes under drawn-together
bushy eyebrows were grim and full of scrutiny as he looked
at his Catholic niece. It rankled sorely that his own brother
belonged to that faith, and he was determined not to allow
his daughter to follow suit by marrying into a Catholic fam-

ily. As meek and pliant as she was, she would become corrupted in no time at all.

Despite his grand title and vast estates, the marquess of Thurlow would have to make his views and opinions on that subject absolutely clear before any vows were exchanged between that particular gentleman and Dorothea at the altar.

It had recently come to his attention that Sir Thomas Blackwell was expected to return at any time to Ashcombe Manor. Should it be proved that the marquess did have Catholic leanings, it was not too late to give his daughter's hand in marriage to someone else—and Thomas Blackwell was eminently suitable. It did not cross his mind to consult Dorothea on the change he might make to her suitor, and he was selfishly insensitive to the fact that she might feel deeply resentful. The advantage would be in having a son-in-law whose religious opinions matched his own.

Lord Carberry greeted his niece stiffly. 'So, Serena, you have come to spend a few days with Dorothea,' he said at length.

'Yes. It's good of you to have me stay, Uncle. Dorothea and I have much to catch up on,' Serena replied respectfully. When she looked into her uncle's cold eyes that glared down at her, she could see that nothing had changed. No matter how agreeable she always tried to be when she came to Carberry Hall, it never would. Because of her religion her uncle did not want her in his house, and only tolerated her presence out of family duty and to please Dorothea.

'And Henry? Am I to expect a visit from him?'

'No, Uncle. Father has been invited to Woodfield Grange by Lord Payne for the hunting. It is expected to be a large affair. I believe Sir Everard Digby and other guests from nearby Coughton Court are included in the party.'

Lord Carberry chose that moment to clear his throat, unable to converse on this matter without sounding contemptuous. He had no particular liking for either Lord Payne or Everard Digby, both of them Catholics. Digby was a handsome, easygoing young man who was passionately fond of every kind of field sport and lived very well with his wife at Gayhurst in Buckinghamshire.

For hunting purposes, Digby had only recently rented the imposing Coughton Court from Thomas Throckmorton, who had gone abroad the previous year—another of his neighbours, Lord Carberry thought with deep condemnation, whose fortunes were heavily depleted by recusancy. No matter which way he turned, he was bedevilled by Catholics.

'We're expecting company in a couple of days,' Lord Carberry told Serena coldly, moving towards the door. 'Lord Brodie, Dorothea's betrothed, is to pay us a brief visit. He will be accompanied by a friend of his, Sir Ludovick Lamont. Sir Ludovick is a Scottish gentleman and highly thought of by King James—although I cannot say as much myself,' he grumbled without enlarging on the fact that he shared the resentment of most of the English for these greedy northerners, on whom King James lavished his attention and had been quick to promote to exalted positions at court. 'No doubt Dorothea will be impatient to introduce you to Lord Brodie. He's a fine man and is highly respected.'

'Lord Brodie and I are already acquainted, Uncle,' Serena stated.

Lord Carberry halted and turned sharply. 'You are?'

'Yes. He came to see Father yesterday to purchase some of his horses. After staying overnight Lord Brodie rode to Woodfield Grange with Father for the hunting.'

Lord Carberry went white. 'Did he, by God!' he responded explosively, his face reddening to the colour of a cock's comb.

'Yes,' Serena replied, undeterred and secretly amused by her uncle's irate response. After what Dorothea had told her about her uncle's unease following reports about the subversive company Lord Brodie often kept, she could well imagine what horrors must be passing through his mind on being told that his future son-in-law was cavorting about the countryside in the company of some of the most notable Catholic gentlemen in the land.

'Lord Brodie shares Father's enthusiasm for hunting and was reluctant to forgo an opportunity to indulge his passion for the sport in this part of Warwickshire, where, as you know, Uncle, some of the finest hunting is to be enjoyed.'

'And no doubt Henry gave Brodie every encouragement,' her uncle growled with heavy criticism, not missing Serena's subtle gibe as he opened the door. His bushy eyebrows drew closer together when he realised his niece was making light of the situation. But it would be wrong of him to unleash his anger on her for Lord Brodie's misdemeanours.

'The enjoyment is lessened if the company is not to one's liking,' he went on. 'It is my opinion that Lord Brodie should stop his foolery and would be better off employed elsewhere. There are those who would be more discriminating than to value the presence of subversives in their midst.'

Lord Carberry retreated to his study, unaware of the unspoken words of indignation that tempted Serena's tongue, for she knew perfectly well that her uncle considered her father to be one of those subversives. But however much she wanted to speak out in defence of her father and their faith, she must not forget that she was a guest in her uncle's house. Any protestations she might make would promptly be considered by him to be of a quarrelsome nature, and he would lose no time in having her dispatched back to Dunedin Hall. This would serve no purpose and only succeed in upsetting Dorothea and angering her own father.

Lord Carberry's sense of disquiet where the marquess was concerned increased by the minute, for it was becoming more apparent to him that he could not be trusted. However, feeling the need for caution, he decided not to raise the matter with the marquess until he had met with Sir Thomas Blackwell. There was no need to upset the apple cart altogether in case Sir Thomas did not find the idea of marriage to Dorothea agreeable and no other suitor was forthcoming.

Lord Brodie and Sir Ludovick Lamont, with their two respective servants, arrived at Carberry Hall on horseback. They were not expected for several hours. Lord Carberry had not yet returned home from visiting an acquaintance the previous day, which meant Dorothea would have to receive her betrothed alone. She was reluctant to meet Lord Brodie—and so was Serena, but for diffent reasons.

If it were not for the fact that the cold fingers of apprehension continued to claw at Serena over her father's activities of late, making her want to ask Lord Brodie if he'd had the opportunity of speaking to him on the matter, nothing would have tempted her to await his arrival, even at the risk of disappointing Dorothea.

Lord Brodie stepped into the hall with an arrogant stride, and when Serena's eyes travelled surreptitiously over him, it was blatantly obvious that he had much to be arrogant about. She noted with some surprise and annoyance the warmth that sprung to her cheeks and how her heartbeat quickened its pace at his presence.

Kit's dark eyes flicked over both young women, locking briefly with Serena's, who felt the impact of his ruthless vitality and pride, but it was on Dorothea that his gaze settled and softened.

Because he wanted to pursue a military career, Kit had always avoided marriage but, when his cousin had died and he had inherited Thurlow in Northamptonshire, at thirty years old he had considered it time he settled down and had put his mind to finding a wife. On meeting Dorothea, he had been appreciative of her in every aspect, and decided that she was a prize worth seeking. Lord Carberry had encouraged the match, and Kit was pleased that he did not insist on a long courtship, for he was impatient to take her to Thurlow. Taking her hand, he raised it to his lips.

'Dorothea! You are well, I trust?'

Dorothea flushed, her serious expression lightening. 'Perfectly, my lord,' she murmured shyly. 'But you are early. Your arrival has taken us by surprise. My father is not here to greet you.'

'Think nothing of it.' Kit smiled, his eyes twinkling. 'I was impatient to see you. I would have sent a note but it would have been a waste of time. The note and I would have arrived together.'

Dorothea turned to Serena, who had taken a stance a little behind her. 'Serena,' she said, 'you remember Lord Brodie.'

Serena stepped forward, her heart tripping a beat when she looked up into the handsome visage, struck by his stern profile. The strength of Lord Brodie's gaze held hers, and for the first time she had a glimpse of hidden qualities that would delight the senses, but quickly dismissed the thought. It was out of keeping with what she really thought of him.

'Of course. How good to see you again, my lord.'

'It is a pleasure to see you again, Mistress Carberry. You are more charming than I remember.'

Kit's tone was natural yet formal—almost ceremonial, Serena thought, experiencing a twinge of disappointment.

Kit turned to his companion. 'May I introduce a good friend of mine, Sir Ludovick Lamont. Ludovick this is Dorothea, my betrothed—and this is Mistress Serena Carberry, Dorothea's cousin,' he said after Ludovick had bowed over Dorothea's hand.

Serena turned her attention to the flaxen-haired gentleman, whose eyes swept over her appraisingly before giving her a decorous, courtly bow. She smiled charmingly.

Ludovick had been unable to take his eyes off Serena since entering the hall. At first he could only stare in mute appreciation—which was peculiar in one usually so bold. Sunlight lancing through the windows drenched her in its glow, caressing and playing on every delectable hill and hollow of her body. He noted her rich abundance of deep auburn hair and large green eyes staring calmly out of a face unblemished and milky smooth, and he found it hard to identify her with the young woman Kit had described to him on their journey to Carberry Hall.

Kit had informed him that she was exceedingly pretty and unattached. When Ludovick had raised an interested brow, his friend had laughed and warned him in mocking tones that it would take a courageous man to take on Serena Carberry. In Kit's opinion she had more mettle than most maids, and was a veritable virago when provoked. Kit had told him jestingly that while he was still in one piece it might be advisable to bypass Carberry Hall after all and continue on their way to Thurlow.

Seeing her in the flesh, Ludovick was all admiration and cocked a practised eye, happily relieved that he'd agreed to accompany Kit instead of returning to London as he had originally planned to do after the hunt. Had he done so, he would have missed the opportunity of meeting this gorgeous creature.

'It's indeed an honour to make your acquaintance, Mistress Carberry,' Ludovick said warmly, bent on winning this beauty for himself. Her smile melted his bones.

Serena considered him to be a buoyant, truly debonair young gentleman, with a bold look not unlike that of Lord Brodie's. His fine apparel, which was the height of fashion, lent him a rakish look. She already knew he was a Scot, so his accent—which was not as pronounced as some she had heard, and was derided by many in England who considered it uncouth—came as no surprise. Prior to his arrival at Carberry Hall, Dorothea had told her he had come south on King James's accession to the English throne, and that he was highly thought of by Their Majesties. Having been a member of their inner circle for many years, like most of the Scots who had come with the king and been given lavish positions of advancements at court, he was extremely unpopular.

Sir Ludovick was not as tall as Lord Brodie and was a little heavier and perhaps a few years younger, Serena thought. Unlike Lord Brodie, who was clean shaven, he sported a small, neatly trimmed square beard and moustache. There was an open honesty in his face and humour in his firm lips, and a quiet amusement in his alert blue gaze that could not fail to draw one's attention.

Serena liked him at once. Experiencing a spirit of mischief and moved by some feminine impulse of coquetry, she favoured him with a dazzling smile, without realising how devastatingly lovely she looked to the scowling marquess.

Kit noticed that she was much taken with Ludovick. Having drawn back a little, he watched his friend's unabashed perusal of Serena with a cocked eyebrow and a careless arrogance to hide a perplexing emotion that troubled him. His irritation began to stir against Ludovick—a man he had been at Cambridge with and who had remained his closest friend ever since. He took stock of this latest feeling, for it surprised him. It was not a feeling he was familiar with, and nor was it one he liked.

'And I imagined life would be dull in Warwickshire,' laughed Ludovick good-humouredly. 'I came to partake of a spot of hunting to enjoy the freedom and escape the confining, plague-ridden city for a few days, expecting to be bored witless and to find the company stilted, yet I have been pleasurably surprised. Not only did I find the hunting splendid—but the company gets better all the time,' he said meaningfully as his eyes quite shockingly raked Serena in her buttercup-yellow gown. 'Your beauty slays me, Mistress Carberry.'

'And you, sir, are a flatterer,' laughed Serena lightly. 'Do you live in London, Sir Ludovick?'

'Yes, I do. My family home is in Argyllshire, but I have taken a house close to the Thames, west of the city at Chelsea.'

'And are you able to indulge your passion for hunting there?'

'On occasion—although a great deal of my time is spent at court.'

'And do you see much of His Majesty?'

'Indeed he does,' Kit interrupted. 'As you will have observed, there is nothing modest about Ludovick. After travelling extensively abroad, he returned to England and the court—which he re-adapted himself to disgustingly quickly, I might add—having become comfortably embedded before the king left Scotland.'

'I protest, Kit,' Ludovick uttered in smiling indignation. 'You'll convince these two lovely ladies that I am idle and good for nothing.'

'And that is precisely what you are, Ludovick.' Kit chuckled. 'Your life consists of one pleasurable round of perpetual entertainment—and where better to find it than at Court. Queen Anne's own love of pleasure makes it a perfect place for a gentleman to be. And I have to say,' he said, looking meaningfully at Dorothea and Serena, who were smiling at this light banter between the two friends, 'that he finds favour with many of the ladies who flit around Their Majesties.'

'And you, sir, are no innocent yourself,' remarked Sir Ludovick.

'I never claimed that I was,' Kit replied with a slight satirical inflection in his voice.

The gentlemen's eyes met and the gentle taunt hit home. 'Aye, well,' said Sir Ludovick in good humour, 'we'll say no more, otherwise you will find the fair Dorothea may ask Lord Carberry to find her another suitor.'

'The court seems a merry place to be,' Serena commented. 'I always imagined His Majesty would be burdened down with affairs of state.'

'Not at the moment. At this present time the king is in Cambridgeshire, also indulging his passion for hunting. He leaves Salisbury and others to preside over the affairs of state.' Sir Ludovick smiled, his eye continuing to peruse Serena. This was beginning to create a deep sense of unease in Kit, although he could not explain why, because Ludovick was behaving as he always did when in the presence of a beautiful woman; it had never bothered him in the past.

'You have made an unsettling impression on Ludovick,' remarked Kit, gazing at Serena with a slightly mocking smile. 'I think he has other things of a softer passion on his mind besides hunting.'

'Not at all, Kit,' said Ludovick with a feigned look of outrage. 'I think of nothing else—although…' he smiled, a warmth entering his eyes when they rested on Serena '…it is hunting of a different kind that interests me just now— and I am certain it will prove to be just as pleasurable.'

Kit frowned with slight displeasure at Ludovick. 'Please ignore my friend, Mistress Carberry, and do not be offended by his boldness. He is quite shameless and a disreputable scoundrel. I assure you he has nothing honourable in mind.'

'Then I shall not take the slightest notice.' Serena smiled. 'And did you enjoy the hunting at Woodfield Grange also, Lord Brodie?' she asked, turning her attention to Kit, her eyes meeting his in questioning intensity, seeking some sign that would tell her all was well, and that what they had discussed on the morning of the ride had been nothing more than their imagination running riot. The quickening in his eyes told her he was not unaware of her train of thought, but all she received was a casual regard with a bland humour concealed in it.

'It was enjoyable,' he answered. Because of the growing concern he felt for Sir Henry, he had begun to feel protective of his daughter of late, and he didn't like the feeling. His mode of life and imminent marriage to Dorothea suited him. She did not pose the same threat to his emotions as her fiery, high-spirited cousin.

Stiffened by pride, Serena managed to dominate her disappointment. 'And my father?'

'He was hale and hearty when he left to return to Dunedin Hall. With such a large hunting party gathered together and deer in abundance to be hunted and caught, you don't need me to tell you that he was in his element at Woodfield Grange.'

'I'm pleased to hear it.'

Kit's dark eyes were unfathomable and seemed to glide over Serena in lingering appreciation, but he looked quickly away, leaving her disquieted. His laconic reply had given her not one glimpse of his inner thoughts and she would have to suppress the questions that burned in her, questions that caused her thoughts and wild imagings to run riot so they had become like a grotesque nightmare.

She must be patient, she told herself, and wait until she found the opportunity of speaking to him alone. This did not prove easy, for Kit kept himself aloof from her throughout the rest of the day and at dinner. But Serena was determined to find a way of speaking to him before they retired for the night. Lord Brodie and Sir Ludovick were to leave at first light, so she may not have another opportunity.

Lord Carberry returned home shortly after his guests had arrived. He was as surly as a bear with a sore head, after over-imbibing of his friend's liquor the previous evening. Presiding at the head of the dining table, he conversed with the gentlemen, but did not exert himself unduly to be pleasant. This brought a questioning frown to Kit's brow, closely followed by a flash of annoyance in his dark eyes.

'I apologise for making my visit a short one, Lord Carberry, and it is with regret that, due to pressing matters at Thurlow that demand my attention, Sir Ludovick and I must leave at first light. However,' said Kit, his eyes coming to rest warmly on Dorothea, 'I shall return very soon to arrange for the wedding.'

The older man considered his future son-in-law's superior size with a baleful glare, regretting the troth made between Lord Brodie and his daughter. 'I am not unaware that you have been in the district for several days now. Perhaps if you had not spent your time ingratiating yourself so well with Robert Catesby and Digby and the like, you would have found more time to spend with Dorothea.'

Kit's reply to the unconcealed rebuke was a sardonic lift to his brows. 'By your tone, sir, I take it that you do not care for Catesby?'

'No, sir, I do not,' Lord Carberry blustered, his temper already inflamed by Kit's disagreeable behaviour over the past few days. 'He's headstrong and a troublemaker—a man who exercises considerable personal influence over his contemporaries.'

'And he also happens to be a Catholic,' said Kit mildly.

'Aye—a Catholic—and a militant one at that.'

'Your worries are unfounded. Perhaps it will ease your mind when I tell you that I have seen neither Robert Catesby or Sir Everard. I went to Woodfield Grange to partake in the hunt on Lord Payne's invitation, and passed a few pleasurable days in the presence of his other guests. I see no fault in that. Neither of the gentlemen you mentioned were present.'

'I'm surprised to hear it—considering the friendship that exists between Catesby and Lord Payne.'

A hot retort rose quickly to Kit's lips but, remembering he was in Lord Carberry's house, he was wise enough to

bite back his words, realising there was more at stake here
than a matter of whose company he kept. Kit had little
tolerance for anyone questioning his behaviour, and Lord
Carberry was no exception. The man's arrogance in assuming he could dictate how he behaved pricked Kit's pride,
and though he made an effort to retain his good manners,
his eyes gleamed cold. He knew perfectly well what was
going through Lord Carberry's mind, for he was giving
every indication that he was beginning to regret the betrothal between himself and Dorothea.

'They did not make a Catholic of me, if that is what you
mean, and nor am I ripe for conversion. I can be very stubborn, Lord Carberry, when I want to be. I see nothing
wrong with the company I keep and will not apologise for
it—and if you are uncomfortable with the arrangement,
then that is unfortunate.' Kit delivered the pointed statement quietly yet firmly.

Whether Lord Carberry was aware of the depth of Kit's
anger or not he gave no sign, but whatever he saw in his
dark gaze made him let the matter rest without further dis-
cussion.

The moment caused a peculiar unease and Serena felt a
little chilled when she looked up and saw her uncle staring
at Lord Brodie. She could not begin to recognise the depth
of the older man's fury, but she saw the taut rage emanating
from every line of his body. There was a look of such cold
calculation in his eyes, which rested on his future son-in-
law, that she felt the cold hand of fear race up her spine.

Alone in her bedchamber, Serena paced the floor in frustration. She heard Lord Brodie and Sir Ludovick come upstairs and bid each other goodnight. Taking a deep breath,
her expression set and determined, and carrying a lighted
taper, Serena left her room. Lord Brodie might be shocked
when he opened his chamber door and found her standing

there, but she didn't care. He had a low opinion of her anyway, so why should she care what he thought.

To be seen entering his room when all the house had retired for the night would do irreparable harm to herself and Lord Brodie, and Dorothea would never speak to her again. But if he could ease her mind by telling her that her father was not involved in a conspiracy against the king, then she would consider her actions well warranted.

Chapter Five

Without hesitation Serena tapped softly on Lord Brodie's door. In a moment it was jerked open and he stood there, his eyebrows twisting dubiously when he saw her. Neither of them spoke; after glancing up and down the passageway, Kit snatched her inside, taking the taper from her and placing it on a chest by the door, a cynical twist to his mouth.

Having discarded his doublet, he seemed larger in the dim light; in fact, everything about him was forceful and exuded brute strength. Serena met his piercing dark stare, seeing something ruthless in that controlled, hard gaze. She stood tense, her back pressed against the door, afraid to venture farther, or to let her eyes wander to the huge four-poster bed which occupied centre stage. Already she realised it had been a mistake to venture into this lion's den.

Feeling compelled and at liberty to look his fill, Kit noted her silken lashes sweeping the soft rosiness of her cheeks, and that her glorious green eyes were dark and limpid in the soft light, her hair a living, dancing flame, with trailing tendrils escaping from the carefully arranged mass. Having removed the small pleated ruff she had worn earlier, he saw that a pulse throbbed gently in the long curve of her throat, rising slender and graceful above her gown of an iridescent blue. She was a fragile image of perfection,

standing before a man who dwarfed her. He met her gaze
with a querying, uplifted brow.

'Why, Mistress Carberry! What the devil are you doing
here? Are you not aware of the impropriety of such a visit
at this hour? Do you make a habit of entering a gentleman's
bedchamber at night?'

'Of course I don't.'

'Perhaps you've lost your way. Is it Ludovick's bedchamber you are searching for? If so, it's farther along the
passageway—although,' he said, a wicked gleam dancing
in his narrowed eyes and an infuriating quirk lifting the
corner of his mouth, 'there is every reason to suppose he
will be in bed by now. However, it will not reduce his
pleasure on seeing you. It comes as no surprise that you
are attracted to my friend. The eccentricities of his behaviour know no bounds and I know he would be delighted to
receive you.'

Serena's face warmed to a vivid hue at what he implied
and her eyes flared with ill-suppressed ire, but her mission
was too important to become sidetracked. 'He is charming,
I grant you, but if you cast your mind back to our first
encounter, as you saw for yourself, Lord Brodie, I am not
the sort to fall for a gentleman's flattery or be swayed by
his persuasion. It is not Sir Ludovick I have risked my
reputation to discuss.'

'Nevertheless, prepare yourself to be pursued. The way
Ludovick danced attendance on you all evening tells me
he'll not delay in calling at Dunedin Hall to ask your father's permission to pay court to you.'

'I don't think so,' Serena replied sharply. 'When Sir Ludovick rides with you to Thurlow tomorrow, I have no
doubt whatsoever that I will become just another woman
he has passed a few pleasurable hours with. The moment
some other takes his fancy he will forget ever meeting me.'

'I doubt it. You have him well and truly hooked. Ludovick is my closest friend and I gave him the best advice

I could. I told him what a hot-tempered little shrew you can be when provoked, but he wouldn't listen.'

A fierce light sparked in Serena's jewel-bright eyes. 'You did what? How dare you abuse my reputation and good name by discussing me with your friend? If Sir Ludovick has any sense at all he will ignore your conceited opinions.'

Kit chuckled infuriatingly, delighting in her indignation. 'He won't. He never has before. Now, tell me why you are here.'

'I apologise for intruding, but I have to talk to you.'

'Talk? How disappointing. I was hoping you might have other, more pleasurable things in mind.'

Meeting his gaze, Serena felt her flesh grow warm. His eyes had grown darker and smouldered with an inner light, passing over her in a simple caress that seemed to strip her bare. His gaze dipped to the creamy swell exposed above the lace trim of her bodice, which brought two indignant high spots of colour to her cheeks.

'Do you forget so soon that you are betrothed to Dorothea, my lord? I find your eyes far too bold and eloquent for my liking.'

Kit arched his brows and gazed down at her with sardonic amusement. 'Forgive me, but it is not often a lady comes visiting me in my chamber like a wraith in the night. You either underestimate your charms by seeking me out in this clandestine manner, or overestimate my ability to resist you, which I shall strive to do because—as you were so quick to point out—of my betrothal to your cousin and my determination not to hurt her. But you must see that you have placed me in an extremely delicate situation. Aren't you uneasy, being here alone with me?'

'I am not afraid of you.'

Kit chuckled softly at the forthright thrust she gave to her chin. 'You give no indication that you are—but perhaps you should be.'

As his gaze leisurely assessed her, Serena could not

imagine what he found that was of so much interest. He was the epitome of the confidant, arrogant male, which made her all the more aware of her own weakness and fragility, despite her attempts to appear otherwise. She was immensely relieved when he appeared to recollect himself and his mood changed. Frowning, he stepped away from her and went to where the fire had burned low and glowed in the hearth. One fist was pressed into the hollow of his waist and his other arm supported him on the stone mantel, one foot placed upon the raised hearth. When he turned the harsh lines of his face had softened, all trace of his former mockery having vanished.

'I'm happy that you did not leave before my arrival,' he said quietly, having unconsciously hurried to Carberry Hall earlier than he had intended, should she have decided to do just that, while telling himself it was his eagerness to see Dorothea that was the cause of his haste.

'You stand at the door like a deer sensing the hunter. Come over to the fire where we are less likely to be over- heard. The situation is delicate enough without making it worse by drawing attention to ourselves and causing a scan- dal in the middle of the night. Even after so short an ac- quaintance, I believe I know you well enough to know that what you have to say must be serious, otherwise you would not be here.'

'The only reason I did not return home was to ask you if you have spoken to my father. Please don't think I re- mained for any other reason. With every sight of you I am reminded of my own folly that day we met, and I deeply regret my stupidity. I had to speak to you.' Responding to his order, she moved warily towards him. 'I realise how it will look if anyone finds me here, but it was a risk I had to take.'

'You are an extremely brave young woman.'

'Bravery has nothing to do with it. In view of everything,

I had no choice. You are leaving early in the morning so I will not have another chance to speak to you.'

Kit indicated a chair close to the hearth. 'Please, sit down. I should have known after our conversation how anxious you would be.'

Serena perched stiffly on the edge of the chair, glad of its support. 'Lord Brodie, ever since our conversation I have been living on a razor's edge. It pains me greatly to have to humble myself in this manner—to you of all people—to discover what my father is up to, but with Andrew in Italy there is no one else I can turn to. The thoughts going through my head are driving me insane. I cannot endure it.'

Kit could see she was full of apprehension and knew exactly what it had cost her to seek him out. He regretted his earlier mockery and should have known better than to make what she had to say harder than it was. He should have made every attempt to put her mind at ease—but after what he had noted on the hunt, he couldn't do that. Regarding her in silence, a deep frown drew his brows together and for a moment he was thoughtful, his gaze holding hers with a penetrating intensity.

'I apologise. I can see my revelations have upset you. It is my fault you are so distressed. Haven't you considered asking your father?'

Serena was sure there was more than the conventional apology in his words. 'Of course I have, but I know he would fudge the issue and tell me it was the wild imaginings of my mind if I were to mention plots to him. Did you speak to him?'

Kit shook his head. 'I'm afraid not. The opportunity never arose.'

Her hopes sinking, Serena was swamped with disappointment, and the sudden gravity of Kit's manner sent a blade of fear stabbing through her. 'But you still believe something awful is about to happen?'

'Yes, I do—and very soon. Parliament is to reconvene in a few days' time. I suspect that whatever is afoot will manifest itself then. The whole event at Woodfield Grange was charged with secrecy and caused me a certain amount of disquiet.'

Serena's heart stopped in sudden fear and she stared at him wide eyed. 'Why? What do you mean?'

'There was a tension in the air. The atmosphere was not conducive for relaxation or enjoyment.'

'But I thought you said—'

'What? That the hunting was splendid and that your father enjoyed himself? I did not speak loosely. He did—as did everyone present who belonged to his faith. Outwardly there was normalcy about the whole proceedings, but there was a tension among the gentlemen—with an underlying violence on leash. Clearly a general level of secrecy has been maintained, but the mouths of servants and wives cannot be stopped.

'My uncertainty leads to speculation about a stir but, as to the precise form of this stir, I cannot name it. There were whispers among certain Catholic wives. They fear some disorder is brewing—that some extraordinary event is anticipated. I fear that Catesby's emphasis on raising a troop of horse to enter the service of the archdukes in the Netherlands is nothing more than a fabrication to distract attention from the true nature of the action.'

'Do you suspect a rising? Is that it?'

Kit didn't answer straight away; when he did, he spoke thoughtfully, picking his words. 'I am assailed by a multitude of questions but I can find no firm answers. I have listened carefully and sought to put myself inside a Catholic mind—but nothing is that simple, nothing is obvious. Given the evidence, there is every likelihood there will be a rising. It is rumoured that it is their intention to deliver the king a petition for tolerance. Perhaps they mean to back it up with force.'

'That does seem plausible.'

Kit nodded. 'I may be wrong. But you are right. At least there is sense in that. I am disturbed that there are so many splendid horses being collected in various stables in the Midlands. If there is to be no Flanders mission, then for what other purpose but a rising, I ask myself.'

'Do you think it will be concentrated in the Midlands— if there is a rising?'

'No. It has to be on a greater scale for it to be of effect. Behind it all I sense Catesby's hand. With his authority reaching into the innermost ranks of the Catholic Order, anything could be manoeuvred by his ambitious scheming.'

'Is he a good friend of yours?'

Kit shrugged. 'He and his associates made me welcome, but I did not become one of their intimate circle.'

'Was he present at the hunt?'

'No—but at every point his name was on everyone's lips.'

Serena shook her head in a helpless gesture as she tried to comprehend it all. 'I wish I understood all this. What can they achieve? If they manage to bring down the king, the crown will pass to his son Henry. How can this aid the Catholic cause? I suppose that, if it does succeed, it will bring about changes for the Catholics.'

'And if it fails the damage and scandal will do their cause no good and will be so great that both here and abroad they will condemned.' Kit frowned. Trying to work out what was going on was like trying to find his way out of a maze without an exit. 'It's a puzzle, I know. The only obvious point about it all is that it's a conspiracy involving Catholic fanatics. They have a long tradition of subversive activity.'

Serena's lips twisted in a wry smile. 'That I do know,' she said, thinking of her father's lifelong dedication to the cause.

'My own concern,' Kit said quietly, almost to himself as he continued to look into the embers, 'is the timing of my visits to Warwickshire—to my taking part in the hunt and even buying horses from your father's stables. I have a distinct feeling that when something does manifest itself, my own involvement—no matter how innocent—will be misconstrued and I shall be brought down by it.'

Serena gasped, horrified by what he was saying. 'No—surely not. You are not a Catholic and have played no part in any conspiracy. You bought horses from my father for perfectly legitimate reasons.'

Kit's mood had darkened and his expression was grim. Although he looked calm and in control, his mind was in a continual turmoil of conflicts. 'Nevertheless, it is possible that I may be suspected of complicity. Anyone connected with plotting against the king will be arrested. Men have lost their heads for less.'

'Then you must distance yourself from all of this.'

'I intend to. But already it may be too late. I am not alone, either. I am not the only one not of their faith to be at their gatherings, and I believe it was to their advantage to have unsuspecting Protestants in their midst in order to deflect suspicion that anything is afoot. Whatever offence occurs, myself and others will not escape suspicion.'

Serena was scarcely able to grasp the reality of it all as Kit's words fell like hammer blows against her heart. As she stared up into his dark eyes a chill seemed to penetrate to her very soul.

'And what about my father? I am so afraid that he is involved—that he is one of those conspiring against the king. Dear Lord! It will ruin him. All his goods and estate will be forfeit to the Crown—and this time he will hang for sure. May the Lord save him,' she whispered.

The prayer was heartfelt and Kit looked at her closely, seeing panic in the eyes of this usually assured young woman. In truth, Kit didn't know if Sir Henry had been made privy to what was to take place, but he had certainly implicated himself by selling his horses to Catesby. Kit would not distress Serena by saying so, but he would not give much for that gentleman's life either. It would be a hard thing indeed to escape the full consequences if he were to be charged with rebellion and treason.

'In my foolishness I hoped that Father would put it all behind him, that no more would he endanger his family and others,' Serena continued, 'but it is not to be. His determination to carry on his crusade and to continue to involve himself in plots and conspiracies was too much to be borne by my mother, who grievously endured many throughout their marriage.'

'You have just cause to be angry and upset by your father's actions, but he loves you well and does not seek to hurt you. If my words have frightened you, I apologise. It was not my intention to upset you.'

Kit's voice was surprisingly gentle and the unfamiliar sound caused an embarrassed flush to sweep Serena's cheeks in a crimson flood. He was looking down at her, and for a moment she fancied there was a strange expression in his face she had not seen before.

'You have not upset me, and do not forget that my sole purpose for coming here was to be put in the picture. It's important for me to know so that I can perceive the danger and act upon it should the time arise.'

'The picture may not be so bleak. I may be wrong.'

'And I am afraid that you may be right,' Serena whispered. She stood up quickly. 'I have stayed long enough. I must go.'

At the door she turned, drawn to his gaze. 'You will take care, my lord?' She didn't know why she asked him this, and she was confused by it, considering how she felt about him, but for some unknown reason it was important to her that he did. There was an intensity in her lovely eyes that clearly conveyed the depths of her concern.

Having followed her to the door Kit nodded, moved by

it. 'Never fear, madam. Don't let it trouble you. I am capable of defending myself if I must.'

The light in the dark depths of his eyes was as enigmatic as it was challenging to Serena and, unexpectedly, she felt a quiver of excitement. The quickening in Kit's eyes told her he was aware of that response. Her rampaging emotions and imaginings when she wondered what it would be like to love such a man disturbed her greatly, and she tried to push them away, but they were to become like mischievous imps playing a teasing game, flitting to and fro through her mind when she least expected it.

The long-enduring ache of suppressed passion stirred Kit's blood. He suddenly wanted to remove the pins from her glorious hair and spill the heavy tresses free of their confinement, to run his fingers through the silky mass. For a moment his resistance wavered, making him pause. It was a small warning, but a warning all the same. Too often of late he had found his thoughts straying to her and he scowled, pulling himself up sharp, determined to keep a tighter rein on his attraction to her.

'Goodnight, Mistress Carberry. Try and get a good night's sleep.'

'I will—and I trust you will do the same, my lord.'

With a rapidly beating heart Serena sped silently along the dark and narrow passageway, which twisted and turned and weaved its way between the rooms of the upper storey of the great house, breathing a huge sigh of relief when no floorboards creaked beneath her feet to betray her presence. Carberry Hall was full of shadows, weird noises in the rafters and wind in the chimneys blowing so loud and fierce again tonight that it rattled every shutter in the house.

The storm had been building up by slow degrees throughout the day, and now the wind had reached its height and went searching over the dark landscape in a frenzied dance. A savage bolt of lightning seared the sky, illuminating the room when Serena entered, closely followed by a loud clap of thunder. Irately she pulled the drapes across the window to close out the storm which, to her anguished and wretched mind, was a harbinger of darkness and doom.

When Lord Brodie and Sir Ludovick had left for Northamptonshire the following morning and Serena had returned to Dunedin Hall, Lord Carberry, even more disquieted by his future son-in-law's recent behaviour, lost no time in sending a message to Ashcombe Manor inviting Sir Thomas Blackwell to Carberry Hall.

Serena listened in silence over dinner while her father enthused about the splendid hunting he had enjoyed at Woodfield Grange and the company he had kept, but she sensed an underlying tension and a nervous excitement about him. Determined to speak to him about the matter which so concerned her, she followed him to his study afterwards. He was standing by the window staring out when she entered and, when he turned, she caught an expression on his face which made her recall Lord Brodie's words of the secrecy and tension he had sensed among those present at Woodfield Grange—a waiting for something to happen.

Sir Henry's expression quickly changed to one of fatherly concern when he looked at his daughter, noticing how pale she looked and recalling how quiet she had been throughout dinner.

'You look pale, my dear. Are you feeling unwell?'

'No. I am quite well, Father. There is a matter I must speak to you about. I am deeply concerned about something which has recently come to my notice.' Impatient to have her say and brave whatever her father told her, the words came tumbling out in a rush. At first he looked so shocked she thought he had been taken ill, but the shock was shortlived. After traversing varying degrees of disbelief, perplexity and horror, his expression became grim, his manner telling her with cold certainty that what she suspected was true and that the unthinkable was about to happen.

'And I need not ask how you came by all this,' Henry said harshly, interrupting her at length. 'This is nothing but conjecture. It is evident to me that Kit has been speaking to you.'

'Only because I asked him. I had suspicions of my own long before I spoke to Lord Brodie—and besides, he, too, suspects something is afoot, but knows nothing as to the nature of it.'

Sir Henry threw her a look of impatience, clearly angry and ill at ease at being confronted with this by his daughter. 'God help me, girl! Suspicions—that's all they are. If you are not sure of anything, don't go jumping to conclusions. These suspicions are in your imagination and as always will come to nothing.'

'No, Father. Not this time,' Serena persisted, refusing to be put off. Defeat was something she would not accept. 'Andrew is aware of something being hatched and is concerned that you may be involved. He spoke of it to me before leaving for Italy.'

'Aye, he said the same to me, telling me that he had it from a reliable source in Italy that something is brewing here in England. But we hear of plots and conspiracies being uncovered every day. Why this sudden alarm?'

'Please, Father,' Serena entreated. 'I am no longer a child, so please do not treat me as such. Just this once be frank with me. I know something is about to happen, and I am deeply concerned as to the nature and seriousness of it. Considering your past record for insurrection you can hardly blame me. I know that much of what you do is for the good of the faith—but can't you spare a thought for me...for Andrew and James? Must you persist in embroiling yourself in plotting and scheming? Must you always solve things so dramatically—so violently? Will you never trust to reason?'

'Serena,' Sir Henry said sharply, surprised and secretly alarmed that any action of his had brought about this unexpected outburst, 'whatever I have done I have done because I considered it necessary and to advance the faith.'

'I know that. But what does it all mean? Has everyone behind this gone mad?'

'How much do you know?'

'Nothing. Nothing at all—only whispers…rumours, nothing more, but they are enough to frighten me. Everyone is so secretive.'

'And that is how it must remain.'

'Father, can you look me in the eye and tell me there is no conspiracy to bring down the king? Can you tell me in all honesty that the horses Robert Catesby bought from your own stable are to go towards raising a troop of horse intended for the Spanish Netherlands?' She waited for the words that would dispel her fears, but they never came. Instead her father's shoulders drooped and he seemed to age ten years before her eyes.

Sir Henry stared at his daughter, seeing the pleading in her eyes, and he felt strangely helpless and ashamed before it. Something of a dark and sinister nature was about to explode upon the nation, but he could not tell her what it was for he did not know the precise nature of it himself.

Despite being a prominent figure in the Catholic community in the Midlands, because he was not in robust health and was no longer a young Catesby or a Digby, when Catesby had come to purchase horses he had done his best to convince Sir Henry they were for the very purpose Serena had just mentioned. Catesby had even gone so far as to suggest that Henry's son James might care to join his troop when he had finished his education at St Omer at Calais.

But Henry had sensed it was a useful piece of dissembling Catesby used with others, and that he and his contemporaries no longer considered him suitable for the engineering of a plot, which offended and pained him greatly. Henry had learned to keep his thoughts to himself over the years. To speak them aloud could lead to disaster, which was why, in this instance, he would keep his own counsel and wait for events to unfold. He had always spoken to Serena of truth and honesty, and of the respect one could earn if one always abided by this and was sincere, but at that moment he was unable to abide by this doctrine he preached to others. He shook his head slowly, avoiding her gaze.

'Nay, lass. I cannot.'

'That is as I thought,' she said quietly. 'Then it is damning indeed, Father.'

When news of the Gunpowder Plot broke—a plot to destroy the Parliament, the king, the royal family and the government—the spirit of vengeance and hatred it stirred within Protestants and those it was directed at made Catholics—both militant and innocent fearing a general massacre—tremble in its wake. A world which had been cruel to them before was about to become sadistic.

It was past midnight at Dunedin Hall and rain was falling heavily when news of it reached Sir Henry Carberry and his daughter. In the silence of the dark hours Serena strained her ears to listen, wondering what had disturbed her. Hearing the sound of thundering hooves heralding the approach of a large party of riders, immediately she was wide awake and out of bed.

Pulling back the heavy drapes, she peered anxiously out of the window, seeing the dark shapes of about thirty men and horses. Fear of unknown things seized her and, grabbing her robe, she wrapped it round her, dashing out of her room and down the stairs. As if expecting the arrival of these horsemen, Sir Henry was fully dressed. He went out to them, ordering Serena to remain indoors.

Obeying his unusually harsh command, Serena shivered

with fear and cold as she listened to their voices over the noise of the beating rain. They were low and urgent, and she was unable to hear what was being said. Soon the horsemen were on the move again, leaving a few tired horses in exchange for fresh ones.

When Sir Henry returned indoors Serena went to him, swallowing hard, for a sudden dryness had almost stuck the sides of her throat together. There was a sudden death-like silence in the house, an absence of sound that was almost audible.

'Father! What did they want?'

Shock and disbelief stared out of his eyes, and also a bleakness Serena had never seen before. She knew that her worst fears were justified and a chill of terror shivered through her.

'Horses,' Sir Henry said at length.

Serena caught his arm when he turned from her. 'Father,' she demanded in desperation, 'tell me what has happened.'

He looked at her hard. 'The plot has been discovered. We are all betrayed.'

'Betrayed! Why—what do you mean?'

'It's a total shambles,' Sir Henry muttered. 'All is lost.' His expression turned from shock and disbelief to one of resignation. 'I speak the truth when I say that I knew nothing of this—but it would seem that I am to be ruined by it. I suspected there was to be a rising in the Midlands— but that was all. I knew nothing about the heart of the treason.'

'And now you do?'

'Yes,' he replied, speaking in an even voice. 'I have just been told that one of the conspirators, with thirty-six barrels of gunpowder, has been found by searchers in a room beneath the House of Lords. The plan was to blow up Parliament House—along with the king, the royal family and the government.'

Serena stared at him in shocked disbelief. 'But—but that is monstrous.'

'The timing of the explosion was intended to be the first action of a greater scheme. It was to coincide with a rising in the Midlands and for all loyal Catholics to rally to the cause—to unite in armed rebellion and seize control.'

'So my suspicions were correct. That was the true reason why the horses were needed,' Serena whispered, understanding at last.

'Yes, but the most important objective was to kidnap the young Princess Elizabeth, the king's daughter housed at Coombe Abbey, near Coventry.'

Serena was puzzled. 'But how would that further their cause? The Princess Elizabeth is a Protestant.'

'It was their intention to install her as a puppet queen.'

'But the king and queen have other children—the five-year-old Prince Charles and the baby, Princess Mary. What was to happen to them?'

'If the plot had succeeded, Prince Henry and probably Prince Charles would have been with the king at the House of Lords.'

Serena felt sick with horror, deeply affected by this. 'And those two small boys would have perished. Oh, Father,' she whispered, 'such violent methods cannot be justified.'

Sir Henry smiled cynically. 'Catesby and his contemporaries long ago rejected passive endurance, Serena. They consider the necessity of the Catholics of such importance that the enterprise would be of sufficient worth to compensate for the innocent deaths.'

'Nothing can justify that.'

'I know. Such an act cannot be condoned. But it was on Elizabeth their attention focused. No baby or small child would suffice. Elizabeth would make a more viable figurehead, and she is ideally placed for the plotters' purposes at Coombe Abbey. It was their intention that she would be raised as a Catholic and marry a Catholic.'

'Then thank the Lord it failed. I assume those gentlemen just now were the fugitives.'

'They were. Most of the leading conspirators, too. It appears that their expectations of gathering support have come to nothing—and the company is shrinking fast as others leave. They came in the hope of acquiring fresh horses, which I gave them. They also took those I sold to Lord Brodie which he has not collected. He will have to be reimbursed, of course.'

A sadness came into his eyes and he placed an arm around Serena's shoulders, leading her slowly back up the stairs, oblivious to the servants who had been woken by the unexpected and unwelcome guests. 'I'm afraid my stables are almost empty now, Serena. It will take a long time to make them what they once were.'

A lump rose in Serena's throat, knowing how dearly her father had loved his horses. Suddenly she turned and looked at him in alarm as a thought occurred to her. 'Polly! They have not taken my horse?'

'No, my dear. In anticipation of just such an event, I instructed John to have both Polly and Monarch stabled separately.'

'Father, did those men ask you to join them?'

'They did—but I'm too old and too battle-scarred to go gallivanting around the countryside in support of a lost cause. And anyway,' he murmured in a voice filled with so much bitterness that it prompted Serena to turn and look at him, making her realise that her father's enthusiasm for the concerted efforts over the years to further the Catholic cause and bring about toleration was beginning to wane, 'I wouldn't have had the stomach for it in the first place, had I been given prior knowledge of the inner workings of this particular plot.'

Serena was relieved and comforted to hear this, but later, when she learned that warrants had been issued for the arrest of those privy to one of the most horrible treasons ever contrived, all her old terrors came back to haunt her.

A hue and cry ensued, having spread from London to the surrounding counties, when government officials suspected that any conspirators in London would have flown. But they had one of the conspirators caught at the scene of the intended crime—John Johnson, an alias assumed by Guy Fawkes—who would be put to the torture to divulge the names of his comrades.

Searches were to be concentrated on the Midlands, where a solid belt of opulent and obstinate followers of the Catholic religion lived. Serena knew it would not be long before attention became focused on Dunedin Hall.

Since leaving Carberry Hall, Kit had been in a dilemma, for no matter how hard he struggled to concentrate on the sweet face of his betrothed, it was no easy matter dismissing Serena from his mind. He saw her as she had been when he had first seen her, courageous and beautiful and filled with innocent, angry passion. He remembered the sensual grace of her body as it had moved as one with her horse when they had ridden together, and how she had told him of her concern for her father with such tender pride.

Kit also remembered how she had looked when she had sought him out in his room, of the sexual aura that surrounded her, and he remembered other things about her, things a man already betrothed to a maid of incredible sweetness should not. But he was like a man on the dizzying edge of an abyss, about to plunge downward.

When news of the inner workings of the Gunpowder Plot reached him at Thurlow, he was as shocked and horrified as the next man, but he was also filled with dread because of the danger it posed not only to himself but also to Sir Henry Carberry and Serena. His concern deepened when he learned that, a few days after the plot had been uncovered, several of its principal members had been killed when

the Sheriff of Worcestershire and a force of men had surrounded and stormed Holbeach House in Staffordshire,
where the plotters had sought refuge.

Robert Catesby, who was suspected of being at the centre
of the plot, and Thomas Percy, a charming, dangerous
knave according to some, were among the four killed.
Those captured had been conveyed to the Tower.

Uneasily aware of his known connection to the plotters,
Kit knew it would be difficult for him to discount any association with the traitors—and, he thought with cynicism,
after this there would be many gentlemen in England less
likely to profess to the Catholic religion than before the
plot was uncovered.

Not yet having brought the horses he had purchased from
Sir Henry to Thurlow, Kit dispatched Robin to Dunedin
Hall to arrange for their delivery, and also to assess the
situation there. But, unbeknown to him, Robin never
reached Dunedin Hall. Nearing Ripley, the unfortunate
young man encountered Thomas Blackwell, who had been
in London since before the uncovering of the plot and had
only returned to Ashcombe Manor late the previous day.

Thomas was accompanied by three government officials—just a few of many who were sweeping the county
with a zealous fervency. They were investigating and
searching Catholic houses for fugitives of the plot and em-
inent Jesuit priests who, it was assumed, indoctrinated the
English Catholics with the belief that they should defend
the supremacy of the Pope to that of King James. So far
their search had yielded nothing but a few terrified Catholics.

Thomas remembered Kit Brodie's servant—in fact, he
remembered every humiliating detail about the day his
pride had been savagely mauled. No matter how fervently
Robin protested, Thomas told his companions that this
young man's noble master was known to have Catholic
sympathies, and that he belonged to a family which had

branches of that faith. He also told them that a good many obstinate Catholic noblemen could be counted among his friends—among them Catesby and Digby.

Knowing this, Thomas's companions were easily persuaded. Deciding that the marquess of Thurlow was worth further investigation, young Robin was dispatched to London and the Tower, where he would undergo interrogation.

Thomas's smile was one of evil, murderous satisfaction as he watched Robin go. From the moment he had heard of the Gunpowder Plot, he knew it was the leverage he needed to topple the illustrious marquess of Thurlow from the elevated height of his pedestal. His ploy was to discredit one of Their Majesties' favourite lords, to tarnish his whiter-than-white reputation, and he was not above telling lies to do so, however farfetched. And yet they might not be lies, he thought, in the light of Brodie's cavorting with Catesby and his compatriots.

And, he thought, a ruthless gleam entering his eyes as he unconsciously fingered his cheek, he had not forgotten that he had a score to settle with that she-cat Serena Carberry. Nor was he in any doubt that Sir Henry had been involved in the conspiracy. Their time would come and he would await it with a good deal of pleasure.

Chapter Six

With the authorities searching houses for information of those involved in the conspiracy, an atmosphere of crisis prevailed.

'Father! I'm so afraid,' Serena said when she found him wandering disconsolately in his now-empty stables. 'You cannot passively wait to be taken. It is inevitable that you will become suspect.'

Sir Henry's eyes filled with remorse at the suffering his actions had brought to Serena. Life had not robbed him of his ambition, but age had distanced him from the young hotheads of this new age. He felt used and betrayed by those he had called his friends—and in particular by Robert Catesby. What Catesby had done was a vile and wicked thing and he had done the cause no good by it.

'What would you have me do?'

'You must go to Flanders. You have friends there, and you will be close to James.'

Sir Henry became thoughtful, and Serena knew precisely what was going through his mind. She was painfully aware of the friend he would seek out on reaching Flanders's shores, but she withheld her comments and kept her feelings on his close association with Mrs Davis to herself.

'I have considered this, but if I go I insist on you going

to Carberry Hall to stay with William. Under my brother's protection the authorities will not touch you if they should come looking for me. Being a woman, you will be spared— and I would be easier knowing you to be safe.'

The split from her father would be intolerable for Serena and her heart was full to breaking point. But she agreed.

Kit became uneasy and concerned when Robin failed to return from Dunedin Hall, and just when he was considering going himself to find out what had happened to his servant, government officials came to search Thurlow under the supervision of Sir Arthur Throckmorton, the Sheriff of Northamptonshire.

Kit was informed that on hearing of Lord Brodie's suspected part in the conspiracy from his chief minister, the earl of Salisbury, the king, feeling disappointed and betrayed by one of his most favoured lords, had ordered his immediate arrest. His Majesty was determined to mete out swift punishment to the traitors who had been set on murdering himself and other members of his family and his government.

Sir Arthur's expression was grim. 'I apologise for disturbing you, Lord Brodie, but I have received information to the effect that you have some connection to the dastardly plot. Accusations have been made against you and I have been instructed by Salisbury to search Thurlow and convey you to London under guard. Have you anything to say?'

'I would say it is ridiculous were it not so serious or so damning. Are you certain that your information is correct?' Kit asked, his voice courteous, while inside he felt that the horrifying menace, which had hung over him since that fateful moment when the plot had been uncovered, had come home to roost.

Puzzled by the order that he must search Thurlow and arrest this illustrious lord, who was a known Protestant and fiercely loyal in his allegiance to the king, a man he himself held in the highest regard and respected for his good sense and integrity, Sir Arthur found this whole business distasteful and was hesitant to believe Lord Brodie guilty of the accusations against him.

'I regret to tell you that the information was so definite and so serious that I was ordered not to hesitate to act.'

'And is it proved that I am an accessory to this crime against the king?'

'No. That is why I must take you to London for interrogation.'

'How was this information against me received?'

'Your servant was waylaid by a gentleman who recognised him. The gentleman was accompanied by a party of government officials who were in the area to search out information about others who may have been involved in the conspiracy. Your servant was on his way to Dunedin Hall to visit Sir Henry Carberry on your behalf—a gentleman who is a well-known recusant in Warwickshire. His eldest son is a Jesuit priest, and it is not known whether he is abroad or in hiding somewhere. Sir Henry is also known to have sold horses to Catesby to aid the cause.'

Sir Arthur's mention of Sir Henry took on a new edge. 'That is correct. Has Sir Henry been arrested?'

'No. He escaped—fled the country, I believe.'

'And his daughter?'

'She is residing at Carberry Hall with Lord Carberry and her cousin.'

Sir Arthur had no idea of the relief that flooded Kit's whole being. Not a muscle in his darkly handsome face gave any indication of this. He looked so cold, dispassionate and in complete control that Sir Arthur could not fail to admire him.

'Why do you ask about Sir Henry?'

'Personal concern for a friend. Nothing more. You may not be aware of the fact, Sir Arthur, but his niece and I are betrothed. Whether or not she becomes my wife, or I suffer the fate of traitors, remains to be seen,' Kit said drily. 'Do you mind telling me the name of the gentleman who recognised my servant?'

'It was Sir Thomas Blackwell of Ashcombe Manor.'

Sharp talons of dread raked Kit's heart, and the muscles of his jaw were taut with a barely controlled rage on hearing this name. 'Blackwell,' he growled. ''That explains your presence here in my home.'

'You know the gentleman?'

Kit nodded. 'The man is a blackguard and of unrestrained, ruthless ambition.'

'I'm not acquainted with Sir Thomas, but I have heard disparaging remarks about him. Wasn't it you who complained about his disgraceful conduct in the Low Countries, which resulted in his regiment being recalled?'

'It was. Our paths have crossed frequently in the past in extremely unpleasant circumstances. It would seem I have just become a victim of his malice. No doubt it will amuse him to see me cast into the Tower and charged with treason.'

'Are you saying that Sir Thomas is lying—that you did not associate with Catesby and his associates?'

'No. In part the information is false—certainly intended to be misleading.'

'In part? Then you don't deny it entirely?'

'Why should I deny it? I have nothing to hide. I confess to having dined on occasion with Catesby and his friends, but that does not make me guilty of collusion. Others were also present who had no part in the conspiracy. Certain branches of my family are Catholic—and there are liberal helpings of Catholic blood in your own, Sir Arthur,' he said pointedly, for the Throckmorton family was one of the most prominent Catholic families in England, 'but that does not make me a Catholic.'

'If what you say is true, I sincerely hope you establish your innocence.'

Kit grinned wryly. 'So do I, Sir Arthur.'

* * *

Still reeling from her separation from her father, news of Lord Brodie's arrest hit Serena hard. The accusations of conspiracy against him were based on Thomas Blackwell's testimony, reinforced by a good deal of evidence. But unbeknown to Serena his captivity was short-lived.

Aware of the gruesome fate awaiting him at the Tower, from the moment Kit left Thurlow he was determined to escape rather than enter the gates of that formidable fortress. His opportunity came late one night—he loosened the bonds that held him when his guards thought he was asleep. With all the stealth of a shadow he slipped away. Fleet of foot, he travelled south-west, hoping to find Ludovick at his home at Chelsea.

It came as no surprise to Serena that Lord Brodie's betrothal to Dorothea was blighted by the discovery of the Gunpowder Plot and his assumed involvement. Not long after his arrest and with undue haste, Lord Carberry, believing he had just cause to cancel his daughter's betrothal to a traitor, joined her in what he considered to be a more successful union to Sir Thomas Blackwell.

Serena was appalled that Dorothea had no objections to the match and would listen to no wrong said about him. The possibility that her cousin might fancy herself in love with the beast that almost ravished her had never occurred to Serena. She had known Dorothea all her life, yet she was beginning to realise that she did not know the inner workings of her mind at all. Nothing she could say would make her cousin change her mind or her opinion of Thomas Blackwell; as for herself, she would never be reconciled to such an unsuitable match, and she hoped he would not give her cousin cause to rue the day she married him.

And so, unable to come to terms with Dorothea's determination to wed Sir Thomas, and feeling that she could not bear to come face to face with the aforesaid gentleman ever

again—which she would have to do if she remained at Carberry Hall—Serena decided to leave England and seek out
her father in Flanders.

She slipped out of the house when everyone had retired
for the night, leaving her uncle and Dorothea a note telling
them of her intentions, convinced that by the time they
woke and read the letter she would be well on her way to
the south coast. Her uncle's fury would be fearsome when
he discovered what she had done.

Quickly she saddled her beloved Polly. It would sadden
her when she had to part with her, but she would sell her
for a good price and find her a suitable stable before em-
barking on her journey across the Channel. Driven by a
compelling need to see her home one more time, she
headed in the direction of Dunedin Hall. She would also
obtain possession of a few things to take with her and make
use of some of James's clothes. Dressed in the guise of a
man, she would be less conspicuous; it would make her
journey less difficult being unencumbered by skirts,

Eventually the ghostly shape of Dunedin Hall came into
view. Stealthily Serena let herself into the deserted house.
An eerie quiet hung over the place, but she had a keen
sense that something was wrong. Lighting two candles that
she found on a large chest, she looked around her, appalled
and pained by the sight that met her eyes. In her absence
the house had been ransacked and looted, although there
had been few articles of any great value left. Dunedin Hall
had held many treasures, and it was fortunate that her father
had hastily arranged to have them removed to Carberry Hall
with his brother's grudging approval before he left.

Despite their differences, Lord Carberry believed in the
old adage that blood is thicker than water and had no desire
to see his brother meet a traitor's death. With his love of
wealth and the finer things in life, and knowing that all
Henry's property and possessions would become forfeit to
the Crown, he had agreed to take anything of great value

and would store it until such a time—God willing and the king's pardon—as when Henry could return to England.

The searchers had shown no respect. Floors had been ripped up and panels removed from the walls in an attempt to uncover any concealed priest holes, of which there were several at Dunedin Hall. As she looked around her at the utter devastation, Serena's only feeling was anger that strangers had entered, violated and defiled this house that was sacred to her, sacred because it had been her home where her family had lived and loved.

Concentrating her mind on her task, she knew speed was essential. Slipping out of her dress, she put on instead hose and breeches she found among a heap of clothes on the floor that belonged to James. He was younger than she, but a tall youth for all that. Putting on a shirt and dark blue doublet and a stout pair of her brother's boots, she then twisted her hair into a knot at the back of her head and placed a wide-brimmed hat on top.

Pushing the dress she had taken off into a bag with one other, some undergarments, shoes and other small items that she would need for the long journey ahead of her, she then collected a few jewels of small value which would be of use to her from her own chamber. They were hidden in a secret drawer in a large chest, which had been overlooked when her father had been arranging his escape.

Clutching the bag, she went quickly down the stairscase, a slight shadow moving stealthily against the wall illuminated by the lone candle she held. Dunedin Hall had become a house of memories. A house of ghosts. Serena was struck by the almost brooding silence, an ominous silence that was like a large crouching beast holding its breath, waiting for something to happen.

Before she reached the bottom step she paused, certain she had heard a sound. On hearing the ponderous approach of footsteps ringing sharply on the stone flags, her heart began to pound. Her eyes were large as she peered and tried to penetrate the gloom, becoming fixed when she saw a dim arc of light down a passageway growing larger and brighter. She had to stifle a cry when a large black figure emerged carrying a lantern, menacing and unreal, almost stripping away her façade of courage as it advanced towards her like a terrifying beast.

Serena fell back, her eyes dilated, all the colour draining from her face as the figure stepped into the light and she realised that misfortune had placed her once more into the hands of Thomas Blackwell. As he set the lantern down on a large chest, its yellow light threw his gigantic shadow against the wall. Clutching a trembling hand to her throat, Serena recalled his violence on their last confrontation. Shaken by the memory, she feared that it was about to be repeated. But this time she was alone and completely at his mercy. There would be no marquess of Thurlow to save her from Thomas Blackwell's brutal hands this time.

Moving down the remaining stairs, she mastered her fear sufficiently to say coldly, 'I might have expected to find you here. Are you responsible for what has happened to my home?'

'I saw a light and came to investigate. The Sheriff had the authority to question the servants and search the house for your father and any other undesirables who may be in hiding here. It's well known that these spacious Catholic houses are honeycombed with passages and riddled with secret holes for priests and fugitives to hide in. Having found such places, it is clear that Dunedin Hall is no different.'

'Then the Sheriff has done his job well,' Serena said scathingly, 'considering the disorder of things and my family's belongings which have been transported away. No doubt the Sheriff will make a considerable profit out of it all.'

'Your father has been declared a traitor. In such cases all properties of the accused become forfeit.'

'Ha!' Serena scoffed. 'Accused! The charge against him has not yet been proven.'

'It will be. Where is he?'

'Somewhere in Flanders. You will not find him here.'

Thomas moved closer, his gaze becoming salacious when they rested on her lips and heaving angry bosom. 'Then perhaps you can explain your own reason for being here. I know you are presently living at Carberry Hall.'

Sir Thomas's leering gaze stripped Serena's blood to ice, and she saw what she had not seen when she had believed herself smitten—the lines of dissipation around his mouth and a chilling arrogance in his eyes.

'This is my home and I can come and go as I please.'

'It is almost midnight and I find your behaviour suspicious.' Thomas's narrowed eyes travelled the length of her. 'Very fetching,' he murmured, taking in every detail of her attire, his hooded eyes heavy with desire. 'Are you going somewhere? Did you think to escape me? Did you think I had forgotten how you thwarted me the last time we met?'

In unwavering response Serena met his gaze directly, her glare conveying her absolute contempt. 'If you touch me I shall scream.'

'Such spirit, such defiance—I like that,' he drawled. 'Go ahead and scream. No one will hear you. You went too far when you tried to make a fool of me, Serena. You touched my honour and now I think I have a duty to punish you— to take what you so fiercely denied me the last time.'

The full horror of what was about to happen to her crushed down on Serena with appalling gravity and brought all her paralysed senses to life. 'You blackguard,' she spat. 'Have you no concept of honour? Lay one finger on me and I swear I shall make you pay for any offence you commit against me.'

An abrasive laugh came from her assailant. 'So, you think you can tease and entice and then dance away to delight yourself with Kit Brodie, do you? Nay…' he laughed '…I'll not have it. I have you now and there is no escape. You will get what you deserve and not forget me in a hurry.'

'And after you have defiled my person—when my uncle hears of this—do you think he will still consider you suitable to marry Dorothea? He'll give you the whipping you deserve more like.'

Thomas's eyes skimmed over Serena with a mixture of angry insolence and hungry fervour. 'He won't, because if you know what's good for you you'll silence your tongue. I'll deny everything and accuse you of leading me on, convincing everyone that what you accuse me of is merely a malicious invention on your part, because of your jealousy that I am to wed Dorothea instead of you.' He moved closer, his breathing becoming laboured as his excitement mounted. 'I intend to make you suffer—to hear you scream—to make you go down on your knees and listen to you beg for mercy—you treacherous, papist bitch.'

And then his iron-thewed arms were around her. He held her fast, his assault conjuring up memories, and Serena remembered the force, the power of this man. Her hat came off and her hair tumbled loose about her shoulders, hampering her as she struggled frantically. Thomas's hands mauled her body mercilessly, and when he lowered his head to clamp his mouth on hers she almost retched, flinging her head from side to side in an attempt to avoid his violation, humiliated and angry that she was having to suffer this torment yet again.

'Stop fighting, damn you—you witch,' Thomas growled as she managed to drag herself away from him, desperate to put an end to the nightmare.

'You beast—you lecherous oaf,' she spat, outraged, lashing out at him in fury, but he caught her wrist cruelly and twisted her arm, forcing her to her knees.

'That—' a voice rang out from across the hall '—is quite enough, Blackwell. Release Mistress Carberry.'

Thomas turned and found himself looking into the muzzle of the marquess of Thurlow's pistol. At first he stared at him in disbelief, but then his expression became one of fury. 'You!' he hissed.

'I am no apparition, Blackwell. If you touch her again I'll kill you,' Kit said, making his presence felt, his voice cold and lethal and his eyes as penetrating as dagger thrusts. 'Do you understand me?'

Glancing uncertainly towards the vision that had suddenly appeared, Serena beheld a face that made her tremble and a gasp rise in her throat. For a split second she thought she was imagining things, that her vision was distorted, that the marquess of Thurlow could not possibly have stepped in to rescue her from Thomas Blackwell's brutal hands a second time. She blinked, but her vision did not clear, and she saw it was indeed Lord Brodie, just as tall, just as handsome as she remembered, his face as hard as a granite sculpture as he glared at his adversary.

His presence stirred memories of a cosy room at Carberry Hall late one night, and Serena's heart pounded with an overwhelming intensity. Ever since their first meeting he had kept intruding into her thoughts when her desire was to keep him out, and now she was unable to suppress the surge of jubilation that raced through her. But how did he come to be here when he should be languishing in the Tower?

As he was consumed with rage, a red haze formed in front of Thomas's eyes. He reached out and tried to deliver Kit a punch, but to his astonishment he found his arm seized by Kit's free hand with a strength that exceeded his own. The pistol in Kit's other hand struck him hard in the belly, then his free hand slammed against Thomas's jaw and bowled him over on to the floor where he lay bellowing like a gored animal. Gasping for air, he struggled to his feet, leaning against the balustrade for support. His hand went to his hip where he wore his sword, but Kit saw the gesture and prevented him from drawing it by raising his pistol.

'I'll get you for this, Brodie,' Thomas rasped with difficulty, his eyes freezing with a piercing darkness promising repercussions. 'I'll see you both in hell before I'm finished with you.'

Kit's eyes took on a steely hardness as he moved closer, still brandishing his pistol. 'What's the matter?' he taunted with an infuriating grin, placing the cold muzzle beneath Blackwell's chin and watching with heightened interest as perspiration broke out on his brow. A soft chuckle of derision went rippling around the hall. 'Did you think I was a prisoner in the Tower, where I would be made to suffer every indignity and every conceivable torture known to man? Did you hope that I would soon be dangling on the end of a rope with my insides ripped out?'

Kit's mood changed suddenly. There was a tensing of the muscles in his lean jaw and a feral gleam in his eyes. 'You have much to answer for, Blackwell. I know you were responsible for the arrest of my servant, and I realise how disappointed you must be to discover I have escaped the not-so-watchful eye of my gaolers after all your efforts to discredit me.'

'Aye, I admit it. I thought I had gotten rid of you, but I never thought you'd have the audacity to show up here.'

Kit smiled wryly. 'I have come to serve vengeance of my own on someone who was not content to settle his account with me in person. Unlike you, Blackwell, I would rather face my enemy than have him at my back. Is there no end to your wickedness? You still ply your skills with ruthless ease against women, I see. Are you so smitten with Mistress Carberry that you must take her by force?'

Thomas sneered. 'To hell with you, Brodie. Why didn't you seek the hospitality at Carberry Hall?'

'I knew what kind of reception I would receive. Through your doing I have been accused of treason against the

Crown, so I could hardly expect Lord Carberry to welcome me now, could I? I've been watching you all day, Blackwell. I followed you here—and it's as well I did,' he said, switching his attention to Serena.

Seeing the strain of her ordeal showing on her face, Kit moved towards her. Reaching down, he took her hand, feeling it tremble as he drew her to her feet. He watched as the flickering light from the nearby candles illuminated her features, which were etched with pure clarity on his consciousness. She looked pale and stricken and heartbreakingly beautiful. His heart wrenched. 'Are you all right?'

She nodded. His dark eyes seemed to bore right through her, the gaze so bold that she could almost feel her heart knocking against her ribs as she struggled against his mesmerising stare. 'Yes. He hasn't hurt me.'

A scowl darkened Kit's brow. 'Not through lack of trying,' he stated.

'I never expected to see you,' Serena remarked.

Kit lifted a sleek, black eyebrow. 'Ever?'

'So soon.'

'I couldn't keep away,' he said with a smile.

Thomas was glaring at them both, hatred burning like a fire within his breast. 'Your concern for this she-cat is touching, Brodie,' he rasped, sensing an advantage as he tried to bring his strident breathing under control. 'You show more for her than you do her cousin.'

Kit glanced at him sharply. 'What do you mean by that remark?' he asked, a coldness congealing around his heart. 'You speak of Dorothea, my betrothed, I think.'

'I realise you are still under that assumption, but that is no longer the case. Dorothea is betrothed to me now. Since your arrest and condemnation as a traitor, Lord Carberry has seen fit to cancel the arrangement made between you.'

Kit spun round to Serena. 'Is this true?'

She nodded, thinking that the icy coldness in his eyes

and hard set to his jaw would have done justice to an executioner.

The windows of Kit's understanding were suddenly blown wide open, igniting all the tapers of hellfire. In two short strides he was in front of Thomas, his face contorted with dark fury as he glared at him. 'By God, what treachery is this? You are to marry Dorothea?'

With venom Thomas smiled smugly. 'I am. She has no objections to the change of groom. In fact, she is in favour. Dorothea has excellent taste and wants only the best. In short, she prefers me to you, Brodie.'

Kit sprang at him, seizing him by the neck of his doublet and giving vent to a stream of oaths and insults that would have done credit to any trooper under his command. His face became convulsed by a spasm of violent rage. The idea of Dorothea married to this depraved animal seared through him like a red-hot blade, bringing a bitter taste to his mouth.

Transfixed by Kit's reaction, Serena had not realised until that moment how much he must love Dorothea, and how hurt and resentful he must be feeling, discovering she was to wed another man. Because that other man was Thomas Blackwell would make it harder for him to bear. As for herself, she was assailed by confusion and lowered her face to hide a hurt she could not confess to.

But Serena wasn't to know that Kit's rage was because something had been taken from him rather than any romantic feelings he might cherish for Dorothea. He pushed Thomas back against the stairs. 'Then marry her and be damned to you, Blackwell. But I have not done with you yet. Because of you and your malicious lies I have been branded a traitor. I will not rest until you have exerted as much effort as you did to discredit me as you will to clear my name. We both know I am guiltless of the crime of treason, and only you can restore me to the king's good graces.'

'Over my dead body,' sneered Thomas contemptuously.

Kit's hard face was wiped clean of any expression. 'So be it. You carry a sword. Prepare to defend yourself, Blackwell. Let us have this out in the open between us with some mark of honour.'

Acceding to Kit's demand for a duel, Thomas nodded, his eyes gleaming murderously. 'My pleasure.'

'No,' cried Serena wildly, rushing forward to try and stop them spilling blood. 'You cannot do this.'

Kit threw her an exasperated glare. 'Stay out of this,' he ordered between his teeth, his face rigid. 'This is between Blackwell and me. It is not your affair.'

Trembling with fright, meekly Serena obeyed and crouched against the wall, feeling physically ill and watching in helpless misery as the two men faced each other, the hatred and contempt they felt for each other vibrating between them.

Quickly Thomas unsheathed his sword and launched an attack. Kit answered the invitation by raising his own, and a clash of swords reverberated around the walls of the cavernous hall as the naked blades met in a shower of sparks. Both men were adept swordsmen of formidable strength, defending and gaining the advantage alternately, jabbing and parrying, the attack aggressive. But Kit's blade began to threaten and Thomas was made to twist and dance to avoid his relentless thrusts; the speed that Kit exerted, encircling, forcing him to move faster. Sweat beaded Thomas's brow as he struggled to dodge the shining length of steel which nicked and snipped, the rents in his doublet becoming bloodied.

With a subtle caress with his clever blade, Kit finally lunged, the tip of the double-edged rapier disappearing into Thomas's shoulder. Thomas staggered back. At first his reaction was sluggish and his eyes widened. His hand gripped his shoulder to feel blood already oozing through his fingers. Appalled, he fell to his knees and stared up at the tall,

noble man, whose lips were stretched across his teeth in a
savage snarl, and Thomas could feel the cold steel of the
blade poised against his throat as Brodie prepared for the
kill.

Serena rushed forward, knowing Kit's fury was so great
he would do just that. 'No,' she cried. 'Please don't kill
him.'

Kit turned his head and stared at her with incredulity.
'What? After what he is guilty of? Why should I spare a
dog intent on rape? He would not have spared you.'

'You saved me,' she whispered, unable to understand
why she should want this monster who had sought to violate her to live. She only knew that she did not want to be
responsible for ending any man's life.

Kit cursed softly and lowered his sword. 'Be thankful
Mistress Carberry has a soft heart, Blackwell. Left to me,
I would finish you now.'

'And add murder to your crimes?'

Kit shrugged. 'Who would know? In a short time Mistress Carberry and I will be in Flanders.' He turned and
looked at Serena. 'I take it that is the reason why you are
attired so strangely? Am I right in assuming that you have
run away from your uncle and that you are on your way to
join your father?'

'Yes. The moment I knew Uncle William intended marrying Dorothea to Sir Thomas, I found it impossible to
remain at Carberry Hall any longer.' Serena glowered at
Thomas, moving closer to him and speaking with derisive
scorn. 'My loathing of you is so great that I could not bear
to be close to you. Because I chanced to smile at you, you
had me figured out for an easy tumble.

'I despise you and can only pity Dorothea. If your abuse
of her is half as violent as it has been towards me, then she
will most likely expire on her wedding night. I would give
ten years of my life to see you lying dead at my feet, and
I only asked Lord Brodie to spare you because of the dire

consequences to ourselves should it become known he killed you.'

Freed from the threat of Kit's blade, Thomas staggered to his feet, clutching his wounded shoulder, his face having darkened to a livid red. Such hatred sparked in his eyes that Serena involuntarily shivered.

'I give you fair warning,' he growled at Serena. 'Hide yourself from me when next we meet.'

Having sheathed his sword, Kit brandished his pistol in front of Thomas yet again, speaking in a tightly controlled tone, his expression hard and cold.

'If you ever touch her again I will kill you. You will not escape me a third time. Take care that you heed my words, Blackwell. I should hate to make Dorothea a widow before she becomes a wife. And yet I might be doing her a favour if I were to blow your head off here and now and spare her the indignities and misery which will be her lot when she becomes your wife. It would not distress me in the slightest, and I only refrain from doing so because Mistress Carberry has asked me to spare you.'

Kit looked at Serena, his dark eyes holding hers in an unrelenting gaze. 'Are you ready to leave?'

She nodded. With trembling fingers she knotted her hair and placed the hat back on her head, grasping the bag with her few possessions in it.

Without further ado Kit bound Thomas hand and foot, ignoring his clenched teeth and sharp intake of breath, which betrayed the pain he was clearly suffering from his injured shoulder. Propping him up against the wall, Kit smiled down at him.

'Forgive me for leaving you in such discomfort. For obvious reasons I cannot allow you to go free. Mistress Carberry and I must be well on our way before you raise the hue and cry. You can be certain someone will come by when it's light to plunder the house further.'

Breathing hard, Thomas glared at Kit and ground his

teeth on meeting the mockery in his dark eyes, hating him, hating the tolerant smile, the imperturbable confidence and unruffled composure.

'You have slept your last peaceful night, Brodie. Mark me well.'

'I am the marquess of Thurlow—and mark *me* well, Blackwell. I will not be mocked.'

In the candles' glow Thomas watched them go, hearing a door shut, closely followed by the sound of their horses' hooves as they disappeared into the dark, wet night, intent on escape.

Unfortunately, the strong current of air that swept into the hall when Kit opened the door to leave blew a lighted candle over. It fell on to some curtains the searchers had left strewn on the floor. They caught light almost immediately, and the house was soon engulfed with flames.

Lord Carberry's rage, caused by his niece's disappearance shortly after she had left the house, was absolute. With a small party of men he was soon in hot pursuit, heading towards Ripley, strongly suspecting that Serena intended calling at Dunedin Hall before journeying south. It was the flames lighting up the night sky that made them proceed with all haste.

Chapter Seven

Serena matched her horse's speed with that of Kit's, neither of them turning to see the red glow in the night sky. She glanced across at her companion, unable to see his features clearly, but she could make out the rigid outline of his jaw and the glitter of his dark eyes as he looked ahead.

'Thank you for arriving when you did,' she said when they slowed their horses. 'It seems that Sir Thomas is determined to pursue me to the bitter end.'

'You may be right, which is one reason why I should have killed him when I had the chance. Blackwell never forgives the slightest wound to his pride, and your determination not to submit to his desire will have dented it badly.'

'He is the reason why I left Carberry Hall. I couldn't bear to watch him dance attendance upon Dorothea.'

When Kit thought of Dorothea's betrothal to Thomas Blackwell, his lips twisted with excruciating distaste. The very idea of the gentle Dorothea being initiated into the joys of love by Thomas he found obscene. There was also something repugnant about Lord Carberry, who was an avaricious man with the finely honed instincts of a horse trader.

'It's plain my betrothal to Dorothea has been blighted by the discovery of the Gunpowder Plot and my assumed involvement, so I'm not really surprised that Lord Carberry has withdrawn his favour,' said Kit, quietly angry and infuriated by Lord Carberry's casual dismissal of his suit. But despite Lord Carberry's betrayal, he would not vent his spite.

'Having chosen to overlook Blackwell's disgraceful conduct in the Low Countries, he seems perfectly satisfied with him since he possesses all the prerequisites of title and wealth—while not forgetting that he is a devout Protestant. But I share your opinion of Blackwell, and my heart quakes at the thought of Dorothea being married to him.'

'She was eager to do her father's bidding and is not marrying him against her will—quite the opposite, in fact,' Serena informed him. 'Dorothea is quite enamoured and cannot wait for the wedding to take place. As for myself— well—I can only hope she survives the ordeal.'

Serena studied Kit's chiselled profile etched against the black night, and if it were not so dark she would have seen there was an angry slant to his brow and a tight set to his lips. She wondered how he really felt about Dorothea marrying Sir Thomas, and how deeply he was hurting.

Absently Kit tried to recall Dorothea's features, but the images were less distinct than the sweet sound of her voice and the gentleness of her nature. He became troubled— even more so when he realised that the thought of the young woman he should have married did not stir as powerful emotions either in his breast or in his loins as did the thought of the vibrant and beautiful Serena riding by his side.

'How do you come to be in Ripley?' Serena asked, breaking into his thoughts.

Kit glanced across at her, wondering how she would react if she knew where his thoughts had wandered, and he smiled speculatively to himself. 'Not only did I return to confront Blackwell—I also came to see you. On my arrest I learnt that a warrant had been issued for your father's arrest but that he had escaped.'

'You were fortunate to escape yourself. Did you come to Warwickshire at once?'

'No. I had need of a horse and some money so I went to Chelsea to see Ludovick. I hid there for a while before heading north. It gave me no pleasure running from the capital like some whipped cur, but the alternative was the Tower.'

'You—you said you came to see me. Why?' Serena asked. For some reason she could not explain she was exhilarated that he had cared enough to seek her out.

'It was important for me to know what happened. Do you know how deep your father was involved with the conspiracy—how much he knew?'

'Nothing. He had no knowledge of the inner workings of the plot. Catesby told him he needed horses to form a troop of horse for the Netherlands and he believed him—but he was uneasy.'

Kit nodded. 'It's as I thought—but I doubt he would be believed by the interrogators who are baying for blood.'

'He knew that, which is why he escaped to Flanders.'

'He was wise to do so. Have you heard from him?'

'No. I don't even know if he is safe. I can't help worrying about him,' Serena said, her voice heavy with concern.

'That is natural. Plans for the intensive interrogation of the conspirators and their allies are being worked out by the government. Information is being sought fervently, and there is a degree of vindictiveness in the way they are going about it. They are making it an excuse to settle old scores with the recusant Catholics—which is precisely what Blackwell is guilty of where I am concerned.

'Having accused me of being mixed up in the conspiracy, he has produced damning evidence to substantiate his accusation. Wives and other members of the conspirators' families are in a perilous situation. Many have been taken to London and housed with the city aldermen where they await interrogation.'

Alarmed, Serena glanced across at him. 'Do you think I am in danger of being arrested?'

Kit met her gaze. 'It is highly probable. If so, your uncle's protection will not save you.'

'I think I am in greater danger from Sir Thomas than I am from the government,' Serena said on a wry note. She frowned suddenly in puzzlement. They had reached a crossroads and it became evident to her that Kit intended taking the road north towards Coventry. 'This is not the way we must take,' she said, bringing her horse to an abrupt halt. 'This is not the road south.'

Kit had ridden on a little way, but came back when he saw she had stopped. 'I have no intention of going south,' he told her bluntly.

Serena struggled to quell her disappointment. 'Then we must part. I must go south. I have to.'

'No. You, my dear Mistress Carberry, are coming north with me.'

Serena's eyes flew to his in alarm. Instantly all her anxieties returned and the camaraderie of a moment before began to crumble. Her heart, which had been curiously touched by his earlier solicitude, hardened, and her face turned mutinous. Kit's words were an order, and she bridled at his arrogant assumption that she would go with him without question. It broke the spell and whipped up her anger.

'I shall do nothing of the kind,' she snapped, her eyes as stormy as the sky overhead. 'How dare you assume authority over me. I've told you I intend following my father to Flanders, and if you try stopping me I shall fight you tooth and nail.'

Kit grinned thinly, his eyes gleaming down into hers like pieces of flint. For the first time a spark of anger flared in their dark depths. 'That sounds more like the Serena Carberry I remember,' he commented coldly. 'I am aware of what you would like to do to me—that you would take great delight in scratching my eyes out—but you can rant and rail all you like. You are too much of a frail and fragile female to substantiate your threats.'

'Ha! Frailty, indeed,' Serena scoffed in outrage. 'Why, you—'

'You are in grave danger and I have no intention of letting you remain here. When Blackwell comes to his senses he will follow you,' Kit said harshly. 'After using you most cruelly to his own ends he will have you arrested—and, believe me, it will be no picnic.'

Serena was so angry she almost flew at him. Remaining adamant, she dismounted, drawing her horse to the side of the road where she was insensible to the rain dripping from the trees on to the crown of her hat and settling in the brim. 'I will not go with you.'

'Yes, you will,' Kit stated in a voice that brooked no argument, also dismounting and going to stand beside her. 'You're in trouble up to your pretty little neck. No display of outraged pride will get you out of it. Face it. Your father is accused of treason and has absconded. Like it or not, there is every possibility that you will be accused of collusion and harbouring a priest.'

Kit towered above Serena. When she looked up at him she felt the full weight of his lethal stare and thought she had never seen him look so tall or so formidable. She stared at him in amazement. 'Are you referring to Andrew?'

'Who else?'

'But Andrew is in Italy.'

'Try making your interrogators believe that. By all intents and purposes he is here in England with other priests in hiding.'

'But he is not. You believe that, don't you?'

'What I believe is not important. It's the law you have

to convince, not me. Now come along. We must be well away from here by daybreak. I would be failing in my duty if I let you go after your father, who would have taken you with him if he'd wanted you to go. You'd be caught long before you reached the south coast.'

'Duty!' exclaimed Serena in spitting tones of venom. 'It is not your duty to take me anywhere.'

'I am making it my duty in the absence of your father. Believe me,' he growled, 'I want no encumbrances on my journey—nothing to get in my way until I've succeeded in my one objective, which is to clear my name of this dastardly accusation against me. But I've said you will go and go you will—like it or not and hate me for it.'

'Do you expect me to meekly abide by your orders and do your bidding? You are either jesting or insane,' Serena scoffed.

Kit raised his brow in an arrogant arch. 'I assure you I am not jesting and I am quite sane. I am deadly serious, and despite my aggressive behaviour towards Blackwell I am not one to mistreat a lady. But if you are going to be troublesome and persist in this foolishness, I shall have no choice but to truss you up and take you with me by force— which will make the journey extremely uncomfortable for you—unless, of course, you abandon your foolish intent to go to Flanders and return to your uncle's care and protection at Carberry Hall.'

'And submit myself to the lechery of Thomas Blackwell? Never.'

'Then what is to be?' Kit asked, trying to maintain his calm, which was proving extremely difficult in the face of Serena's anger. 'Do you accept my proposal? The choice is yours.'

'Choice? Proposal? Forgive me if I appear to have a queer misunderstanding of words, my lord, but it sounds decidedly like an order to me.'

Serena gave Kit a slanted glower, trying to dominate her

fury. Kit was looking down at her in the dim light and his hard gaze neither flinched or wavered. Her eyes blazed defiance and she bestowed on him a look of such ire and burning intensity it should have reduced him to a cinder, but he merely smiled scornfully and infuriatingly into her snapping eyes and shrugged, turning towards his horse.

'Be reasonable. Calm yourself and make up your mind. The hour grows late and it's my intention to be well on my way before dawn. It may have slipped your mind, but I, too, have been accused of treason and have a care for my neck. I have no wish to be caught and hanged and my body cut to pieces and spiked on top of every gate in London before I've had a chance to clear my name and redeem my honour.'

'Then leave me.'

Kit's eyes narrowed dangerously and his face darkened with brooding anger at her continued defiance. When he spoke his voice had an edge of sarcasm. 'Believe me, madam, I have no wish to saddle myself with a troublesome female. Nothing would give me greater pleasure than to send you on your way—be it to Flanders or back to Carberry Hall, for that matter—but should you come to harm I shall have Sir Henry to answer to. Have you any idea where to look for him in Flanders?' he asked.

Serena threw back her head defiantly. 'Not exactly, but I will find him. I can ask. I have a tongue in my head.'

'Aye—and were I a man of sense I would have you permanently clapped in a scold's bridle to silence it,' Kit growled.

Affronted by his remark, Serena glowered at him. 'Oh, you beast.'

Seizing her arms and thrusting his face close to hers, Kit forced her to look at him. 'To embark on so perilous a journey unprotected, you will fall prey to all manner of dangers from barbarians who set upon lone travellers. If you thought the treatment you received at the hands of

Blackwell was harsh, then believe me you can expect far worse. Now get on your horse. We are wasting precious time arguing.'

Kit's voice bore a tone of command that would tempt obedience from the most reluctant soldier, but from Serena it drew a further outburst of rage. With fists clenched by her sides, she glared at him. 'You cannot force me to go with you.'

'Try me,' he growled. Suddenly he became alert, his eyes drawn to the road down which they had just ridden. Without a word he gathered the horses' bridles and took her arm, dragging her unceremoniously away from the road and into the dark, enveloping wetness of the trees.

When Serena would have spoken he placed a finger firmly to her lips, urging her to be still and silent. Straining to listen, she heard the distant drumming of horses' hooves fast approaching. The sound grew more distinct, and peering through the foliage they saw the dark shapes of several horsemen appear and pause at the crossroads, trying to still their restless mounts as they discussed which road to take. Voices became raised and words were whipped on the wind to where they stood, and Serena shuddered when she recognised that of her uncle.

'To the south,' he shouted. 'They can't be too far ahead. Sir Thomas told us they were heading to the coast.'

'Aye,' said another voice. 'They'll not escape. With your niece safely returned to you, milord, we'll have Brodie dispatched to London where his neck will stretch for certain for this night's work. Sir Thomas was lucky to escape with his life.'

Unconsciously Serena was holding her breath, her eyes wide as she watched the horsemen clatter past in their haste to catch the fleeing couple. Kit cursed softly under his breath and she turned, aware of him standing very close with his hand still gripping her arm.

'As luck would have it, it would seem your uncle has

discovered your disappearance sooner than you hoped. Clearly he went to Dunedin Hall and found Blackwell, who alerted him to your destination. So now what do you say, Mistress Carberry? I fear we are both caught in a trap that is not easily resolved. For obvious reasons you cannot travel south, and to return to Carberry Hall you will be subjecting yourself to the lecherous persecutions of Blackwell.'

'And by your aggressive and arrogant manner,' Serena flung at him scathingly, 'you are beginning to resemble him in many ways. Your tricks and threats may be more subtle than his, but in the end they are the same.'

Kit's stare was cold and uncompromising, and there was a hard edge to his voice when he spoke. 'Accuse me so if it satisfies you,' he said irritably, his lips curling over his white teeth, which gleamed in the darkness, 'but I have never forced my attentions upon a woman when she has made it plain they are not welcome. I have always considered myself to be a gentleman in my dealings with the opposite sex.'

'A sentiment held entirely by you,' Serena mocked.

Kit's jaw tightened and his features became even harder as he tried to restrain his anger. Never had he met a woman who set him on edge like she did. Her stubborn determination to be as awkward as she possibly could was beginning to aggravate him beyond words. The softer hues of Dorothea's gentle nature and sweet face were far more favourable in his memory and easier to exist with than this tempestuous, venom-spitting female who would test the patience of a saint.

'What is it to be?' Kit damanded, his patience nearing breaking point. 'Are you to come with me or return to Carberry Hall—which I shall only allow you to do after you have given me your word that that is where you will remain and that you will abandon your foolhardy intention of going to find your father?'

'What choice do I have?' Serena flared, snatching her arm from his grasp. Jerking Polly's bridle from his other hand, she drew her out of the trees into the road. Everything was going wrong and she had the heartbreaking thought that in going north with Lord Brodie she might never see her father or her brothers again. Her throat constricted painfully and she felt the sudden need to cry. But pride forbade her and she swallowed down her tears, turning fiercely to face Lord Brodie when he came to stand beside her.

'Is this all the thanks I get for offering you my protection?' he asked crisply with an arrogant lift to his brow.

Serena's eyes widened at his audacity. 'Thanks? You expect me to thank you for preventing me from going to my father? Oh, no, sir. I think not. You'll get no thanks from me.'

'Do you give me your word you will not try and escape me?' Kit asked firmly, approaching her as he would an untamed rabbit that threatened to bolt and scramble down the nearest hole at any minute. 'Do we have a pact? The journey will be more bearable if you cooperate.'

'Yes,' she hissed, glowering at him, her eyes shooting green fire. 'You have it—at least for the duration of the journey, when I shall then expect you to put me aboard the first available ship for Flanders. But I swear I will give you no peace. You'll rue the day you forced my hand and issued orders to me.'

Kit raised a mocking brow, meeting her gaze squarely, cynically trying to ignore the protective need she roused in him, a chord no woman had ever touched before. 'Madam! Is this a declaration of war?'

'Yes,' she flared, surreptitiously fixing her eyes on the man she had come to regard as her tormentor. 'If you like.'

'Then so be it. You have it.'

Hoisting herself into the saddle with an agility that both astounded and impressed Kit, Serena gritted her teeth and steeled herself for the ride ahead, refusing to betray her trepidation and unaware of the great distance she would have to travel alone with this bullying, arrogant man before they reached their destination.

Climbing on to his horse, with a frown Kit contemplated the vituperative minx he had saddled himself with—she had a waspish tongue that could flay the skin off a man's back better than any cat. The state his life was in, he had no time for entanglements of any kind—and especially not with Serena Carberry, despite her winsome looks and soft, ripe body that would pleasure a man into eternity, a woman who would rejoice in his weakening and laugh in his face. But then Kit smiled into the dark, intent on teaching this tenacious wench a lesson about men she would not forget in a hurry during the time they would be together.

Touching their heels to their horses, they sped on. The wind had gathered in strength and the rain fell heavier than before, making riding extremely uncomfortable. Serena knew the area well, but as they rode farther north towards Coventry the territory became unfamiliar.

To add to her discomfort the icy rain was relentless and beginning to penetrate her sodden cloak. She was also extremely cold and her healthy young stomach was beginning to growl with hunger. Her hands and feet were numb and aching, and on top of all these discomforts her teeth were beginning to chatter. It was sheer will-power and stubborn pride not to show weakness to Kit that kept her astride her horse. But Kit could see Serena was suffering and that she would rather expire in the saddle than complain. He admired her stubborn courage.

To avoid drawing attention to themselves, they took a route away from the main thoroughfares. It was dawn when they reached the outskirts of Coventry and Kit called a halt to their flight. There were no other patrons at the inn they stopped at, which was mean and shabby and in dire need of a good scrubbing from top to bottom in Serena's opinion, but it was warm and the food was good, and she attacked it with relish.

'Am I allowed to ask where you are taking me?' she asked Kit when they had eaten and sat facing each other beside the fire.

Having removed her boots, Serena sat with her stockinged feet outstretched to the heat of the fire, looking across at Kit petulantly. Everything about him stirred her resentment and she was determined to thwart him at every turn, for only by doing so would she be able to retain her sanity until it was time for them to part.

Steam rose from their sodden cloaks which were draped over an iron guard on either side of the huge fire to dry. Feeling the dampness beginning to leave her bones and a tiredness wrapping itself around her, Serena had not realised until then the depth of her fatigue. She would dearly like to close her eyes and sleep, but Kit's gaze, which never flinched or wavered from her face, kept her alert.

Feeling relaxed after the meal they had shared—in silence, for Serena had not spoken one word to him since leaving Ripley—Kit relaxed into the corner of the settle. Idly he gazed at her with a good deal of pleasure, for in spite of her man's garb she was a sight to heat any man's blood. With her face flushed to a soft pink glow and her eyes two sleepy orbs of emerald green, she was all temptation and he felt the blood pump rapidly through his body. He acknowledged her question with a bland smile, his eyelids dipping languidly over his dark eyes as he continued to study her at length, musing in rueful reflection over their predicament.

'I told you. We ride north.'

'How far north?' she pressed. 'Nottingham? York?'

'Much farther than that.'

Lifting her gaze, Serena stared at him in a rising panic. 'You mean we are to leave England?' she asked aghast, her eyes pleading to be told she was wrong. 'Is it your intention for us to go to Scotland?'

'Edinburgh is to be our destination, but I wish to stop in Northumberland first. If the going doesn't change for the worse, we should be there in a few days.'

'If we live that long,' Serena jibed, her chin rising in a gesture of unswerving tenacity. 'If we venture from the main routes, there is every danger that we will be set upon and murdered by highwaymen.'

'And if we don't stay out of sight there is every possibility that I shall be recognised. Besides, the main routes will be congested. The roads will be so churned up we will be up to our girths in mud, which will hamper our progress.'

'Then why go all that way?'

'As a precaution.'

'You must have a lot of courage to take me there. I promise I will be no compliant captive.'

'You are not my captive.'

'Are telling me I am free to leave?'

'At your peril, madam.'

'Forgive me if I appear a little confused. On one hand I am not your captive—and yet on the other I am. It would seem we are in for a wonderful time,' Serena responded, her tone heavy with sarcasm.

Kit's handsome eyebrows gathered together with annoyance. 'I certainly don't call it wonderful being arrested, having my property taken from me and my betrothed's father no longer considering me a suitable husband for his daughter.'

'Then you should do something about it.'

'I intend to.'

'You cannot be in too much of a hurry if you are to hide away in Scotland—to take to the hills like a fox being chased by the pack.'

'Northumberland, initially,' Kit corrected.

'What's the difference?' Serena snapped sullenly. 'It might as well be the outer limits of Mongolia to me.'

'And it is not in my nature to hide from anything or anyone. I am merely biding my time,' Kit told her coldly. 'When the time is right and things have cooled down, and with a little help from Ludovick, who will keep me informed as to what is happening in London, I shall return to England to clear my name.'

Serena glanced at him questioningly. 'Sir Ludovick knows you are going to Scotland?'

'Yes.'

'I see,' she said, sighing deeply. 'So I have to endure weeks, if not months, in that godforsaken place until you think the time is right to return. If I request to join my father, what will you say?'

Kit's stare became glacial, his tone harsh, annoyed with himself for allowing her irritating persistence on this matter to effectively get under his skin. 'That it is impossible. To consider such a journey unprotected would place you in great peril.'

Kit sounded angry, but Serena detected a note of real concern underlying the rebuke and was confused by it. As she met his eyes, a wry smile curved her lips. 'And there speaks a man who has travelled and seen much of the world. However, if things should change, is there no port or coastal village where I might obtain a passage on a vessel bound for the Low Countries?'

A corner of Kit's lips lifted roguishly as he pinned his eyes to hers. 'Northumberland can boast almost forty miles of wonderful coastline, with ports where vessels sail to all parts of the kingdom and the world. But we shall be away from the coastal areas and, with the onset of winter and the threat of snow, it will be a dangerous trek overland to Berwick or one of the other ports. Besides, the North Sea is a challenge to all seamen at this time of year.' His eyes narrowed and his smile became provoking. 'So you see, like it or not, we are stuck with each other.' He frowned suddenly. 'Have you really no idea where your father might have gone?'

Serena's eyes clouded. 'I know where he will most likely be, and I wish with all my heart that it were not so.' She swallowed, looking down at her hands, knowing her father would have sought the comforts of Mrs Davis, and strongly suspecting her own discomforts would be much harder to bear than his. 'Please don't ask me,' she said quietly.

Kit considered her, observing the despairing look that entered her eyes as she looked away, and he frowned, respecting her request not to pry. But what she left unsaid obviously troubled and pained her greatly.

'I only hope we arrive at our destination before the snow sets in. It has often been known to last until May,' he murmured casually, knowing what Serena's reply would be—amused when it came in an explosion.

Her head snapped up and she stared at him aghast, stung once more into awareness and alarmed by his casual words. 'May? You mean I will have to remain with you until May?'

To her consternation and irritation Kit laughed outright in the face of her anger, stretching out his long booted legs to the heat of the fire. 'Maybe you will.'

'Considering what has befallen you, my lord, you look disgustingly relaxed and at ease,' she said waspishly, glowering across at him. 'And where are we to stay when we reach Northumberland? Are we to be alone the whole time?'

'That troubles you, does it?' Kit asked calmly, his eyes probing hers, answering her question with another.

'Of course it troubles me. I have no wish to be alone with you.'

'Then let me set your mind at rest. My mother has land and property in the north. It is my intention to go there for a while.'

Serena felt a sudden stirring of interest, realising how little she knew about him. 'Your mother is alive?'

He grinned. 'Very much so.'

'And she lives in Northumberland?'

'No. At least, not all the time if it can be avoided. She hates the isolation of it. Since my father's death she prefers to live in Edinburgh.'

'When my uncle fails to find us, how do you know he will not direct his attention to the north?'

'Lord Carberry knows very little about my mother's estate in Northumberland, and besides,' Kit murmured, a wicked gleam glimmering in his dark eyes and a cocksure grin lifting one corner of his lips, 'he will need the instincts and the nose of a wolfhound to track us to where we are going.'

He fell silent, leaving Serena to wonder with considerable apprehension at this place of such isolation he was taking her to.

Gazing at the dancing flames licking feverishly at the logs, Kit was content to bask in the warmth, feeling comfortable with Serena's company, despite her antagonism and shrewish tongue. He settled back, reluctant to resume their journey until the rain had abated.

As she too basked in the glowing heat, Serena availed herself of the chance to take account of her companion. Her gaze leisurely observed his lean yet muscular thighs, and she allowed it to wander upwards over his padded breeches to his narrow waist and powerful shoulders, her eyes settling on his dark features. He had nothing wanting in looks or bearing. Mentally she tried imagining what it would be like to be loved by such a man. Exquisite sensations sped through her veins at the mere thought, but she squashed the wayward feelings with a determined frown, knowing it would do her no good to let her mind go wandering along those lines.

Beneath lowered lashes she found herself meeting his

gaze once more and flushed softly. The tug at his lips and the narrowing of his brooding dark eyes told her he had read her thoughts.

'Please believe me when I tell you that I only have your welfare at heart,' he said softly.

'You have a strange way of showing it,' she quipped.

'Then I shall try harder, Serena,' he murmured, ignoring the questioning lift of her brow at his use of her name. 'We must both try to make the best of a situation not of our making.'

Serena was not so easily mollified. 'You are wrong, sir—'

'My name is Kit. If we are to share each other's company for a length of time, I think we should dispense with the formalities.'

'Then if we are to remain here for a while I would be obliged if you would be quiet and let me rest. I am heartily sick of arguing. My bones ache and I am extremely tired. And I have no wish to venture out until the rain has stopped.'

'I too am wearied of argument,' said Kit, rising to his feet to go and have a word with the landlord. He stretched and yawned, respecting Serena's need to rest. 'It was a cursed hard ride. You are right to close your eyes. I, too, have no wish to travel farther in this confounded rain.'

With her feet in the hearth, Serena settled back and closed her eyes to shut Kit out, but they flickered open when he rose, drawn to him by his sheer physical presence. For a moment she felt her resistance waver, but then she rebuked herself, bringing her mind to a grinding halt. For her peace of mind she must not let him get beneath her guard. On a sigh she closed her eyes and was soon drifting into the realms of sleep.

After a brief rest Kit thought it was time to leave. Serena was sound asleep, her feet drawn up onto the settle and her head resting on her arm. Her hair tumbled about her face and her eyes were closed, her gold-tipped lashes lying like soft shadows on her rose-red cheeks. Her sweet lips were parted as she breathed softly, her chest rising and falling evenly beneath her doublet, which hid the tempting roundness of her breasts. As Kit was about to wake her he lingered, looking down at her in wonder, savouring this moment of peace and reluctant to wake her, when she would once more become an injured, hissing cat.

Studying her carefully, Kit thought that in sleep she looked more like a child than a woman, harmless, innocent and uncommonly lovely. Although there were similarities between her and Dorothea, Dorothea's qualities were of the pale kind, in sharp contrast to Serena, who was a vision of fire and beauty.

Serena felt a hand on her shoulder and someone gently shaking her awake. Opening her eyes, she looked up into the dark, brooding eyes of her captor.

'Come,' he said gently. 'It's noon and time we were on our way.'

Still extremely tired and aching in every limb, Serena forced herself to sit up and struggled into her boots. 'Has it stopped raining?' she mumbled tiredly, knotting her hair beneath her hat.

'For now. We'll find another inn before dark and bed down for the night.'

Before Serena could utter another sound, Kit had picked up her now dry cloak and placed it around her shoulders. Mutely she followed him outside, coming awake the moment she felt the cold, icy blast of wind on her cheeks. Taking a deep breath, she mounted Polly and followed Kit out of the inn yard, continuing to head north towards Northumberland.

Chapter Eight

Northumberland lay between the Tyne and the Tweed and on a tilt towards the North Sea. Its countryside was of rivers and forests, where the Celts, Romans and Normans had all left their own particular mark. From the south the traveller was able to take in the whole of the north borderland of England, mile after mile over fell and vale, across the long ridges to Cheviot and the Solway, where streams and burns meandered in timeless grace between the hills and centuries old deep clefts.

Kit and Serena had been travelling for five days, and the farther north they went the biting cold deepened. It was on one such night, at a busy hostelry in Teesdale, when Serena had her first alarming and embarrassing encounter with Kit. Retiring for the night, she was too exhausted to notice that she had drawn the attention of one of the patrons. With a keen interest the man had watched her eat her meal and say goodnight to her companion, taking particular note when he heard her say that she would see him in the morning.

Serena was deep in slumber when the knocking began on her door. Responding with an objectionable groan, she pulled the covers up over her head, too tired to acknowledge it. When it persisted, her eyes heavy with sleep, she padded across the floor, shivering when she felt the cold air assault her bare flesh. Clad only in a shift, it was in moments like these when she would have given anything for the protection of a robe.

Sounds of people still about drifted up to her from the ground floor of the inn, indicating that the hour could not be all that late. She yawned. It must be an important matter for Kit to feel the need to wake her—but, she thought with a feeling of annoyance, if it was his intention to share her bed, she would give him short shrift.

Suddenly the door was thrust open and she fell back with a gasp. In the dim light a man pushed past her and shut the door. It was difficult to see who it was, but of one thing she was quite certain: it wasn't Kit. Suddenly she was wide awake, outraged at the man's audacity to force his way into her room. Breathing heavily, he made a grab for her, but she evaded his groping hands.

'Come now,' the man hissed as she moved away from him, eyeing him warily. 'I've had my eye on you ever since you entered the inn.'

'Get out of my room before I scream,' Serena ordered through gritted teeth.

'Nay—be nice to me, now,' the man crooned, his tongue sloppy with drink. 'I saw you downstairs and right fetching you looked in those boy's breeches. Let's see what tasty bits they concealed, shall we?'

Breathing hard, the man lunged for her again. Anticipating his move, Serena made a dash for the door, but he reached out and grasped her hair, making her cry out in pain as he pulled her back, grabbing her round the waist, flinging her on to the bed and swooping down on her. A fierce struggle ensued between them. Serena lashed out and kicked him with all her strength, her stomach heaving at the stench of his sweat and the foul breath on her face.

With panic born out of desperation, she managed to reach out and grasp a candlestick standing on a table beside the bed. Raising her arm, she hit her assailant hard on the head with the heavy object with utter disregard to the consequences, hearing him grunt before going limp against her.

With her heart pounding and blood drumming in her ears, quickly Serena disentangled herself from his limbs and flew towards the door, pulling it open and dashing across the passageway to Kit's room. Slipping inside, she pressed herself against the panels—and, at the sight that met her eyes, immediately wondered if she might not have jumped out of the pan into the fire by seeking this particular sanctuary.

Kit was stark naked, having just finished washing. The candles burning in the room cast a mellow light around him, and he turned on hearing the door open, far from disconcerted when he saw Serena. Her skimpy shift outlined her perfect shape. Pressed against the door she was breathing hard, her face flushed and her hair a wild tangle about her bare shoulders. Kit stared at her, his eyebrows arched in surprise. In embarrassed confusion Serena quickly turned her head to avoid looking at his nakedness, and with a soft chuckle of amusement and casual unconcern, Kit picked up a towel and wrapped it around his waist.

'I—I'm so sorry,' Serena gasped, flaming tides of hot colour sweeping over her face. 'Please forgive my intrusion.'

'I'm surprised that you of all people would enter a gentleman's bedchamber without knocking,' Kit drawled. 'As you can see—I wasn't expecting you.'

Serena didn't want to see. She didn't want to look at him at all, and she was thankful of the curtain of hair that hung down the side of her face, shielding her view. 'There's a man in my room,' she blurted out. 'When he knocked on my door I thought it was you.'

Kit frowned, no longer smiling. 'So you let him in?'

She gulped and nodded. 'Yes. He—he is an ill-mannered

oaf and quite drunk. He tried to force himself on me—and we—we fought.'

Kit immediately strode across to her and took her shoulders, gripping them hard, his expression grim. 'Look at me, Serena,' he demanded in a tone that prompted her obedience. Slowly she turned her head to look at him. 'Did he hurt you?'

She shook her head, oddly touched by his concern. 'No. But I think I may have hurt him. I only hope I haven't killed him.'

Kit's eyes narrowed speculatively. 'Why? What have you done?'

'I—I hit him on the head with a candlestick.'

At the vehemence with which she spoke, Kit had great difficulty in repressing a grin. 'Poor man. Had he known he was about to face a voracious hawk instead of a docile, domestic dove, he would have avoided your door like he would a thousand plagues. Wait here. I'll go and see.'

Drawing her to one side, he went out, just in time to see a man stumbling quickly away down the passageway groaning and holding his head as if all the serpents in hell had invaded his skull. Scowling, Kit watched the pathetic wretch go, sorely tempted to go after him and beat him to a bloody pulp for daring to lay hands on Serena, but he thought better of it. Nothing would be achieved by thrashing a drunken man and drawing attention to themselves.

Kit returned to find Serena standing with her arms crossed firmly over her chest. 'Rest assured that you did the man no harm,' he told her, going to the window to draw the curtains. 'He's already stumbling down the passageway in search of his own chamber. In the morning when he wakes he will be unable to remember what hit him.'

Unconsciously Serena's eyes were drawn to Kit as he turned from her to pull at the curtains, her gaze settling on his back. She found herself admiring his wide shoulders and narrow hips with the towel draped snugly around them. The sight of his semi-nakedness caused her heart to quicken with excitement. The sinews of his bare back rippled as he moved, and there was a sensuality that sparked the hot blood within her. It was difficult for a young woman not to admire a man who was built with such perfect proportions as he was.

Kit turned and caught her watching him. Meeting his level gaze, she flushed crimson and turned her head away. Slowly he moved towards her with a lopsided smile on his lips and a purposeful gleam in his dark eyes.

'I'm happy to learn you would be willing to open your door to me, Serena—should I come knocking in the middle of the night,' he murmured huskily, his eyes burning into hers as he reached out and lightly brushed away some wisps of her hair that clung to her face. 'And you cannot really blame the man—whoever he was—for seeking you out, looking as you do. I can well understand how he felt.'

'There's no excuse for his behaviour,' Serena retorted hotly, doing her utmost to hold on to her crumbling composure and keep her eyes above Kit's waist. 'And I trust you will not have need to come knocking on my door in the middle of the night. If you have anything to say to me it can wait until morning.'

She walked past him towards the door, but suddenly Kit's arm went round her and he pulled her back against his naked chest.

'You don't have to go,' he said, his voice low and urgent.

'I—I must.'

'No, Serena,' he murmured, turning her round to face him and slipping his fingers through the hair on either side of her face. 'I have needs. I need you.'

'Need!' she gasped, seeing the workings of his mind and unable to say more, because at that moment he stopped her mouth with a kiss, shocking her senses alarmingly.

Kit's lips moved hungrily over hers, bruising and demanding, warming her to the core of her being, and beneath the onslaught of his fervour she felt herself go limp against him, feeling her body's betrayal as it began to respond shamelessly. She felt his hand boldly slipping inside the neck of her low bodice and lightly cup and caress her warm breast, feeling and teasing the hard nipple between his fingers. His mouth left hers and travelled down her throat, finally coming to that object which was giving him so much pleasure. His mouth sought and caressed it, the heat of his lips scalding her through the thin protection of cloth.

Again Kit found her lips, his hands moulding themselves to her buttocks and pressing her to him until she could no longer ignore the evidence of his burgeoning passion. The warmth of his naked flesh penetrated the delicate material of her shift, and as she felt his fingers grow bolder and begin raising the hem, she pulled back.

'No, Kit,' she gasped, her senses reeling. 'It will serve no purpose.'

'No?' he said, his voice oddly strained, unable to hide his annoyance on finding his lusts thwarted. Her nearness had aroused him to such a pitch that he had a sudden need to rearrange his towel.

Ignoring the plea in Kit's dark, compelling eyes, Serena tore herself from him and returned to her room, locking the door and seeking the warm sanctuary of her bed once more. She struggled to blot all that had just happened from her mind—of the stranger's pawing hands and the disgusting smell of him. But nothing could stop her thinking of Kit and how he had looked in his nakedness when she had entered his room. The magnificence of his masculine body had almost proved too much for her virgin eyes. His broad shoulders and muscular chest, his flat belly and his manhood, and every other disconcerting feature about his perfect body, had been scorched and were branded on her memory for all time

* * *

On what Kit hoped would be their last night on the road they spent at an inn close to the church and the market place in Corbridge, a bustling trading town on the southern border of Northumberland. The town, approached from the south, appeared as a compact huddle of stone houses and slate roofs above the banks of the River Tyne, but as they drew closer it became clear to Serena that it was an important commercial centre—its trade, Kit explained, mainly in leather, hides and iron.

Outside the inn Kit dismounted and helped Serena down. Usually when he offered his assistance she coolly and stubbornly rejected it, afraid of coming too close after that night in Teesdale. But this evening, having ridden farther than during any of the days they had been on the road, she was more fatigued than usual and almost fell into his arms in her eagerness to find a bed, where she might creep beneath the feather comforters and sleep until dawn.

The following morning Kit rose early and went to wake her, intending to make an early start. Usually she was up and ready to leave as soon as they had broken their fast, but this morning when he tapped on her door there was no answer. The door opened slightly at a push and he paused and looked inside, thinking she must have risen before him and gone downstairs, but the sight that greeted him made him catch his breath. Serena was only half dressed and humming a soft, lilting tune as she washed herself over a bowl.

Her arms and shoulders were bare, her thick auburn tresses fastened on her head in wild confusion. Rubbing soap on to her creamy skin, she was so absorbed in her task that she was unaware of Kit's presence. Utterly bewitched and enchanted he stood perfectly still, unable to drag his eyes away from this treasure that was indeed a sight for sore eyes. Everything about her was untamed and passionate, and every move she made was a sensual invitation to his starved senses.

What little there was of her shift moulded itself to her body with endearing delight, and Kit's eyes devoured the loveliness she displayed, every nerve in his body coming alive and responding to her as she leaned over the bowl to wash her face. His gaze followed tiny droplets of water as they trickled slowly down her throat and disappeared between the curves of her fully ripened breasts, their roundness and rosy peaks invitingly exposed and beckoning his hungry gaze as her skimpy white bodice scooped open to reveal all.

Remembering what it had been like to feel and kiss those exquisite orbs, Kit felt a rush of blood to his temples and his stomach quivered. Unaware of his quiet watchfulness, Serena reached for the towel and began rubbing herself dry, still humming softly to herself. Kit was tempted to rush inside and clasp her in a fierce embrace but, knowing she would explode in a storm of rage for daring to look at her in her state of undress, he smiled crookedly and stepped back.

Unwittingly, he must have made a sound or she sensed his presence, for with a gasp she turned towards the door, swiftly placing the towel in front of her to conceal her nakedness. Her eyes widened with furious rage when they went beyond the door and focused on Kit's smiling, impertinent face. She flushed scarlet, but then her chin came up and she burst into life like an erupting volcano.

'Kit Brodie!' she lambasted. 'Have you no manners at all that you must come prowling and spy on me like an impertinent sneak thief!'

Standing there half naked she tried to protect her modesty with a damp towel, finding it ironical that their roles should be reversed from the night she had come upon him stark naked in his chamber.

She looked so adorable and desirable to Kit that he could

not resist taunting her. Brazenly he pushed the door open
and stepped inside, closing it behind him to protect her
from the eyes of other patrons staying at the inn. He
grinned, pure devilment dancing in his black eyes as they
travelled from her flaming face to the towel she clutched
to her bosom.

'I did knock—which is more than can be said of you
when you sought me out in my chamber,' Kit reminded
her, his eyes resting on her full, soft lips. 'The door was
off the latch so I thought I'd wake you. Recalling how
fatigued you were last night, I thought perhaps you might
need a little encouragement to get out of bed.'

'As you can see I am wide awake and getting washed,
so kindly have the decency to leave,' she snapped. 'How
dare you intrude on my privacy? I'm sure you have seen
enough to appease your ardour.'

Kit's teeth flashed like a pirate's in his swarthy face.
Settling his hands on his hips, he slowly advanced towards
her, the torment of wanting her almost unbearable. 'Indeed,
you are extremely fair to look upon, Serena. My eyes have
not seen nearly enough and ache to see more.'

Something in his expression made Serena shrink back.
She was conscious of his height and how his mere presence
seemed to fill the small chamber. Because he was fully
dressed in his black doublet and thigh-length boots, she was
extremely conscious of her own state of undress, and she
was also conscious and alarmed that she was stirred by his
masculinity. But she refused to surrender to the call of her
blood and crushed these treacherous feelings that threatened
to weaken her. Glaring at him, her green eyes were vibrant
and burning with ire and indignation.

'Don't you dare lay a hand on me, Kit Brodie. Come
any nearer and I swear I shall scream the place down.'

Kit's bold gaze continued to openly rake her body but,
recognising the merits of restraint, he checked himself and
advanced no farther. What had begun as teasing was in

danger of turning to something more and getting completely out of hand if he touched her, because he knew if he did he would be unable to conquer his desire and would drag her on to the bed and make love to her. He chuckled and turned from her.

'Fear not, Serena, I shall not abuse or take advantage of you in your moment of weakness. However,' he murmured, turning and drinking his fill of her comely shape behind the towel once more, 'I can only hope my act of mercy will in due course reap its own rewards.'

Serena recognised the meaning behind his words. 'You beast!' she flared. He was laughing as he moved towards the door and her lips formed every conceivable insult she could throw at him as she gave vent to her anger. Bending down, she picked up her boot, hurling it viciously at the door as he passed through. Unfortunately it missed and hit the wood instead with a resounding thud before falling to the floor, and still she could hear his laughter as he went along the passageway.

Kit derived immense pleasure from the memory he carried with him downstairs, and not even the landlord's succulent breakfast could compete with the comeliness of Serena's adorable assets. On a more serious note, he knew he must fight to keep tight rein on his desires where she was concerned. He was in no position to form a serious relationship with a woman of her background until he had cleared his name of the evil he had been unjustly accused of, and his property and titles had been restored.

But, he thought, smiling quietly to himself, there was no reason why the time they had to spend together could not be pleasurable.

After a long angry moment Serena calmed down enough to finish her toilet and dress for the day's journey. Dreading the moment when she would have to face Kit, she was sorely tempted to leave him at the inn and find her way to the coast, despite having given him her word that she would do no such thing. But she knew she would get no farther than the end of the street before he discovered her absence and came after her.

The sky was heavy with snow as Kit and Serena continued northwards. Knowing there would be no inn in which they could spend the night, there was a need for haste. It was Kit's intention to reach their destination before nightfall.

The countryside became wilder and more desolate. They followed drovers' and packhorse tracks, tracks that had been followed for centuries. Serena was uneasy, certain they would lose their way and become lost—or worse. They might be set upon, robbed and murdered by thieves. But she found her fears easing gradually as they progressed, feeling a strange security in the presence of her companion—despite his conduct earlier. Kit knew the area well and, looking large and forbidding astride his large dappled brown horse, with a pistol at his belt and a sword hanging from his saddle, he would instil caution in the meanest robber.

A lightening of spirits seemed to come over them both. Perhaps it was because they were conscious of nearing their destination or because the place itself was weaving a spell around them but, whatever the reason, Serena felt a whole new world inviting her to explore, becoming pleasantly aware of the beauty and strangeness all around her, the smell of the crisp, cold air, the sodden grass and rich damp earth which, like a drug, all seeped into her skin.

Following Kit along the tracks, she listened in silent admiration as he ardently pointed out places of interest to her, enthusing at length about every one of them, telling her about the moorland ridges and the North Sea to the east, and the gently undulating Cheviots in the north. Serena saw her first shaggy cattle and black-faced sheep, and she laughed with Kit when they heard the chuckling grouse in the heather, watching in admiration as ptarmigan and wild duck took flight on being disturbed, and commented on the inquisitive black cock, whose sharp eyes would follow them until they were out of sight.

It was clear to Serena how much Kit loved this country, that it was like wine to his soul, and how loath he must be to leave it for the south. They were in a valley sheltered from the buffeting wind that scudded the heavy snow clouds across the sky when they stopped for something to eat. A wide stream tumbled its way through the centre, in a hurry like themselves to reach its destination. Unfastening the bag containing the food they had purchased in Corbridge from Kit's saddle, they left the horses to graze and found a secluded spot beneath some boulders.

Serena perched on a rock, munching her bread and cheese in silence. Appreciative of the view she gazed along the length of the valley. Enthralled, a feeling of peace engulfed her. Having lived all her life in a turmoil, the quiet was foreign to her. In a sense she became like someone who had fallen under some kind of enchantment. Unbeknown to her the wind had brought colour to her cheeks and her face had softened, her magnificent eyes glowing jewel bright.

'It's a magnificent view,' she commented softly, turning to look at her companion, and when she caught his eye she sensed he was feeling exactly as she felt, that the place had cast its own special enchantment on him, too, but unlike her he was familiar to it.

Kit was sitting with his back against a rock watching her, an arm resting casually on his raised knee. Something in his expression made Serena's breath catch in her throat and look away. A warm glow spread inside her and she felt a brazen longing to be close to him, a feeling not unknown to her, having experienced it before when they were together like this.

'I have to agree with you, Serena,' Kit replied, using her

name easily now. It sounded so perfectly natural to Serena
that she failed to notice it any more.

Kit tore a piece of bread from a loaf and began eating it
slowly, contemplating her profile. For most of the time he
had been purposely quiet and tolerant of Serena's capri-
cious moods, knowing the loss of her home and her father's
plight in the Low Countries were still very fresh in her
mind. But she had withstood the long journey well. He
would have expected her to look pale and drawn after the
long days on the road, but amazingly she seemed to thrive
on it.

Gazing at her in rueful reflection, he recalled how she
had looked earlier when he found her half naked. The rec-
ollection stirred and raked the red-hot embers in his mind.
She had been totally at ease and unaware of the watchful
interest of his gaze. He recalled the moment when she had
bent forward and the neckline of her bodice had gaped open
to reveal the soft plumpness of her breasts and high peaks
of the lustrous, rose-red nipples, hardened by the cold water
she had splashed on her chest.

His eyes dark and brooding, leisurely he leaned back
against the rock, his memory expanding, the vision bringing
a smile to his lips and a narrowing to his eyes, and he could
see in his mind's eye the look on her face when she had
turned on him, her eyes as vindictive and sharp as a snipe's
beak that could pick a man's bones clean. But now he saw
how soft and flushed her face was in repose, her thick
lashes making soft shadows on her cheeks and her hair a
glorious halo of auburn light.

'What time do you think it is?' Serena asked, breaking
into his thoughts, mercifully unaware of the direction in
which they were travelling.

'Around noon, I imagine. Why do you ask?'

'Will we be at our destination before dark?'

Kit frowned, glancing up at the leaden clouds hanging
low over the hills and noting the strong, snow laden gusts

of wind whipping across the landscape. He hoped the snow would hold off until they reached Addlington Hall, his grandmother's old home. 'Hopefully. If the snow holds off, that is. But the sky bodes ill. Eat as much as you can now because I don't want to stop again.'

Prodigiously hungry, Serena was eager to comply and unashamedly cut herself another large hunk of bread and cheese. When she was replete she went to the stream, noting the ice-crusted edges as she scooped some of the freezing water into her hands and drank. With a ghost of a smile on his lips, Kit never took his eyes off her, silently admiring and contemplating her every move.

'I'm impressed,' Serena said, wiping the water from her chin with the back of her hand and resuming her perch on the boulder, a little smile dimpling her cheeks. 'How could I ever have imagined we would become lost with you as our guide? You follow the tracks like a true native.'

Kit grinned. 'That's because I am. I was born and raised in Northumberland at Minton Hall—several miles south of Coldstream on the Scottish border.'

Serena was surprised, not realising until then that he came from the north. 'And is that where we are going?'

'No. I'm taking you to my maternal grandmother's home, Addlington Hall, which is not quite as far north as that.'

'Who lives there now?'

'No one. Apart from a couple of servants my mother employs as caretakers, that is. Under the entailment and because there was no son, the house and land came to my mother on my grandmother's death, which was quite recent.'

'And will it be yours one day?'

Kit's expression hardened. 'In the event of recent happenings and my assumed involvement in the Gunpowder Plot, that depends on what happens to Thurlow and if the king sees fit to redeem it to me. It became forfeit to the

Crown on my arrest. I inherited Thurlow when my cousin died. My father grew up there but, being the younger of two sons, he did not inherit the estate.'

'Are the Brodies not a Scottish family?'

'Yes. But it's a large family and became scattered, some going south during my great-grandfather's time. Thurlow came into the family about then.'

'And is your mother Scottish?'

'Like my father, she has an equal smattering of both English and Scottish blood. When my father married her, he was fortunate that her family held many properties in the north—one of them being Minton Hall, which was where they chose to live,' Kit explained. 'I was very close to my maternal grandmother and spent my youth between the two houses. But much as I love Northumberland, Thurlow was where I chose to live when I inherited it from my cousin.'

Serena looked at him curiously, realising that she did not know this man at all. He had looked so very much at home in Warwickshire that she'd imagined he'd spent all his life in the south and close to the court. Yet he seemed completely at home here in the wilds of Northumberland as well. She noted that a faraway look entered his eyes as his gaze swept down the valley.

'Between a man's intention and what actually happens, lies a distance that must be measured in fathoms,' he said quietly, 'which I have come to find out during these last weeks. I had planned to live each day at Thurlow in wedded bliss to Dorothea, but I soon found that this would be impossible. Events over the past weeks have prevented that.'

'And if Thurlow is redeemed to you, what will become of your grandmother's house? You cannot live in two places.'

'I have a brother and a sister. Melissa is eighteen years old and lives with my mother in Edinburgh for most of the time. It's possible that when she marries, she—or Paul, for that matter—might favour living at Addlington Hall. It depends on what my mother intends doing with the estate. I would like you to become acquainted with them while you are in the north—if it isn't asking too much.'

'No, not at all. Thank you. I would like that. And where is your brother?'

'Paul is doing military service in the Low Countries.'

'Like his brother before him. I can see that you love Northumberland, and I fail to understand how you can bear to leave it feeling as you do,' said Serena, trying hard to understand, never having lived anywhere other than Dunedin Hall. Her face was puzzled. 'How can you belong by blood to one place and yet feel at home in another? Evidently you have the ability to belong to wherever you happen to be.'

'That is true. But here I can be myself.'

'Yes,' she said. 'I can see that.'

The intensity, the warmly intimate look in Kit's dark eyes held Serena transfixed, its warmth igniting a flame within her blood. Her delicately beautiful face was framed by her halo of hair blowing in the restless wind, and the effect of Kit's gaze was vibrant and alarmingly alive. She tried to imagine him as a boy riding these hills and fells, seeing him little different to how he looked now, with his unruly black hair blowing in the wind, riding his horse with nobility and pride, as rugged and hard as the landscape over which he rode.

'No matter where I am I shall always regard Northumberland as my home,' said Kit. Standing up and moving towards her, he grinned suddenly, sparkling devilment dancing in his eyes when he looked down into her upturned face, his heavy-lidded gaze speculative. 'One day you will thank me for bringing you here and widening your horizons.'

Taking her hand, Kit drew her to her feet, keeping hold of it far too long for Serena's comfort. His warm strong grip and probing dark gaze disturbed her, making it more difficult for her to regard him as an enemy, but the arrogant self-assurance of his expression made her suddenly wary of him and she bristled. His words reminded her with harsh clarity that he was the one responsible for preventing her from going to her father in Flanders, something which had momentarily slipped her mind. Resenting his easy dismissal of her grudge against him, she found it difficult to remain civil.

'I could have widened my own horizons just as well in Flanders,' she told him sharply, her eyes sparking as she tossed her head with a flippant air and snatched her hand from his grasp. 'With people of my own choosing. You may yet live to rue the day you insisted I accompany you to Northumberland.'

Having roused the vixen he had come to know and love, a corner of Kit's lips lifted roguishly and his eyes pinned hers until he saw a flush of ire mount her cheeks. 'Why? Do I abuse you?' he asked. 'Is my treatment of you so agonising that you do not take stock of your surroundings and admire and glory in them. You must forgive me,' he chuckled softly, 'but I was of the opinion that you were beginning to enjoy seeing Northumberland almost as much as I do myself.'

'Yes, you abuse me constantly and should die of shame for bringing me here against my will,' Serena berated him angrily. 'And despite the beauty of the place it does not compensate for the cold and damp that is beginning to seep into my bones, numbing my mind so I can scarcely think or feel anymore. Nor do I like the discomfort of riding mile upon mile along endless tracks, fit only for goats rather than men and horses, where we may be set upon at any time and rendered helpless by outlaws.'

'My dear Serena, when were you ever helpless?' Kit laughed. 'And God help any outlaw if they should dare attack you.'

Conspiracy of Hearts

Anger choked any words Serena would have uttered and, turning from the amusement in his wickedly dancing dark eyes and infuriating grin, she flounced off to where they had left their horses, just as the first flurries of snow began to fall.

Dismayed to find their horses had wandered to the other side of the fiercely tumbling stream where they were contentedly nibbling at the grass, she looked down at the water, reluctant to wade across. It was deep in places and would be sure to come over the tops of her boots, and she had no wish to continue the rest of the journey with wet feet. Calling to Polly to come back, the usually obedient horse merely glanced at her and carried on munching the grass, infuriating her further.

Having noted that Kit's skittish, high-spirited stallion had whickered and pranced and courted her beautiful Polly since the moment they had first become acquainted—and that the stallion's behaviour bore an uncanny resemblance to its master—she was certain that the wicked beast had something to do with her docile mare's change of temperament and disobedience.

Having collected the remnants of their meal and placed it back in the bag, Kit threw it over his shoulder and came to stand behind her.

'Allow me. Let me assist you. I think we will have to go to them,' and without further ado and before Serena could object, he caught her up, placing one arm beneath her knees and the other round her back, holding her so close she could feel the hard rack of his muscular chest, and the firm-as-a-rock steadiness of his arms.

But placing his booted feet on the rocky bed of the stream, Kit slipped—whether accidentally or on purpose Serena had no way of knowing, but she gasped, fully expecting to find herself immersed in the cold tumbling water. To her relief he regained his footing.

'Put me down,' she demanded. 'I can make my own way across.'

Kit laughed, having no intention of relinquishing his hold on this delectable baggage when he'd managed to draw her close at last. 'Just bear with me and cease struggling. I should hate to drench us both.'

Realising her arms had locked themselves about his neck, and having closed her eyes in panic the moment he had slipped, Serena now opened them cautiously, finding his face so very close to her own, his eyes staring into hers, plumbing their emerald depths with a leisured thoroughness as he splashed through the water.

Serena felt warmth spread unbidden over her face beneath his close perusal, embarrassed at finding herself held so close. They reached the other side of the stream and, after what she thought was an unnecessarily prolonged moment that set her teeth on edge, Kit lowered her to the ground, sliding her body down his slowly, determined to play his act of possession out to the very end.

Serena turned slightly, catching her breath in surprise when she felt the light touch of his hand against her breast. The contact sent a rush of excitement crashing through her, and it was somewhat surprising to realise that her breathing and her heartbeat were affected by his touch. She had only ever skirted on the fringes of sensual awareness, and it was astounding how quickly her body could respond.

Beneath her clothes her breasts became warm, pleasurably so, she was ashamed to realise, as her gaze fastened on Kit's. The glow of his dark eyes probed deep into hers, penetrating and questioning. They stood quite still, their gazes arrested, magnetised in the silent communication of sexual attraction, which was unlike anything Serena had experienced before. Her breath became snared in her throat, for she was absolutely astounded that he had the ability to scatter her wits and dismantle her defences so easily. The heat of a flush suffused her, her face becoming the colour of crimson. Again she met Kit's dark, warm eyes filled with challenging amusement, daring her to accuse him of any misdeed. But she knew he had a propensity for being mischievous and did not like being made sport of.

'Thank you,' she said stiffly, regaining her aloofness and stepping back. 'But whatever it is you have in mind where I am concerned, I would advise you not to trifle with me. Unlike Dorothea, I am not as easily taken in by a man who takes her fancy—although it is clear to me that you do not grieve over her loss.'

What she said was true. Dorothea had become just a pale shadow of Kit's past. 'It's unfortunate that our plans went awry, but I do not grieve for her. I was fond of your cousin but nothing more,' Kit readily admitted, secretly grateful to Lord Carberry for disclaiming his suit in the light of the Gunpowder Plot. If he hadn't done so, Kit wouldn't be here in total isolation with Serena.

Despite their differences and her determination to stand against him at every turn, even when she was enraged and taunted and goaded him in a way no one had dared to do before, Kit enjoyed being with her more than with any woman he had known. He was intrigued by every aspect of her. Never had he met a woman who could match her for fire and spirit, and if ever she opened her arms to him he would be hard pressed to remember any of them who had gone before.

Serena's mere presence could tantalise and awaken his lusting desires to the point of madness, while she was absolutely oblivious to what she did. She was too innocent and unworldly to realise she had been born with the wiles of a temptress.

'Weren't you a lovesmitten young woman once—when you fell prey to Blackwell's charms?' he taunted.

The emerald green eyes flashed with sparks of indignation. 'What my feelings were for that reprobate is none of your business, and I would be grateful if you would refrain from mentioning his name to me ever again.'

She turned from him and was about to move towards Polly when, suddenly, long fingers closed tightly upon her upper arms and Kit pulled her back against his hard chest, his breath warm on her cheek when he spoke, his lips so close to her ear that it set her body trembling in alarm. Without turning, she knew that his face had become warm and sensual.

'Please let me go,' she begged, her voice quavering, shock and surprise stiffening her body, anticipation of what was to come slamming against the self-control she was fighting to keep intact. She tried to struggle, but he held her firm.

'I will,' he murmured behind her, his voice deep and husky, teasing her ear with his lips, the touch so light she could have imagined it. 'I will respect your request, Serena, and I can only rejoice that you did not reject my touch as violently as you did Blackwell's.'

'Dear Lord,' Serena whispered in alarm, closing her eyes and leaning helplessly against her tormentor, feeling that it was like falling into the open jaws of a mantrap which would snap shut at any moment. 'Please don't do this to me. I want none of this.'

'I think it's a little late to start praying,' Kit teased huskily. 'Do not deny what you feel or try to forestall what your heart knows to be the inevitable. There may be conspiracies at work in the political sphere, Serena, but there is another kind of conspiracy working between us, between our hearts, that neither of us will be able to escape when it reaches its height.'

'How can you know my emotions when I have not expressed them to you?'

'I am attuned to what a woman thinks. I know perfectly well the effect it had on you when you felt my hands slide slowly down your body when I set you on the ground. It was my pleasure, Serena, I do assure you,' Kit said, his voice as seductive and soft as thick velvet. 'I look forward to the day when I will break the bonds of restraint which bind you—so for mercy's sake, do not fight me as you did Blackwell.'

Serena felt his lips drag themselves across her cheek when she pulled away from him. Without turning and quite perplexed, she moved towards Polly with wooden legs as she struggled to regain her composure, piece by shattered piece, feeling his eyes on her all the while.

What was happening to her? she asked herself, cursing the lure she had felt in the strength of Kit's arms, dauntingly aware that she would be unable to fight the desires his touch had aroused in her if they were to remain alone for much longer. How could her treacherous heart have betrayed her so readily—and with a man she told herself she had no particular liking for? The resentment and dislike she felt for him would need careful nurturing if they were to survive.

Trembling in every limb, she mounted her horse. As she began to ride on she tried not to look at Kit again, but she found it impossible not to, having to pass where he was waiting for her on his horse to cross to the other side of the stream. The cold stare she intended to fix on him melted when she faced him once more, and though she searched his face to find something there that would stir her resentment, there was nothing but a strange tenderness in the dark depths of his eyes.

Chapter Nine

The snow, which they had hoped would refrain from falling until they reached their destination, offered them no such respite. It began falling heavily during the afternoon, swirling in a sharp wind, and had soon formed a thick veil over the landscape. The path they were following disappeared and their tracks were soon filled in, with nothing to mark their passing. The horses moved at a steady pace, picking their way with care, but they would soon lose their ability to keep moving altogether if it got much deeper.

With the fading light it became bitterly cold. Their breath formed a cloud of vapour in the frosty air and their vision became limited. Serena's gloved hands, her feet, and even her mind, grew numb. There were moments when she had the absurd feeling that she was floating along. And then she knew it was nothing but a weak fantasy when her eyes focused on Kit's large figure just in front of her.

Had he been alone Kit might have carried on the three miles or so to Addlington Hall, but it was evident to him that Serena was chilled to the bone and nearing exhaustion. The light was fading fast and it was imperative that they found shelter soon, otherwise she was in danger of freezing to death. As they topped a ridge, Kit paused and turned to her before they made the descent.

'Stay close to me,' he shouted above the wind. 'It's treacherous at the best of times riding down this side of the hill. At the bottom we'll be on level ground and close to a place where we can stay the night. Hopefully we'll soon have a roof over our heads. It's not the destination I had planned, but we'll never make it there tonight.'

Serena's teeth were chattering so fiercely that she couldn't have replied if she'd wanted to. Slowly she followed Kit down the steep hill, feeling Polly slip and slither beneath her, praying she wouldn't fall out of the saddle. If she did, she would never manage to climb back up again.

Kit looked back to make sure she was all right, unable to see her face which was hidden beneath the large hood of her cloak. 'It's just a little farther,' he assured her. 'Stay close to me.'

An odd, disconnected shape appeared like a ghostly apparition out of the curtain of snow. Straining her eyes, Serena saw it was an ancient tower-like structure, just one of many she'd seen dotting the Northumberland landscape.

'Take care,' shouted Kit, the wind whipping the words from his lips. 'The tower used to be enclosed by a ditch. You can just see the traces of it where the snow hasn't quite filled it in.'

Picking their way across a narrow bridge, Serena's heart was in her mouth, fully expecting it to give way beneath them and send them tumbling into the ditch below. The wind chose that moment to go crazy, coming at them from all sides and blinding them with driven snow. Once across, Kit dismounted and went to Serena, his only thought being to get her inside the shelter of the tower as quickly as possible. Reaching up, he dragged her from the saddle, holding her tightly against him. Feeling her tense nerves responding to his touch, he struggled against the buffeting wind, fully aware that she was frozen through as she strained through the deepening drifts beside him, scarcely able to lift her feet.

The tower house, built by Kit's ancestors, was a strong structure with three storeys. Uninhabited for decades, it was almost derelict, but it would provide them with much-needed shelter for this one night. The basement was for stock, where Kit would stable the horses, and the entrance to the upper storeys was at first-storey level up a flight of stone steps, precariously covered with snow. Managing to surmount these and still holding Serena close to him, Kit put his weight to the broken timbers of the door, relieved when it swung open with a loud creak on its rusty hinges.

Their eyes did a broad sweep of their surroundings, able to make out tattered shreds of hangings on the walls encrusted with dirt, and the odd shapes of rotting and broken furniture. A small, gaping window was set high up in the wall through which snowflakes danced. Filthy, mildewed rushes were strewn on the floor, and there was a pile of half-charred logs in the raised hearth, no doubt left over from when some other traveller had sought shelter within these walls.

'Good Lord,' said Kit. 'I apologise for the sorry state of the place. It's dismal, I know, but it will have to do. We will not be too uncomfortable once we have a fire going and can feed our appetites.'

Serena stared around her in stunned disbelief. She had not expected him to bring her to a grand house, but this was dreadful. The cold had penetrated so deeply into the tower that she doubted even the fiercest furnace could warm it. Dread settled over her heart at the thought of having to spend the night in this foul-smelling, hideous place.

Drawing her farther inside, Kit sat her down on a broken settle. 'At least there's a fireplace. I'll get a fire going as soon as I've stabled the horses below. There's a bag of oats fastened to the saddle—not enough, but it will have to suffice until we get to Addlington. Will you be all right until I return?' he asked, drawing back her hood and peering into her face, which was as white as the snow outside.

Having lost the power of speech, Serena could only stare at him in disbelief, the thought of being alone in this awful place causing panic to well up inside her. When Kit moved towards the door she flew after him, intending to go with him, but he turned quickly and thrust her back down on to the settle, trying not to dwell on those mesmeric, terror-filled eyes.

'For once in your life do as you're told, Serena,' he ordered sharply. 'And don't give me that angry, defiant look,' he chastened when he saw her jerk up her chin a notch. 'In your present state you're too weak to stand against me. Now wait here. There's no one here so you'll be perfectly safe until I get back.'

In numb silence Serena watched him disappear into the swirling snow, wondering why he wasn't as cold as she was. He had such strength, such confidence. Was he some superhuman who could withstand the cruel elements?

Exhausted beyond measure she sighed, relieved to be under cover, but as she stared at the mess around her she shuddered with distaste. In alarm her eyes flew upwards when she heard sounds coming from the upper storey, all her senses reverberating through her. It sounded like the flapping of hundreds of tiny wings, causing her heart to stand still. Dear Lord, she prayed, please don't let them be bats.

Taking a deep breath, she closed her eyes, trying to suppress a persistent shiver, unable to believe that Kit had brought her to this gruesome place. She was floundering on the brink of exhaustion, bone weary, wet and cold, and after such a long journey she had expected to be welcomed by servants who would be waiting to cosset her, where she would find warmth and a meal, a bath and a comfortable chamber to sleep in, not this godforsaken derelict tower in the middle of a snow-covered wilderness. It was a world away from reality, one frozen in time where she could see nothing ahead of her but everlasting cold. Absolutely demoralised, she wanted to cry, but even her tears were frozen.

Kit was soon back, carrying the bags of food, an old rusty bucket he had found, and a lantern and tinderbox fitted with a flint and steel that he had miraculously discovered on a ledge in the basement where he had stabled the horses.

'The horses should be all right until morning,' he told her. 'At least it's dry down there. There's some peat heaped up if we should need it. As soon as I have a fire going I'll melt some snow down for water.'

After rummaging in one of the bags, he came towards her with a small vial and, after removing the stopper, placed it to her lips. 'Here. Take a sip of this brandy. It will warm you and put some life back into your frozen limbs.'

Weak and in no condition to refuse, Serena took a sip of the liquid, coughing and almost choking when the fiery liquid reached the back of her throat, but she was glad to feel its warmth spreading through her when it reached her stomach.

Despite the grim aspect of the stronghold, Kit directed himself to the task of building the fire. Collecting some of the dry rushes from the floor, he heaped them in the hearth for kindling. Piling the half-charred logs on top, he placed a light to it. The dry rushes soon took hold and began to blaze, feeding the hungry flames. When he was satisfied that it wouldn't go out, he turned his attention to Serena, perched on the edge of the settle. Going to her, he took her hand and raised her to her feet, drawing her towards the heat and dragging the settle after her.

'Here. Sit close to the fire. You'll soon begin to feel warmer.'

Doing as she was told and resuming her seat on the settle, Serena looked down at her hands. They were so painful she couldn't remove her gloves. Kit's eyes missed nothing. When he saw her glance helplessly down at her hands he became touchingly aware of the pain she was experiencing. Squatting down, he smiled at her as though she were a child and he was trying to coax away her anguish and fears.

'Here, let me,' he murmured, taking hold of her hands with a gentleness Serena had not expected of him.

He removed her gloves as if her fingers were so fragile they would break if he was unduly rough. Freeing them from their confinement, he enfolded her small hands in his own and tried to rub the circulation back into her frozen veins. With his head bent and intent on his task, he raised her hands to his lips, holding them there in the hope that the warmth from his mouth would help with the thaw, leisurely caressing the cold flesh with his lips.

Wholly dependent on him, Serena watched in rapt amazement. A pulsating heat began to throb in her hands, spreading outwards, and she felt shooting, tingling sensations travelling to the tips of her fingers. With her hands still enfolded in his, Kit's gaze swept upwards and regarded her in silence, and for a moment his eyes held hers with penetrating intensity.

The mysterious depths were as enigmatic as they were silently challenging, and unexpectedly Serena felt an answering response. The darkening in Kit's eyes warned her that he was aware of that brief response and his eyes narrowed, a hint of a smile tugging at his lips. No words were spoken, but in the glow of the firelight their eyes locked, each probing and searching the innermost thoughts of the other. When she would have pulled her hands free Kit refused to relinquish his hold. Taking one hand in each of his own, he placed them against his cheeks.

'Are they warmer now?'

Her lips trembled into a smile of thanks, bringing a glow to Kit's eyes—it was a smile that warmed him to his soul. 'For a smile like that I would sleep with Lucifer himself if I knew I could be the recipient of another like it,' he murmured.

There was so much sincerity in his voice that Serena felt her pulses quicken. Her confusion deepened and slowly she pulled her hands from his, afraid of what she was feeling. 'I don't think you need go to such lengths,' she replied softly.

Standing up, Kit took the bucket and went outside, returning a moment later with it filled with snow, standing it close to the fire to melt. Serena shuddered when she heard the flapping noises from above once more. A suffocating sensation came over her. Her eyes travelled up towards the ceiling with terror, and an unpleasant trickle of cold sweat ran down her spine. The excruciating horror that bats might come down the stairs en masse in a fearful black cloud ate into the deepest crannies of her mind, resurrecting awful memories of her childhood when she had become fastened in an old building where they roosted. Her fear-filled eyes flew to Kit's, who was faintly amused by her alarm.

'Heaven help me if there are bats up there,' Serena whispered. 'I would rather chance my luck with the elements outside than that.'

'Don't be alarmed. It's just birds roosting you can hear,' he told her. When he saw she wasn't convinced, he picked up the lantern and went to the narrow steps against the wall which led to the storey above. 'If it will allay your fears and make you feel easier, I'll go and see.'

The upper storey was as bleak and comfortless as the one below, the air stale and the wooden floor boards thick with bird droppings. The culprits, roosting in the rafters above, flapped their wings and squawked loud their annoyance at being disturbed, having entered through large holes in the roof through which snow flurried.

'I was right,' he told Serena when he returned. 'Only birds.'

'Are there no bats?'

He shook his head. 'Take my word for it, there's not a bat in sight. Why are you so afraid of them?'

'As a child I had an unpleasant experience when I found myself fastened in a disused stable where they roosted during the daylight hours. It was pitch-black but I could feel them. They were everywhere—in my hair, touching my face with their awful fluttering wings.' Serena shuddered at the memory. 'I was locked in that place for what seemed like an eternity—in fact, it was just a few minutes before John heard my screams and came to let me out.'

The terror Kit saw in her eyes was so touching that he felt a deep compassion. 'It must have been a terrifying experience for a young girl,' he sympathised, finding it strange that, in the light of her determination to stand firm and defiant against much stronger forces that threatened her, she should show such a profound fear of so small a creature.

Serena relaxed in the knowledge that there were no such creatures above. 'It was, which is why I have a fear of bats to this day.' Her eyes moved to the bags of food he had placed on the floor. Wanting to do something to help, she forced herself to rise. 'I'll see what we have left in the bag to eat. We might both feel better with some food inside us.'

Serena set about preparing them a meal whilst Kit took the bucket of melted snow down to the horses in the basement. There was cold meat and bread and cheese, which they could wash down with melted snow. When Kit returned they sat down to eat, she on the settle and Kit perched on the edge of the hearth; they ate in companionable silence, careful to leave some food for morning.

As the wind continued to buffet the tower, Serena, feeling considerably warmer removed her cloak and hat, releasing her hair from its knot and pulling out the tangles with her fingers. Giving the rich heavy tresses a hard shake, she was unconscious of the seductiveness of the casual gesture, unaware that Kit, standing perfectly still with his booted foot up on the hearth, was studying her intently.

She looked like a gypsy wench, he thought. This young woman was far more appealing to him than the glamorous Serena Carberry in all her fine clothes. Every nerve in his body was aware of her sensuality. His gaze followed her every movement and he felt his body respond.

Sensing his look, Serena stopped what she was doing and glanced up at him. She often found him gazing at her with a look that was at once questioning and much too personal, almost possessive. It disturbed her greatly for she could not ignore it. She could feel the power within him, and sensations of unexpected pleasure flowed through her. However, she had too many complications in her life just now and had no intention of becoming emotionally entangled with Kit Brodie. At this time of uncertainty she could not afford to.

'Do you feel better now?' Kit asked at length.

'Much better, but I would not like to have to remain in this place for any length of time,' Serena murmured, sitting back on the settle and trying to avoid a broken piece of wood, which was extremely sharp and had an annoying habit of prodding her in the back.

'I suspect many a weary traveller has sought shelter here at one time or another and been glad of it. Still, we'll only be here for tonight.'

'What if it doesn't stop snowing?'

'We'll have to wait until it does.'

She shuddered at the thought. 'Heaven forbid. What is this place?'

'It's called Hawk's Pele. Pele—or Peel—meaning a defensive enclosure within a ditch or mound,' Kit explained. 'Originally the term was applied to the enclosure and not the tower built within. They can be found scattered all over Northumberland—many of them are still inhabited. They were built as a stronghold for defence against destructive raids from over the border.'

'And who built this particular one?'

'My ancestors after the Battle of Bannockburn—when Scotland gained its independence from England over two hundred years ago. In those days it would have provided the family with a reasonable degree of comfort. Such a building was an essential structure for any man of property in the old days. Because Hawk's Pele was considered to be too remote and liable to be cut off, it was abandoned many years ago when Addlington Hall was built.'

'I can well understand that,' said Serena. 'Does no one come here anymore?'

'No. Only the odd traveller seeks its shelter. My grandfather used it as a hunting lodge—and myself on occasion after his demise.' Kit's eyes lingered on the cheerless, unwelcoming grimness of the place. 'Having no further use anymore, no doubt it will be demolished eventually.'

He turned to bank up the fire with some blocks of peat he had carried up from the basement. He placed them on top and around the glowing logs and the eager flames began to lick at the compact brownish fuel. The heat relaxed Serena's limbs, making her feel extremely tired. Kit was gazing absently down into the heart of the fire, his features etched against the glow, and there was an aureole of light around his dark head.

He unfastened his doublet and the whiteness of his shirt emphasised the blackness of his hair falling carelessly to his broad shoulders. It was one of the reasons why he was so striking. There was an aggressive arrogance to his sternly handsome face and ruthless set of his jaw, which bore the dark shadow of a beard. He was one of the most striking-looking men Serena had ever seen and, as he leaned forward, the front of his doublet gaped open; her eyes were irresistibly drawn to the corded muscles of his neck and the coarse, dark hairs on his chest. There was something too masculine, too earthy about him for her peace of mind.

Out of the corner of his eye Kit was perfectly aware of what Serena was feeling. Curving his lips into a satisfied smile, he turned his head and met her gaze. His dark eyes were fathomless, their intensity increasing the longer they looked, and Serena could not refrain from blushing as she felt herself undergoing the selfsame scrutiny she had just given him, feeling a sharp stab of annoyance when she noted the smug smile on his firm lips, which told her he was feeling assured of a willing conquest.

'I think you should try and sleep,' he said softly. 'You've got to preserve your strength if we're to make it to Addlington Hall tomorrow.'

'Why didn't you go straight on to Edinburgh?'

'For purely selfish reasons. I had a hankering to see Northumberland again. I couldn't pass by without calling at my grandmother's house. It depends on the weather how long we stay there. But it's my intention to go on to Edinburgh eventually to stay with my mother and Melissa—which is where I arranged to meet Ludovick when he journeys to Scotland some time during January or February.'

Serena looked at him questioningly. 'Why on earth would Sir Ludovick travel all the way to Scotland at this time of year?'

'To visit his family in Argyllshire—although he often travels to Scotland on diplomatic missions for the king. He is to bring me news of events following the arrest of the conspirators of the Gunpowder Plot. He also hopes to find proof to verify my innocence, and on my behalf present my argument to the king.'

'As I recall, Sir Ludovick was also present at the hunt at Woodfield Grange that day. Why isn't he suspected of colluding with the conspirators?'

'Simply because Blackwell has nothing against him and has no reason to have him implicated.'

'But what if you are seen and recognised in Edinburgh? Aren't you afraid of being arrested and sent back to London?'

'It's possible, but it's a chance I shall have to take. I intend keeping a low profile just in case.'

'Is Sir Ludovick the only person who knows where you can be found?'

'Yes—and I trust him absolutely. Ludovick and I have been friends too long to have secrets from each other. However, if this weather persists, we may have to remain at Addlington Hall until the thaw.'

Serena's delicate brows lifted in question. 'Alone?'

Kit arched his brows and smiled, amused at the consternation this prospect obviously caused her. 'Does that bother you?'

'Not really. But you must realise that eventually I must go to join my father in Flanders.'

A flash of annoyance crossed Kit's features. He kicked fiercely at a log which had fallen foul of the fire onto the hearth. 'So, you still persist with that foolishness.'

Serena's jaw set mutinously, and Kit could see the light of battle was back in her eyes when they met his in wilful defiance.

'Yes, I do. Where else can I go? Do not forget that my home is no longer accessible to me. Besides, I can't bear to think about the bleakness of a future without my father. He might have fallen ill somewhere and have need of me,' she said, knowing as she spoke that this was most unlikely, thinking with much bitterness that, in the event of him falling ill, he would be well taken care of by Mrs Davis. 'I *shall* go to him eventually, however hard you try and stop me.'

Moving close, with blazing eyes Kit leaned forward slightly, fully vexed. She had a propensity to spar with him and render him exasperated to the point of madness by remarks that could pierce his armour like the sharpest blade. 'It's out of the question at this present time so, like it or not, you will have to put up with my hospitality— whether it be this place, Addlington Hall or Edinburgh. I feel a certain obligation to your father to make sure you are safe—and I intend to do exactly that.'

Serena's vivid green eyes flashed with fiery sparks as she thrust her face forward. 'I believe you. But that does not give you the right to appoint yourself as my guardian—or perhaps I should say my keeper,' she flared with heavy sarcasm, standing up and beginning to roll her cloak into a pillow for her head to rest on, her vigorous actions indicating that she intended trying to sleep and had no wish to converse with him further. But Kit was determined to have the final word on the matter.

'Whatever title you attach to me, Serena, you will remain with me until I consider the time is right for you to go to your father—or if he sends for you. If he does, then I shall not stand in your way.'

'How can he do that when he doesn't know where I am?' Serena cried in angry frustration. 'How is he to know that you have brought me to this dismal abode in the middle of an abominable wilderness?'

'Because when I discovered he had evaded arrest and escaped to Flanders, I asked Ludovick to make enquiries as to his whereabouts.'

Serena immediately stopped what she was doing and stared at him in amazement. 'You did?'

'Yes. When we meet Ludovick in Edinburgh, if he has managed to locate your father then I shall write informing him that you are staying with my mother. If it is his wish that you join him in Flanders, then I promise I shall see you get there safely.'

Serena didn't know what to say. She was overwhelmed and touched that, despite the seriousness of his own situation, he would go to so much trouble on her behalf. Feeling a flood of warmth towards him, her expression softened. 'Why didn't you tell me this before?'

'I didn't want to raise your hopes in case Ludovick is

unsuccessful in locating him. I knew how disappointed you would be.'

'But why were you interested in my father's whereabouts in the first place?'

Kit's lips twisted in a wry smile. 'If I find it necessary to flee the country, I shall need as many friends as I can muster across the Channel.' Combing his hair back from his brow, he sighed wearily. 'Now try and get some sleep. With any luck the snow will cease and the wind will have blown itself out before morning. If so, we'll make an early start.'

He chuckled humorously when Serena drew her legs up on to the settle in an attempt to make herself comfortable. 'Unfortunately there is no guest chamber here,' he murmured, 'so I'm afraid you are going to have to make the best of it.'

'I realise that,' she answered, placing her feet on the floor once more while she tried to arrange her cloak in a more comfortable position for her head to rest on. 'Where will you sleep?'

'Since you occupy the finest bed in the house, my sweet,' he smiled with a hint of mockery, making a sweeping gesture with his hand at the rush-strewn floor, 'where else but the floor.'

Their world existed within the warm yellow circle of light, and Kit watched Serena in admiring speculation. 'I can truthfully say that I have not had so lovely a companion to pass the long cold hours of a winter's night,' he murmured softly.

Serena met his gaze. 'Then it's a pity the setting is not more cosy.'

His eyes gleaming like black coals, Kit leaned against the fireplace with his arms folded. 'And you like it less because you are here with me—alone,' he murmured, his words more of a statement than a question.

'I didn't say that,' she answered softly.

'You don't have to. But whatever thought is going through your mind, I must stress that I want to be your friend, not your enemy.'

'I don't think I like the kind of friendship you are suggesting.'

'Why? Are you afraid of me, Serena?'

'Have I reason to be?'

'Don't be evasive. That was not what I asked. Are you afraid of letting me come too close? Are you afraid that, because I have you here alone, I will force you to submit to my evil desires and rob you of your innocence—with no one to come to your aid should you scream?'

The husky resonance of his voice almost snatched Serena's breath away and she trembled, suddenly unsure of herself. 'Yes, I am,' she admitted, staring into his shadowed face. 'After your earlier assaults on my person, I believe I have good reason to be concerned.'

Kit laughed, his teeth flashing white from between his parted lips. 'At least you're truthful. But I didn't assault you, Serena,' he murmured, a tender, smouldering glow entering his eyes.

'It felt very much like it to me at the inn in Teesdale.'

'Then I apologise if you saw it that way. I did not lay a finger on you in Corbridge—but I was tempted. And later, I acted as any gentleman would when he sees a lady in distress. I merely picked you up and carried you across the stream.'

Recalling exactly how it had been, how he had held her firmly against his hard chest and caressed her ear with his warm and dangerous lips, how his hand unintentionally brushing her breast had rendered her almost helpless, Serena felt her cheeks suffuse with hot colour.

'I was not in distress—besides, it was more than that and you know it,' she told him with a trace of indignation and amazing candor. 'For the duration of our being together, I would be obliged if you would restrain your ardour and do not behave in that way again.'

'But you were tempted.'

Kit's smile was infuriating, and the warm sensuality of his voice almost stole Serena's breath. If he was trying to destroy her resistance he was succeeding admirably. At that moment some indefinable alchemy made them extremely aware of each other and their eyes became caught in that age-old way of would-be lovers. Serena's vulnerability was laid bare for him to pierce the guard she had resolved to keep on her emotions.

'I could feel it in your response, Serena, so do not try denying it.'

'Am I so predictable?'

'You are to me. It is not my intention to embarrass you,' Kit said, speaking softly, his eyes continuing to peruse her lovely face, 'and I promise that for the time being I shall try to keep my ardour under control and my hands to my-self—no matter how my desire might overwhelm me. I do not have to beg for favours and this is hardly the most suitable place to ravish a maid. But if it was my intention, would my advances provoke you to attack me as viciously as you did Blackwell?'

'I—I cannot answer that. Sir Thomas got what he deserved.'

Kit's black eyes danced across at her with unconcealed merriment. 'Aye! Never have I heard a man abused and vilified in such colourful detail,' he chuckled. 'It would have made a hardened soldier blush. In your anger you have a most unladylike turn of phrase.'

Serena blushed scarlet, mortified that he should remind her of that. 'And being a gentleman, sir, you should know better than to embarrass me by referring to an occasion I would rather forget.'

'I seem to recall you telling me in graphic detail that my claim to being a gentleman is a sentiment held entirely by myself,' he mocked. 'Have I done something I am not aware of to redeem myself to you?'

'No, not that I know of,' she retorted coldly, wishing he would cease fencing with her in this way. 'When I said you were a gentleman it was merely a slip of the tongue. However, you asked me what I would do if you made advances towards me, and I will tell you that I am different from most women of your acquaintance. I may not react in the way you are accustomed to expect.'

'How do you know what I expect?'

'I—I don't—I assume. Having led the same kind of existence in the Low Countries as Sir Thomas, I realise you might have much in common with him,' Serena said, unable to resist the gibe and satisfied when she saw it hit its target.

Kit's eyes narrowed. 'Then you don't know me very well.'

'Well enough to have formed an opinion.'

'We—could get to know each other better.'

Serena looked at him steadily. She knew what he was suggesting and was ashamed of the temptation this presented. The days on the road spent alone with him had rubbed her emotions almost raw, and the solid wall she had built around herself in their defence was beginning to erode. One look from him could do immense damage to her mind, which was already a battleground of emotions.

'When I agreed to come north with you I thought I would be safe.'

'I give you my word I will not hurt you. I told you from the very first that I have only your best interests at heart.'

'Your idea of that is open to a good deal of personal interpretation. If we are to remain together, I think we should observe all the proprieties and conventions.'

'Why? To protect your reputation?'

'Yes.'

'I think it's a little late for that.' He chuckled. 'After

spending the past few days alone with me I'm afraid it will be damaged beyond repair. No one will believe you are unsullied, no matter how fiercely you protest the truth.'

'I will know and that is what's important. Now I think we should go to sleep. This conversation is getting us no-where.' Drawing her feet up on to her uncomfortable bed, Serena rested her head on her rolled-up cloak with every intention of going to sleep.

Chapter Ten

The wind howled throughout the night, relentlessly battering the walls of Hawk's Pele, cleverly finding every hole and crack in the ancient structure which was like a ship adrift on a storm-tossed sea. To Kit and Serena's immense relief when they woke after an uncomfortable night, it was to discover the wind had passed westwards taking the snow clouds with it.

Eager to leave the tower and be on their way, they embarked on the few remaining miles of their journey to Addlington Hall. Serena felt a lifting of her spirits as she rode beside Kit and they picked their way with extreme care among the snowdrifts. They were deep in isolation and a million miles away from Warwickshire and conspiracies.

Eventually they came to the small hamlet of Addlington, with its huddle of snow-covered dwellings. Addlington Hall was a mile from the village. Eventually some tall iron gates loomed out of the whiteness. As they approached a man emerged from a small cottage just inside the grounds, hurriedly thrusting his arms into the sleeves of his jacket as he came to identify the visitors and open the gates.

He was a thick-set middle-aged man with a shock of sandy-coloured hair, and as he came close and peered up at them through the iron bars, his features broke into a grin on recognising Kit. Immediately he opened the gates, having previously cleared away the obstructing snow, and as they rode through he tugged his forelock, pushing the gate shut after they'd passed through. Kit leaned down and spoke to the man, who replied with a heavy northern dialect that was quite incomprehensible to Serena. She turned to Kit after the man had scuttled back inside the cottage.

'What did he say?'

'That was Samuel Gilby, the caretaker,' Kit explained as they went on their way. 'The house has been unoccupied since my grandmother's death, but fires have been lit daily to keep the place aired, should my mother and Melissa suddenly take it into their heads to visit. Mrs Gilby, Samuel's wife, is there now. There are no other servants so we will have to manage as best we can.'

'Can't you employ a couple of women from the village?'

Kit shook his head, his features set in a grim expression. 'No. The risk to ourselves is too great. It's amazing how quickly gossip travels, even in an isolated place such as this.'

'Can Mr and Mrs Gilby's integrity be relied on?'

'Absolutely. They have served my grandmother with unswerving loyalty for many years and can be trusted not to gossip to the locals.'

They proceeded up the snow-covered drive lined on either side with lofty trees, their branches heavy with snow. Eventually the rambling, many-turreted Tudor house came into view when they rounded a bend.

'There you are,' said Kit with a note of pride. 'Addlington Hall—the house in which my mother was raised.'

'It looks very grand,' murmured Serena, who could denote from Kit's tone and the fondness of his expression when he looked at the house that it meant a great deal to him. 'I recall you saying that your parents made their home near Coldstream.'

'Yes, I did. But I was not as fond of Minton Hall as

Paul, who had a hearty dislike for the isolation of this rambling old structure. You'll like Mrs Gilby. She's a good woman with a kind heart—but she is a bit strait-laced.'

'Aren't all housekeepers?' Serena remarked, fondly remembering Eliza.

'I'm not sure how Mrs Gilby will receive you—arriving with me alone. Where young ladies are concerned she is a firm believer in the authority of their families and absolute decorum at all times.' He grinned, returning to his carefree manner, his eyes full of mischief. 'When you arrive in the guise of a man and looking for all the world like a hoyden, she will be appalled and may think you are my paramour.'

Serena stiffened with immediate response. Lifting her chin, her green eyes gleamed with a feral light when she looked at him. 'That is exactly what I wish to avoid,' she snapped. 'We both know she will be mistaken and I leave it to you to explain and protect my good name. I know I shall appear ugly when she sees me dressed like this, but I fully intend to remedy that at the earliest opportunity.'

Kit laughed in the face of her anger. 'You have my word that I shall do my best to convince her of your respectability, Serena—but as for your male attire…well…in my opinion I find it rather fetching,' he said with a seductive lowering of his lids and an infuriating grin.

Serena merely glowered across at him before fixing her eyes on the huge building looming large in her sights.

Mrs Gilby came out of the house to greet them. To Serena's relief, she could understand Mrs Gilby very well, unlike Mr Gilby. This was due to the fact, Kit explained, of Mrs Gilby having come from the south before her father had brought her to Northumberland to work on the Addlington estate, where she had met and married Samuel.

Mrs Gilby was a small, plump woman with warm, yet piercing, eyes. She beamed with delight on seeing Kit and studied Serena as she would a curiosity, from top to toe, with her mouth compressed in a thin line. What was passing through her mind when her eyes dwelt too long on Serena's soiled and unfeminine breeches, Serena could only guess at.

'Mrs Gilby, may I introduce Mistress Carberry,' said Kit when they entered the hall. 'I know you will find it rather strange that she arrives here with me alone, but for reasons beyond our control—which I shall explain to you and Samuel later—she had no choice other than to come with me.'

Mrs Gilby glanced up at Kit with a worried frown. 'Trouble is it, my lord?'

'Yes. And I must ask you not to speak of our presence at Addlington Hall to anyone. Is that understood?'

'You have my word.'

'Thank you. We intend staying until the thaw, when we will ride on to Edinburgh to stay with my mother. Have you heard from her recently?'

'I'm afraid not, Lord Brodie. What with the wet weather and now this snow, goodness knows when she'll be able to visit. I keep rooms ready for her and Mistress Melissa just in case.'

'Very sensible, Mrs Gilby. Now—I know it's short notice but we require food. Whatever you have available. I do realise that our arrival has taken you unawares and that you will not have anything prepared, but we have ridden a long way and we are both ravenous—isn't that so, Serena?'

Serena nodded. 'Yes, but…would it be too much trouble for me to have a bath before I eat?'

'No trouble at all. I'll show you to your chamber,' Mrs Gilby said, casting a sideways, disapproving glance at Serena's mode of dress. 'Forgive me, Mistress Carberry, but have you nothing else to wear?'

Mrs Gilby didn't see Kit arch his eyebrows at Serena with an 'I did tell you' smile curving his handsome lips, which she ignored.

'Yes. I brought a couple of dresses with me. They're in a bag fastened to the saddle of my horse.'

'I'll bring it in when I've seen to the horses and had a word with Samuel,' said Kit, disappearing to do just that.

Following Mrs Gilby, Serena was pleased to find that the apartments allotted to her were comfortably furnished, warm, and the bed aired. She looked at the huge four-poster bed with silver-and-pale-blue brocade hangings with longing. After the previous night's discomfort spent trying to sleep on the broken settle, she couldn't wait to crawl under the bedcovers and draw the curtains.

When Mrs Gilby had disappeared to the domestic quarters to prepare something to eat, Serena was amazed when Kit arrived at her door carrying two large pitchers of hot water. His white linen shirt was casually open at the throat and a devilish smile played on his lips.

'For your bath, my lady,' he said, his voice laced with humour. Pushing his way through the half-open door into the room, he was followed by Samuel carrying two more pitchers. Samuel poured the steaming water into a bathtub which he dragged out of a closet before disappearing, whereas Kit preferred to linger, watching Serena with close attention.

Self-consciously she looked at him, unable to imagine what he found to be of so much interest, unless the impertinent rascal expected her to remove her clothes in front of him. Kit met her gaze, a corner of his lips lifting roguishly as his gaze dipped to an opening at the neck of her doublet, which she had already unfastened in pleasurable anticipation of her bath. Meeting her gaze again, Kit lifted a querying black eyebrow. Serena could only wonder at his thoughts as she struggled to maintain her composure beneath his perusal.

'Well?' she asked, impatient for him to leave. 'What are you waiting for?'

'Have you everything you need?'

'More than enough, thank you.'

'Would you like me to stay and assist you?'

'Certainly not,' she replied, irritated by his dalliance and, taking his arm, pulled him towards the door. 'Out you go, you pompous oaf, and leave me alone. My bath is private and I intend to soak for at least a week.'

Kit paused and looked back at the steaming tub in subdued, wistful vein. 'What a pity to bring all that water up here for just one person when it could just as well serve two.'

Serena flashed him a look, seeing a flurry of wicked thoughts coursing through his mind. Without more ado and on a note of gentle laughter, she pushed him out on to the landing. 'Out, you compromising rogue. Go and fetch your own water.'

Feeling positively filthy after the long and wearying days of travel, Serena lingered over her bath, washing her hair and luxuriating in the hot soapy water, feeling the tension in her body melt. Afterwards she donned one of the dresses and clean undergarments Mrs Gilby had kindly ironed and brought to her, enjoying the feel of stockings and petticoats about her legs once more. Sliding her feet into a pair of low-heeled shoes, she was glad she'd had the presence of mind to bring them along.

Drawing the brush through her still-damp hair, she smiled at her reflection in the mirror, carelessly allowing her mind to dwell on Kit and unable to deny that she found their encounters challenging. She was enlivened by them, enlightened, and there was an element of danger, which added to the excitement. Being with Kit was stimulating and never dull; the prospect of spending some time at Addlington Hall with him made her heart pound.

Serena sighed despondently at her reflection in the mirror, for this was not the way she had expected things to turn out when she had agreed to come with him to Northumberland. It was not what she had wanted. Perhaps they had been alone together too long. It would be a relief when the thaw came and they could leave for Edinburgh, where they would part. When she met up with her father again, she would forget all about Kit Brodie and their time together in Northumberland.

But would she? she asked herself, calmly meeting her own candid gaze in the mirror. Would she be able to forget the most fascinating man she had ever met?

With her hair hanging down her back in heavy, luxuriant waves, she set the brush aside and stood in front of the long mirror to survey her appearance and look for flaws, oblivious to the wide, brilliant green eyes looking back at her which were capable of setting a man's blood aflame, or the healthy glow of her face which the constant exposure to the fresh air over the past few days was responsible for.

Biting her lip nervously, she frowned when she looked at her plain-coloured sapphire blue gown, the less flamboyant of the two she had brought with her. Not wishing to arouse censure in Mrs Gilby, she thought that perhaps the scooped neckline revealed too much of her cleavage than was proper, but no matter how she struggled to pull it up it persisted in going back to where it wanted to be. Sighing with resignation, she shrugged, having no choice but to leave it as it was.

Lacking the necessary stays, the bodice clung tightly to her body, and the full skirts had no hoops to lift it out, so it would just have to do. However, Serena secretly thought she looked quite fetching without the invisible and harsh appliances. The gown emphasised both the natural slenderness of her figure and her firm breasts, their defiant curves swelling above the delicate lace-edged bodice.

Kit was patiently waiting for her at the top of the stairs, having bathed and changed, and looked wonderfully attractive. The rich cloth of his doublet was a deep mulberry colour, his freshly washed hair wavy black and gleaming. Before Serena reached him she smiled, a wonderfully engaging smile, her cheeks pink and her eyes extremely bright. Impulsively she spun round in her dainty shoes, her long tresses and voluminous skirts spinning out to reveal her slender ankles.

'What do you think? Is this an improvement on my former attire, my lord?'

Kit arched a brow and looked at her appraisingly, thinking he had never seen her look more lovely. But the sweetness of her expression was greatly at odds with the minx he had come to know and love. 'Do you need to ask? You look like an angel, you vain wench. I can see the lady has changed her plumage.'

'It's easy for any woman to change from a sparrow into a swan with fine clothes,' Serena countered. 'Am I to understand that you approve of the transformation? Do I look less like a lad and a more fitting companion in my dress?'

'A very fitting companion. But I'm not blind. Even in your breeches you never looked less like a lad. But it's a pity such perfection is only skin deep. I am not deceived, madam.' He grinned with mock severity. 'Your cheeks may bloom like the fairest of roses—whereas inside sprouts the thistle reminiscent from across the border.'

Feeling too light-hearted to be intimidated, Serena smiled up at him sweetly, a look of such innocence on her face that it would melt the largest glacier, but Kit was not deceived.

'Don't play the coquette with me. I know you too well, don't forget. But I compliment you,' he murmured, his glowing dark eyes openly raking her from top to toe. 'You look ravishing.'

'And you would like to—is that not so?' Serena remarked with a playful hint of sarcasm.

'I meant it as a compliment.'

'That's what worries me.'

'You took your time.'

'I told you, I wanted to enjoy my bath. I had practically a full week's dirt to wash away.'

'You removed a considerable amount at Corbridge as I

recall,' he murmured pointedly, taking her arm and escorting her down the stairs.

Serena flashed him a sharp glance. 'You recall too much.'

Kit laughed softly down into her upturned face. 'You look adorable. Your eyes are sparkling most outrageously. If I didn't know you better, I would say you were in love.'

'With you?'

'Why not?'

'Because I have far too much sense to allow myself to love a pompous rogue like you.'

'And I have a voracious appetite. I shall try to make you change your mind.'

'You can try—but you will be wasting your time.'

His eyes gleamed determinedly. 'We shall see.'

'Are you telling me that you find my company pleasant after all?'

'Only when you aren't being stubborn and temperamental.'

'I am never temperamental,' Serena objected, pouting prettily.

'Yes, you are. Most of the time, in fact.'

'And you, my fine, incorrigible, stubborn lord, have all the makings of a monster.'

Kit grinned most attractively, his gaze raking hers. 'Only if you drive me to it. But perhaps when you see how charming a host I can be, how attentive to your every need, you will melt towards me.'

Serena's lips curved in a slow smile. 'Charm is often an effective weapon, my lord, but I am not so easily won over.'

'Kit,' he corrected with a scowl. 'Do you forget so soon that my title as well as my property has been confiscated? Besides, I thought we had agreed to dispense with the formalities between us.'

'We have. I just like to put you in your place now and then.'

'Don't criticise. I've been very patient and proper under the difficult circumstances given to me.'

'You brought them on yourself—and you will continue to be patient and proper until the time comes for us to part.'

He chuckled. Having reached the bottom of the stairs, he paused and looked down into her upturned face. 'Don't you ever give up, wench? Don't tell me you didn't enjoy your journey to Northumberland with me.'

'It was most illuminating. But whatever you have in mind where I am concerned, I will tell you now that you are wasting your time.'

Kit raised an eyebrow, amusement dancing in his black eyes when he looked at her. 'Kindly explain yourself, madam. What are you saying?'

'That because Dorothea is no longer available to you, I suspect you are looking for a replacement. If it is your intention to embark on a course of seduction now you find yourself alone with me, I would advise you to reconsider. I have no intention of being a diversion—or of becoming the easy victim of a philanderer.'

Kit laughed outright, amused by her open honesty. 'I have been accused of being many things, but never a philanderer. Where the fairer sex is concerned, I am always extremely serious in my intentions. I think you misunderstand me.'

Serena raised a delicate eyebrow. 'On the contrary. I understand you very well, and I would ask you not to attach any significance to our being together for so long.'

Kit gave her a slanted smile. 'Come along. We will carry on this conversation over dinner,' he said and crooked an arm. Serena placed her hand into it, feeling how strong and firmly muscled it was. They walked down a long passageway towards the room where a carefully laid table had been set by Mrs Gilby. 'We must be careful not to shock Mrs

Gilby too much. She may look like a mild, sweet-tempered woman, but where morality is concerned she is absolutely respectable.' Kit looked down at her, his eyes twinkling with pure devilment. 'I think her husband will miss her company in his bed this night.'

'Oh? Why is that?'

'She is hardly likely to leave us in the house alone now, is she?' Kit chuckled softly. 'Mrs Gilby would consider herself to be failing in her duty if she didn't supervise your stay at Addlington Hall.'

Serena glanced up at him sharply. 'You are a virile man and—'

Kit raised his eyebrows and looked down at her in mock amazement. 'I'm glad you think so,' he cut in quickly. 'I was beginning to think that perhaps you had failed to notice.'

Serena gave him a snapping glance of irritation. 'Oh, do be quiet. I was about to say that clearly Mrs Gilby knows you better than I, and that she may have cause to be concerned. You can be assured that my door will be well and truly locked tonight and every night while I remain under the same roof as yourself.'

'That will not deter Mrs Gilby from playing the chaperon and, if either of us puts one foot out of line, we can be sure to feel the sharper edge to her tongue.'

Serena tossed her head assuredly. 'I've met worse women than Mrs Gilby. I'll have her on my side before the week is out. You see if I don't. I don't believe she's the ogre you would have me believe.'

Kit grinned, not doubting what she said. 'You've seen nothing yet.' He chuckled quietly as they entered the dining room, where Mrs Gilby was busily arranging the food she had prepared for them. 'There's worse to come. Much, much worse.'

'Oh?'

'Wait until you meet my mother.'

Serena uttered a faint gasp, her eyes flying to his as she was about to ask him what he meant by that remark, but Mrs Gilby chose that moment to summon them to the table so she had to be content with a not-so-reassuring smile. Serena was surprised to experience a genuine feeling of alarm at the prospect of meeting the Dowager Lady Brodie.

Behind the huge iron gates, Addlington Hall seemed a world away from the reality of what was happening in London. Time seemed to stand still for the two people who had sought sanctuary within its walls as one week slipped into another and the harsh, frozen white world held them trapped within its icy grip.

By sheer dint of will and refusing to yield to her anxieties, Serena had made a concerted effort on her journey to Northumberland not to dwell on the violent nature of the Gunpowder Plot and the zealous men responsible for bringing it about. But now she wondered how the conspirators who had been arrested were faring in the Tower.

At these times her thoughts would turn to Kit, for no matter how he always tried to appear unconcerned, she knew he was plagued by anxiety over his servant Robin. There was no way of knowing what tortures he was being subjected to, to force him to divulge information about his master.

Torture in England was in theory reserved for exceptional circumstances, and since treason was considered an exceptional circumstance, there was every possibility that young Robin might have the manacles inflicted upon him, a method most favoured by the authorities for extracting information out of a suspect. Serena fervently hoped not, for it resurrected painful memories of her father, when he too had spent some considerable time in the Tower and been subjected to the pain inflicted on him by the manacles.

He had been hung up by his wrists against a wall and the iron gauntlets gradually tightened; the support beneath his feet was taken away so that he had been left dangling in this cruel manner for hours on end. Those who survived such torture were, like her father, permanently maimed. The manacles were considered to be the gentler torture, the worst the rack. There was only one such instrument in England and that was housed in the Tower. This instrument was so feared that the mere sight of it was enough to make the bravest and strongest man confess.

The feeling of apprehension that came over Serena when she imagined Kit's whereabouts being discovered was almost impossible to quell. It was hard to believe she could feel such concern for a man who had forced her to come to Northumberland, and at times had treated her no better than he would a servant. And yet, the thought that he might be arrested, tortured and hanged for a crime he was innocent of, filled her with inexplicable dread. She prayed that the king would grant him the opportunity to present his argument, to produce proof to verify his innocence, whereby with the king's grace all his properties and his good name would be redeemed.

This should have been an idyllic time, but far from easing the tension between Kit and Serena, it did entirely the opposite as they were drawn closer together. Serena knew she was falling under Kit's spell and at first felt no fear, believing she knew the sort of man he was and that she possessed the common sense to deal with it. But with time on their hands everything began to change, and the more they learned about each other, the more the days became a confusion of shifting emotions for them both.

The alchemy between them had nothing to do with reason, but they were both wise enough to recognise the imminent dangers of forming a different relationship to the one they already had and both stepped back. They became like polite strangers, their conversations commonplace, yet Kit was always solicitous and sensitive to Serena's needs— too much so, she thought, when she remembered how volatile he could be and how their conversation had always been laced with challenge. He became quiet and serious, moody almost, with no interest for light banter.

Mechanically they went through the motions of living in the same house, but Kit began spending more and more time away from it. Usually Serena would breakfast alone, but Kit would always present himself for dinner at noon and supper at six o'clock. For her part Serena could scarcely wait for the meal to end so she could escape his steady gaze, unable to read his expression or his feelings. All she could see was the darkly handsome figure sitting across from her at the table. Neither of them were prepared to be the first to break the deadly, dangerous current of attraction that flowed so strongly between them.

On a day that was fine but cold, Serena ventured outside, walking farther away from the house than she usually did. Small white clouds hovered over the peaks of the surrounding hills, the snow stretching in a relentless, white expanse over hill and vale. Breathing deeply of the sharp air, she pushed back the hood of her cloak, feeling a gentle breeze stir and gently lift her hair. Seeing a large dark-winged, white-crested bird go soaring high into the sky, she paused, shading her eyes from the sun with her hand the better to see it.

Serena recognised the bird as being a peregrine falcon, a bird much favoured by her father for its grace, precision and speed in flight. He had been a keen falconer and had kept several such birds, taking great pride in training them himself to return from flight to a lure or to hunt prey on the wing. Captivated, she watched it in flight, seeing it climb above a flock of pigeons which had flown up from their roost in a nearby copse.

Instinct told Serena that the clever and crafty peregrine had selected its intended victim and, holding her breath, she watched it plummet downwards at a terrific speed, suddenly slowing its flight to attack and striking upward to sink its long talons into the pigeon's flesh before bringing it to earth.

Two men hurried towards it, the jingling of the tiny bells fastened to the peregrine's feet guiding them to the location. Serena recognised the two men as being Kit and Samuel. Bending down, Kit took the peregrine on to his gloved hand, gently stroking its dark feathers with the other. Serena's heart was revitalised with joy and soared at the sight of him.

Kit's eyes went directly to her as though the compulsion of her intent gaze was strong enough to tell him she was there. She was standing some distance away, motionless and solemn, her hands held loosely at her waist, her cloak falling in a circlet around her feet. For a long moment they looked at each other over the distance that separated them, direct and steadily.

Handing the peregrine and the glove to Samuel, Kit moved towards her. She was an unforgettable vision of pure perfection to his hungry eyes, and his arms ached to hold her. Beneath the sun her hair was the colour of burnished oak, her cheeks soft and gloriously pink, her magnificent eyes glowing like emeralds. Serena was very quickly becoming an obsession. With a deliberate effort of will he had tried to close his mind against wanting her, and though he had not always been successful he had done his best. It was a constant battle, one he was tired of fighting.

Hot, embarrassed colour stained Serena's cheeks when they faced each other. Kit's sternly handsome face had an odd, contemplative expression on it as he gazed down at her, his dark hair blowing in the breeze, his leather jerkin open at the throat to reveal the strong muscles of his neck.

'So this is what keeps you so well occupied,' Serena said with the hint of a smile, a little self-conscious at being caught watching him. 'I'm sorry. I didn't mean to interrupt.'

'Don't be. We're finished for today. Samuel will take the bird back.'

'It's just that I can never resist seeing the peregrines in flight.'

'Then I apologise for not asking you to come along before. I should have realised your need for a little light diversion.'

'You must enjoy flying them.'

'I do. When he was alive my grandfather taught me the skill. Your own father is a keen falconer, too, as I recall.'

'Yes, although he doesn't hold his peregrines as high in his affections as he does his horses.' Serena's eyes clouded over at the memory and she sighed dejectedly. 'Perhaps now—after all that has happened—I should speak in the past tense. Not only has my father lost his home, but his horses and his peregrines also.'

'No doubt he will acquire more in the future.'

'If he has a future,' Serena murmured, her voice tinged with sadness.

'While ever he remains in Flanders he should be safe enough,' said Kit gently in an effort to erase the doubt from her eyes and ease the pain she so clearly felt. 'Maybe when it's discovered that he had nothing to do with the inner workings of the conspiracy, and that he sold his horses to Catesby with the belief that they were to be sent to the Netherlands, he will be pardoned.'

Unbidden tears gathered in Serena's eyes. 'I wish with all my heart that I could believe that. But I have an odd feeling that even if the king does grant him a pardon, he will not return to England.' She turned away, unwilling to let Kit see how deeply her father's association with Mrs Davis in Flanders affected her, and how worried she was that at this time, with his home lost to him and unable to return to England, he would succumb to Mrs Davis's entreaties to marry her.

His expression serious, Kit put his hand gently on her

arm and turned her to face him, finding himself looking into a pair of eyes the colour of wet grass, with tears sparkling on her long dark lashes, tears she was too proud to shed.

'And you're sure of that, are you?'

'Yes. As sure as I can be.'

A rogue tear spilled over Serena's lashes and traced a line down her cheek. Kit was overcome with a wild desire to kiss it away but, knowing it would be his undoing, almost immediately produced a snow-white lace handkerchief with a dark trace of blood on it, the blood Serena had dabbed from a scratch on her wrist inflicted during her first skirmish with Thomas Blackwell.

'Here. Dry your eyes,' he said softly, handing it to her. 'But I insist on you returning it to me.'

Serena dabbed at her wet face and held it out for him to take, but then she gasped, a teary smile curving her lips when she recognised it. 'Why,' she breathed, touched that he should have kept the handkerchief, 'this is mine. You still have it.'

With a grin he took it from her and returned it to the pocket inside his doublet. 'Yes—and I intend to keep it for posterity.'

Chapter Eleven

'Sometimes I find it hard to accept all that's happened,' Serena said, falling into step beside Kit as they returned to the house. 'If my father remains in Flanders—either by choice or because he can't return to England—I shall have no alternative but to make it my home, too.'

Kit regarded her with serious intent. Whenever she mentioned leaving England he felt a hollow sensation in the pit of his stomach. They were walking along a path which ran beside of the house when suddenly he stopped, taking her arm and turning her to face him.

'Serena, listen to me. There is no reason why you have to go.'

Kit's eyes were dark with torment. His voice was hoarse, his look that of a man about to break a bond he had made with himself and plunge headlong into disaster. Serena wanted nothing more than to let desire have its way and surrender herself to the silent demand in his eyes, to forget the vow she had made to herself not to become entrapped by him. But if she intended going to Flanders to prevent her father entering into a marriage with Mrs Davis, which could happen whilst he was in such a vulnerable state, then she must not weaken.

'I have to, Kit. Nothing is changed.'

As she was about to draw away, unexpectedly Kit took her hand and placed it against his chest. 'I have time to change your mind.'

'No, Kit. My mind is made up.'

'I know I don't have the right, but what if I said that I cannot live without you?'

His words pierced Serena's heart. 'I would know that would not be true,' she answered quietly.

Placing his hands on her shoulders, Kit drew her into the shadow of the house, pressing her back against the bark of a tall tree. 'And what if I said I did not want you to go for no other reason than I want you to stay with me? That I want you to stay for purely selfish reasons? That I cannot bear the thought of never seeing you again?'

Serena was unable to believe he was saying these things to her. 'I would still go,' she whispered, her lips trembling, unable to resist his eyes as they probed the depths of her being and her heart streamed into his. She stepped aside to pass him by, but he moved quickly to stand behind her, his firm hands coming to rest on her waist as he turned her back to him.

Unable to restrain himself a moment longer, suddenly Kit put his arms around her and drew her against his hard chest. Serena's breath dragged in her throat and the scent of him, of leather and pine, filled her senses. Before she knew what was happening, his lips took possession of hers with such accomplished persuasion that she felt a stir of pleasure sigh through her as her body responded to his kiss. Unresisting, she closed her eyes, aware of nothing in the world but the hard rack of Kit's chest as she was crushed against it, feeling the tense muscles under his leather jerkin as his arms locked about her. His lips tantalised and teased, deliberately touching, caressing, as light as thistledown, stirring her passion.

By slow degrees his mouth parted more to pluck the sweetness from her own, sipping, savouring and sampling, until Serena began to feel intoxicated, roused by an answering response so that his tongue became a fluttering firebrand as his mouth consumed hers with a hunger that would not be appeased. With a strangled gasp she pulled back, dragging her lips from his and turning her head aside, but he forced it back with his hand, his arm curled about her waist, refusing to let her go.

'No, Kit. Please don't do this,' she entreated. 'Let me go.'

'Nay, not yet,' he murmured. 'I have waited too long for this moment.' He looked down at her, feeling the heat in her body reach out to him, seeing the regret in her lovely eyes was sincere.

'I remember asking you not to try to seduce me.'

'And I remember telling you that you might be persuaded. Don't resist me, Serena,' he breathed, his gaze fastening on her lips. 'Please spare me the maidenly protests and just relax. It's quite easy, you know.'

Staring at him in dazed confusion, Serena watched his finely moulded lips hovering just above hers. 'I—I'm quite sure it is—only…'

Kit responded with a questioning lift to his eyebrows. 'What's the matter, Serena? Are you afraid to find out?' he asked quietly, the softness of his voice weaving a strange spell around her.

'Please,' she breathed, her breath fanning his lips enticingly. 'Please don't play with me, Kit.'

'It's hard not to, when you are so skilful an adversary,' he murmured, his dark gaze fastened on her lips. Plunging his fingers into her hair, he cupped her face between his hands, his gaze penetrating and probing the depths of her emerald eyes. 'When I'm alone I swear to myself that I will not touch you, but when we are together and I look at you, all my good intentions crumble like dust. You want me as much as I want you. I can feel it when I touch you, see it when I look into your eyes.'

He drew her closer, his lips tenderly brushing her cheek, feeling his pulse quicken. He told himself to let her go, that he should turn aside and release her with a commonplace remark and repress the desire racing through him, but blood was pounding in his temples and he was like a man besieged by a dizziness on the edge of a precipice.

'Have you any idea what it's like for me, being with you day after day, night after night, knowing you are so close and not being able to touch you? You affect me deeply, my love. I have developed a patience I didn't know I possessed. There is something magical and tantalising about you—a dark, sultry promise which emanates from you like a sensuous aura that has held me in its thrall from the very first.'

Kit's voice was low, urgent and compelling, and Serena felt a flame within her flicker to life and go coursing through her veins like liquid fire. Suddenly his mouth clamped down on to hers once more in fiery demand. Her mouth became yielding, soft and pliant as it was seized with a passion that took her breath away. Kit's lips were greedy, taking anything that she gave, his arms refusing to let her go, and Serena felt herself pressing herself against him, consumed by him. He aroused yearnings inside her that were completely alien to her maidenly heart.

It was Kit who finally raised his head and drew back a little, a tormenting hunger in his eyes when he gazed down at her. 'Sweet mercy, what have you done to me? How can I be content after a kiss like that? I can think of nothing except my need for more.'

Putting a finger to his lips, Serena's eyes had increased to a luminous intensity. 'No, Kit,' she said, her voice hardly above a whisper. 'This will serve no purpose. It will destroy what we have. If I come to your bed now, the pain of our parting will be too great for me to bear.'

'It needn't be like that.'

'It will be. If we were to become lovers, what do you

think would happen then? I would be unable to leave you. It would be impossible—and I would lose all respect for myself…and for you, too, perhaps.'

Kit's eyes locked on to hers and his breathing slowed. 'I want you, Serena—and I know you want me. I've had you close by me these past weeks and you have roused me to heights of such torment I thought I could not endure it. But, God help me, I shall not force you.'

'Thank you,' Serena whispered. His eyes were filled with such weariness that she was deeply shaken. 'I fear that my will would not be strong enough to resist you.'

'And nothing I can say will persuade you to remain in England—or Scotland, for that matter?' he asked, tracing the line of her jaw with his finger. 'Wherever we happen to be?'

Serena caught his hand for it weakened her beyond measure. 'No. I can't, Kit. For pity's sake, if you have any feeling for me at all, please do not ask me again. Can't you see that I have no choice? We have been alone too long, you and I. What you feel is frustrated desire and nothing more. We are friends. If we become lovers it will spoil everything.'

Kit's eyes were dark with torment. 'That's nonsense. It will never be like that between us.'

'I will not take the risk,' Serena said heavily, easing herself away from him, and as she did so Kit could feel her tension tinged with sadness and regret. Each word she uttered felt like a ramrod being thrust down the barrel of a musket. Her misty green eyes mirrored his own sense of pain and impending loss.

Without another word Serena turned and fled from him, trembling and shaken, afraid of where her passion had been about to lead her. She knew what Kit wanted, and she was ashamed that it presented some temptation. But if she did yield herself to him and they became lovers, where would it lead? she asked herself. Unable to tear themselves apart, they would stay at Addlington Hall where they would indulge themselves in a torrid love affair, which would serve no purpose to either of them.

And how long would it last? A week—a month? And then what would she be left with? Kit had not suggested marriage. He had told her at the beginning of their journey together that he wanted no encumbrances, nothing to get in the way of his one objective, which was to clear his name of the accusations made against him. But how was she to endure the time they were forced to remain together when she wanted him so much?

With tensed jaw, but making no attempt to follow her, wretchedly Kit stood and watched her go, controlling himself with an effort of will which whitened the knuckles of his hands clenched by his sides. He was shocked to discover how close he had come to losing his self-control, having vowed that his passion, his need, for this woman, his emotions, would never be allowed to get the better of him. At least, not until he had brought honour back to his name and he had something to offer her.

But without her the future yawned before him as dark and cold as the Atlantic Ocean. A gnawing emptiness filled the centre of his being and nothing in the world could ever fill that gap. After a moment he followed her, clinging on to what remained of his sanity like a drowning man might cling to his one hope of delivery.

Kit made no further moves to draw Serena close. He neither spoke of it nor gave any indication that he remembered it, remaining aloof and unemotional at all times—but the truth of it was that it was the only way he had of keeping a grasp on his sanity.

Eventually the snow melted enough for them to leave for Edinburgh, Scotland's capital city to the north. The journey would be extremely punishing and treacherous in places with flood waters after the snow having filled the rivers and streams to overflowing.

The first night of their journey was spent at Minton Hall, Kit's family home at Coldstream; they left early the following morning. Kit had undertaken the journey several times in the past, so he was familiar with the terrain and hostelries. He knew the uplands and each twisting pass well, but it was a route which would not be advisable for anyone to take who was not familiar with it.

On reaching Scotland's capital city it was nightfall and they had been in the saddle since the grey light of dawn. Edinburgh Castle, built on sheer cliffs and dominating the town with its massive structure, could be seen as a dark and ghostly shape through the driving rain. The cold and damp invaded their clothes and seeped into their weary bodies.

Lady Mary, Kit's mother, rented a large establishment in the Canongate, amidst other aristocratic dwellings in that narrow thoroughfare. The spacious, well-sited gardens at the back led down to Holyrood Park and looked up to the great crag of Arthur's Seat. In a bedraggled and exhausted state, Kit and Serena presented themselves at the house to an astonished and extremely surprised Lady Mary.

She received them without fuss, but her relief on seeing the son she believed was incarcerated in the Tower in London was immense. The depth of love she felt for this tall, handsome man could be discerned deep in her dark eyes, which were so like his. Serena had been a little sceptical about meeting Lady Mary, but soon began to relax, realising that she was a woman with a strong personality, practical and forthright. In her early fifties, she was maturely beautiful, in a quiet, assured way, being tall and slender, dark-haired and fine-featured.

News of the Gunpowder Plot had reached Scotland; learning of Kit's assumed involvement and arrest, Lady Mary had become extremely concerned and distressed.

When the roads became passable she had fully intended leaving for the south to be close to him, and to take proper account of the events which had led to his arrest. Not that she would believe them. Knowing her son and his absolute loyalty to King James, she knew there must have been some mistake and that he had been falsely accused.

'Come over to the fire while I order a chamber and a bath made ready for you, my dear,' she said to Serena. 'We must have you out of those wet clothes before you take a chill. What a night to be abroad. How far have you come?'

'Originally from Warwickshire. Due to the severe weather we were forced to spend some time at Addlington Hall,' Kit told her. 'As soon as it was possible we set off for Edinburgh. Now I hope to meet up with Sir Ludovick Lamont, who will inform me on events in London following the arrests of the conspirators. I have much to tell you, Mother.'

Lady Mary fixed her son with a steady gaze, the matter much too serious for her to become upset about any transgression in his behaviour with this young woman whom he had brought alone with him over three hundred and fifty miles to Edinburgh. 'I am out of touch with what is happening in London, but I have heard about the wickedness of the Gunpowder Plot. But we will talk later, when you have both been taken care of. Just tell me this. Are you still in danger?'

Their dark eyes met in grave confrontation. 'I'm afraid so.'

His mother nodded. 'I thought as much.'

After soaking in a hot tub and being provided with some of Melissa's clothes to wear, which fitted her well and for which she was extremely grateful, Serena felt human again. The damp had seeped into the few clothes she had brought with her. Only when they had eaten and were sitting in front of a cheerful blaze, did Lady Mary allow her son to present her with the bare facts of his predicament: his as-

sumed involvement in the Gunpowder Plot, which had resulted in Lord Carberry withdrawing Kit's suit for his
daughter's hand in marriage.

She listened calmly, an authoritative and assured woman,
her face serene and attentive, showing nothing of the inner
turmoil and distress she suffered on hearing Kit tell her all
he was accused of. 'And what did you hope to achieve by
coming here? How can you hope to clear your name when
you are so far away from London?'

'I was given little choice. When the plot was uncovered,
such a frenzy gripped everyone that if I had been re-
arrested, I would have been declared guilty and hanged,
such was the determination of the authorities to seek out
the traitors and administer the severest punishment.'

'But what could Sir Thomas Blackwell possibly have
against you that would make him blacken your name so
damnably?'

Quickly Kit recounted Thomas Blackwell's disgraceful
conduct in the Low Countries and Kit's own intervention,
which had resulted in Sir Thomas's disgrace. 'There has
also been two particularly ugly confrontations between us
of late,' he said, his eyes meeting Serena's calmly, 'which
increased Blackwell's determination to avenge himself. The
Gunpowder Plot provided him with the ammunition to do
so.'

'But I cannot believe the king would listen to the malicious outpourings of this vindictive man and think you
guilty of treason.'

'I have no way of knowing what His Majesty thinks, but
I would lose my life before betraying him. I thought I
would stand a better chance of proving my innocence when
I've gathered evidence in my defence—and when the mood
of hysterical madness subsides. I must remain in Edinburgh
until Ludovick arrives with news of what is happening in
London—which should be any time now, roads and
weather permitting.'

Lady Mary's eyes were drawn to Serena, who was quietly listening to Kit. One would have to be blind not to see the looks she exchanged with her son, but Lady Mary would not wonder about the depth of their relationship, or the significance of it, at present. 'How do you come to be involved in all this, my dear?' she asked with a gentle smile. 'Kit mentioned that when your father left for Flanders, he left you in the care and protection of his brother at Carberry Hall. Why did you leave your uncle?'

'It was my intention to go to my father.'

'Alone?'

'Yes.'

'But wasn't that a reckless venture to embark upon—a young woman alone? Weren't you afraid of the dangers?'

'No, Lady Mary. The dangers that threatened me were at home and greater by far than any I would encounter on the road to Flanders.'

'Perhaps I should explain to you that because of Sir Henry's indirect involvement with the conspirators, his estate also became forfeit to the Crown,' Kit told his mother. 'Unfortunately, the house was ransacked and Serena herself in danger of being arrested and taken to London for interrogation—which is what has happened to the relatives and servants of the accused.'

'Then how is it that Serena is here with you?' Lady Mary asked her son pointedly. 'What prevented her from going to her father in Flanders?'

'She was being pursued by her uncle who was determined to have her brought back.'

'Which was only right and proper if that was where Sir Henry wanted her to be. Surely under her uncle's guidance and protection she would have been safe from the authorities.'

'Lord Carberry would not have been able to protect her from being arrested.'

Lady Mary looked keenly from one to the other and was

not deceived. There was something they were not telling her. 'You are keeping something from me. I can always tell, Kit.' She looked at Serena for the answer, who met her gaze calmly.

'You are right, Lady Mary,' Serena admitted. 'Unfortunately, it is a matter of some delicacy—and embarrassment.'

Lady Mary raised her delicate dark brows in question. 'To whom, Serena? You or I?'

Serena folded her hands quietly in her lap, knowing that Lady Mary's gentle probing would persist until she had drawn every sordid detail out of her. 'To myself. You see, Sir Thomas is not only determined to destroy Kit, but myself also.'

'But why?'

'Because I rejected his advances.'

'He wanted to marry you?'

Serena's lips twisted with irony. 'Nothing so honourable, Lady Mary. Sir Thomas abhors all Catholics, and because I am of that faith he considers me fit for one thing only.'

Lady Mary smiled softly, admiring Serena's forthright manner. 'You have no need to feel uncomfortable about your religion in this house, my dear.'

Serena's lips smiled her gratitude. 'Thank you. You are very understanding.'

'Perhaps that is because I too belong to the old faith.'

Surprise and astonishment widened Serena's eyes. 'You do?'

'I have been a Catholic all my life.' Lady Mary smiled. 'And before you ask, my husband had no objections just so long as I was quiet about it.'

Serena relaxed and laughed lightly. 'Isn't that the case in every Catholic family?' She looked to where Kit sat. 'But—Kit—you—'

'Kit and Paul took my husband's faith, Melissa mine,' Lady Mary explained. 'And do not forget that Queen

Anne—who made me an honoured member of her entou-
rage during her time in Scotland—became converted to Catholicism before she left for the south.'

'That I know,' Serena said softly with a trace of reproach
and a small, indignant thrust to her chin. 'It's a pity the
king does not show the same kind of tolerance to his Catholic subjects as he does his wife.'

'I understand your bitterness, Serena,' Lady Mary said
on a serious note. 'None of it is fair. But there is something
I must ask you.'

'Of course.'

'Tell me more about Sir Thomas Blackwell. He seems
to be a thoroughly obnoxious man.'

'He is. Sir Thomas, like his father before him, is looked
on as being a fine, upstanding man where I live. He is a
man of wealth and property, with many connections at
court.'

'He also has the ear of the king's chief minister, Robert
Cecil, who is a crafty statesman *par excellence,* and not
without malice,' Kit went on coldly.

Frowning, Serena glanced at him. 'Why have you such
a low opinion of Robert Cecil, Kit?'

'The man's unpopularity goes back a long time—towards the end of Elizabeth's reign when court rivalries
were bitter and destructive. A struggle for power ensued
between the second earl of Essex and Robert Cecil—Essex
being handsome and charming—'

'And I believe the old queen doted on him,' Serena remarked with a little smile.

'Precisely. But she would not be dominated by him.
When she appointed Cecil her principal secretary of state—
a position Essex had hoped to secure for one of his followers—Essex grew resentful and frustrated, becoming wild
and irrational and eventually breaking into rebellion. To the
public he had always been a hero, and they blamed Robert
Cecil for his downfall. Cecil became an object of hatred,

and after Essex's execution he was more reviled than ever. Yet, despite the public's profound dislike of him, his position became unassailable. With Essex out of the way, there was no one to challenge his preeminence with the Queen.

'As everyone now knows, before her death he secretly entered into a correspondence with King James in Scotland, earning his gratitude by advising him on his dealings with Elizabeth, and ensuring that the transference of power went smoothly on her death when James took the throne. James was so delighted and impressed by his efficiency that there was no question of him discarding Cecil, whom he later made the earl of Salisbury.'

'But he still does not rate highly in your esteem,' stated Serena.

'I admit he has a shrewd grasp of policy and is a man of untiring industry, who can justly congratulate himself for the difficult transitional period when James came to the throne. But he is a puny man with a sly sense of humour, who knows how to amuse the king—and how to manipulate him.

'Cecil resents my closeness to King James, and would be eager to listen to what Blackwell had to accuse me of. My removal from court would be to his satisfaction—and not only my own, I might add. Since James took the English throne, there are those in Parliament—and many Englishmen—who harbour a strong dislike for the Scottish supporters who followed him south because he bestowed lands, houses and offices on them.'

'But you have an equal measure of both Scottish and English blood flowing through your veins, and you spent a good deal of your time in the Low Countries following your military career,' protested his mother. 'You did become marquess of Thurlow by right.'

'Nevertheless, Cecil resents the fact that I was in James's train, and his resentment was increased when I returned from the Low Countries and my cousin died, making me his heir to Thurlow. So far Blackwell's machinations to bring me low have gone undetected by the king, who set about with fervour to have the conspirators hounded and thrown into the Tower.'

'Do not judge the king too harshly, Kit,' said his mother. 'By nature he is not a violent man and lives in constant fear of assassination. He saw many a bloodthirsty deed done throughout his adolescence. When you take into account the many plots and counterplots which took place before he went to England, then it's not surprising his experiences have left an indelible mark on his mind. This latest conspiracy by all accounts is the most vile, because not only did it threaten his own person, but also those of his wife and children.' On a sigh she spoke to Serena. 'Tell me, Serena, couldn't your uncle protect you from Sir Thomas Blackwell?'

'I'm afraid not. When my uncle learned of Kit's assumed involvement with the conspiracy and harbouring a fierce dislike for anyone belonging to the Catholic faith, he believed he had just cause to cancel Dorothea's betrothal to him and united her instead with Sir Thomas. So you see, Lady Mary, I had to get away. I could not endure living in such close proximity to a man I have every reason in the world to despise, and who would carry out his threat to harm me.'

'I can sympathise with that. It must be difficult for your uncle having a brother who belongs to the Catholic faith if he abhors it so deeply.'

'I confess that it has been the cause of much contention between him and my father over the years.'

'Has Sir Thomas harmed you in any physical way?'

'No, but he has attempted to violate my person twice. It was fortunate for me that Kit came to my aid on both occasions.'

'But not so fortunate for Blackwell,' growled Kit.

'Why?' asked Lady Mary.

'We fought, and I left him with a sword wound to his shoulder and a huge dent in his pride.'

Lady Mary frowned, displeased to hear this. 'You fought a duel?'

Kit nodded gravely. His mother strongly disapproved of this method of settling a quarrel or a point of honour, but at the time he'd had no alternative. 'Because of his malicious lies to discredit me I had been branded a traitor. After my escape I sought him out and asked him to go to the authorities and clear my name, but he refused. What would you have had me do, Mother? Pardon the man?'

Kit switched his hard gaze to Serena, recalling how enraged he'd been when he'd seen what Blackwell was about to subject her to, wanting to tear the man limb from limb because he had dared lay his hands on her yet again. 'And after his attempt to violate Serena, it was not just my own honour for which I fought.'

'I can see that,' Lady Mary said softly, 'and thank goodness you arrived when you did. But whatever differences are between you and Sir Thomas, Kit, you know I do not hold with duelling.'

'I made a point of not killing him. If I had, when I do return to England—which I have to do if I am to redeem myself—he would be unable to retract the slanderous accusations he has made against my name with utter disregard for the truth.'

'Then we must be patient and wait for Ludovick to come to Edinburgh,' said Lady Mary. 'But in the meantime it is essential that you are not seen about the town, Kit. If word gets out that you are here, news will travel fast to London.'

'I think everyone believes Kit and I managed to escape across the Channel, Lady Mary,' said Serena. 'At least, that was the impression we gave Sir Thomas when we left him at Dunedin Hall—and it was where I intended going even then.'

'It was never my intention to flee the country,' explained Kit. 'When Lord Carberry gave chase, we left the road and concealed ourselves until he had disappeared on the road to the south. Sir Henry Carberry is a good friend of mine and I felt duty-bound to take care of his daughter. I could not let Serena go on alone to Flanders, so I persuaded her to travel north with me.'

'Persuasion is hardly the word I would use when you appointed yourself as my guardian,' uttered Serena quickly, shooting Kit a disparaging look. It was a look which did not go unobserved by Lady Mary's sharp eyes.

'It can't have been easy for you, my dear. You are too young…too weak and delicate—which,' said Lady Mary with a trace of irony, shooting a meaningful glance at her son, 'if you will forgive me, is how we of the female sex are often described by our superior male counterparts—to be involved in the many things that have become a part of your life. It cannot have been easy travelling so far in this awful weather with Kit—who I know can be quite impossible; he often forgets he is not commanding an unruly regiment of soldiers.'

Because she spoke with a certain amount of gravity, Serena thought Lady Mary was being serious, but on observation she saw her eyes were twinkling, making Serena realise that she enjoyed teasing her handsome son. Briefly Serena caught Kit's eye, aware that he was watching her intently. A sleek black eyebrow slanted upwards to accentuate his expression of profound scepticism, which she totally ignored and, turning back to his mother, favoured her with a sweet smile.

'I consider no man my superior, Lady Mary,' she replied, trying to avoid looking at Kit.

Serena had felt, rather than seen, the black eyes roll with amusement when Lady Mary had called her weak and delicate, knowing he would be sorely tempted to raise an argument in contradiction despite the presence of his mother.

Having suffered her vicious verbal attacks on numerous occasions, Kit knew for a fact that there was nothing weak or delicate about her.

'I have fared well enough as it happens,' Serena continued calmly. 'It was good of Kit to befriend me—and I can assure you that his behaviour towards me at all times has been courteous and cannot be faulted.'

Lady Mary smiled indulgently at Kit, the hint of mockery directed at her son that she sensed behind Serena's words not lost on her, and she wondered just what had occurred between the two of them on their lone journey to Edinburgh. Kit certainly didn't seem disturbed or distressed in any way over his loss of Dorothea.

'Then I can only hope it will continue. And do you still intend going to your father, Serena?'

'Yes. Kit has promised to help me. He is to write to my father, informing him of my whereabouts and what I intend.'

'If you have any idea where the letter can be sent, Serena, I will write immediately,' Kit offered. 'Perhaps you would like to enclose a letter yourself.'

'Yes, I'll do that. I think it best to have the letter delivered to James at St Omer. Father is bound to visit him some time. If not, I am sure James will know where to forward it to. Where will you send it from?'

'The port at Leith. Ships are always leaving for the Low Countries.'

'And for the time being you are welcome to stay with us for just as long as it takes, Serena,' said Lady Mary. 'It will be good for Melissa having someone of her own age to talk to.'

'Thank you, Lady Mary. You are very kind.'

'Melissa is in Perth just now staying with friends. I expect her back in Edinburgh in a week or so. Although,' said Lady Mary, a wistful smile curving her lips, 'she has become quite fond of a young gentleman who lives in Perth, and may decide to extend her visit. But tell me—why didn't you tell your uncle about Sir Thomas's assault on your person? After all, if Dorothea is to marry him, she should be aware of his violent nature.'

'Uncle William would never have believed me. I—I did try to warn Dorothea about his character, but she was so besotted by him her ears were deaf to anything I had to say.'

'Sir Thomas must be an exceptional man to be able to replace Kit in your cousin's affections so quickly. We can only hope she sees the dark side to his character before she marries him.' Lady Mary focused her attention on Kit. 'Was everything in order at Addlington Hall, Kit? Mr and Mrs Gilby are well, I hope?'

'Everything was fine. But what will you do with it, Mother? The house cannot remain empty indefinitely.'

'I'm thinking of renting it out. Would you approve? I have enough of travelling between Coldstream and Edinburgh—and you know how I much prefer living in town.'

Kit shrugged casually. 'You must do what you will with the house. It is yours, after all. If Paul has a hankering to live there, then all well and good—or Melissa. If she marries a man without property, she may be happy to live there.'

'And then there is you, Kit,' said Lady Mary, her gaze searching her son's face with a mixture of desperation and hope. 'If Thurlow isn't redeemed to you, wouldn't you like to live at Addlington Hall? I know how much you always loved it as a boy.'

Kit knew his mother was trying hard not to let him see how deeply anxious she was for him, but he was very conscious of it. 'No, Mother. Thurlow will only be redeemed to me if I can clear my name of the crime against me. If I can't, then by all accounts I shall be guilty of treason and unable to live anywhere in England or Scotland.' His eyes were steady as they settled on his mother's strained face.

'I think we know the penalty I shall have to pay if I am found guilty of that particular crime. If I manage to escape, I shall be forced to live in exile abroad.'

Lady Mary drew a shaky breath. 'Then let us pray it does not come to that. Tell me, Serena, do you have many brothers and sisters?'

'I have two brothers, Lady Mary. James, who is thirteen, is a pupil at the Jesuit school at St Omer, near Calais, and Andrew, who is older than me, is a Jesuit priest—presently at the Vatican in Rome.'

'They sound pious young men. St Omer has become extremely popular since it was founded twelve years ago, and has attracted children from several Catholic families that I know of. Does Andrew manage to come to England? I know how difficult it is for priests in the present climate.'

'He came home last summer, but stayed no more than a few weeks.'

Searching the depths of the lovely green eyes looking into hers, Lady Mary discerned how they softened with sorrow, and she realised just how deep Serena's own suffering was for her family. 'Your faith must be strong, Serena,' she said gently, 'for you to withstand what has happened to your family.'

'My faith has both depth and permanence, Lady Mary. I will never change.'

Lady Mary smiled softly. 'No one would ask it of you, my dear. Tell me—when did you last go to Mass?'

'Perhaps two months ago.'

'That is much too long. I shall arrange it.'

'Thank you,' Serena said with a grateful smile.

Chapter Twelve

Walking restlessly about the room, Serena glanced to where Kit was sitting on the window seat looking out at the murky weather. He was lost in thought, his mood quiet, but Serena's uneasiness and her apparent inability to be still intruded into his thoughts and brought a frown to his brow.

'What is it, Serena, that makes you scowl like that?' he queried. 'Is it because we've reached our journey's end and you miss riding with me? Or has something displeased you? My mother, perhaps?' With his long, thigh-booted legs stretched out in front of him he sat back, folding his arms, his eyes dark and languid as he continued to peruse her.

Serena stopped her pacing and looked at him, contemplating her answer for a moment before she spoke. 'I am not scowling—and I am relieved not to have to ride any farther with you—and no, Lady Mary has not upset me. She has been very kind,' she answered loftily.

'I'm happy you think so. But?'

'It's just—this matter concerning my clothes,' Serena told him hesitantly.

'What about them? Mother is to sort out some of Melissa's gowns for you. She has ample. You are about the same height—and figure,' he said, cocking a handsome brow as he gave her a lengthy inspection, his eyes sweeping lazily downward over her rounded bosom to her narrow waist, before coming back and meeting her eyes, an impudent smile curving his lips. 'Although, perhaps you're a mite fuller and rounder here and there than Melissa...' he murmured, his voice trailing off.

The suggestive, casual boldness of his gaze sent Serena's indignation spiralling. 'Kit,' she reprimanded sharply, her green eyes flashing with fiery disdain and hot colour flooding her cheeks. It was the first time he had made any forward remark to her since that day he had kissed her at Addlington Hall. 'You are outrageous and quite shameless.'

The twitch of his mouth revealed his amusement, and he arched a brow as he made a silent, appreciative perusal of her angry face. 'Am I?'

'Yes, and quite insufferable. Do you have to ogle and undress me in that objectionable, ungentlemanly manner? It's most unseemly. What if someone should come in?'

'Since when has gazing at something as lovely as you been an offence?' Kit chuckled softly, lights shining in his black eyes as he met her angry glare. Unconcerned by her irritation, he contemplated her with half a smile. 'Since you took it into your head to spurn my advances, to look upon your beauty is the only means I have of feeding the hungering ache inside me, which gnaws away at me constantly. To imagine what delights you conceal beneath all those hoops and layers of petticoats is the only comfort I can gain to appease my yearning.'

Showing no sign of softening, Serena lifted her chin primly and continued to glare at him, placing her hands firmly on her slender waist. 'Then you will just have to be satisfied with what you see because it's as far as you'll get. It's about time you found something else to occupy yourself with to help quell your carnal appetite,' she told him, her tone having sharpened to a cutting degree, while all the time she was trying to still her racing heart and hold on to her crumbling composure.

Kit was not done with her. A brooding warmth entered his eyes, and there was an animal gleam to his white teeth showing between his parted lips. 'When I found myself cast adrift with you on our journey north, little did I know I would fall victim to a vituperative female, who could set me so effortlessly on edge and rob me of the ability to act and think clearly. Circumstances have played a heavy part in the way I feel for you. You are a temptation—a temptation I find difficult to resist. I've had a taste of what you have to offer and I find myself wanting more.'

'Then you must endure it as best you can.'

'Aye, madam, I will endure it,' Kit murmured, lazily watching the tension and emotion play across her expressive face. 'But don't deny the truth. Can you tell me you didn't feel what I felt when we kissed? That you didn't tremble and quiver with passion? Your craving was as great as my own. Can you tell me you didn't want me to make love to you?'

Serena was relieved that he hadn't left his perch to stand next to her. His voice was soft and came across to her as a caress, sending a swirl of sensations rushing into the core of her being and tearing holes in her composure. A livid blush covered her cheeks. Unable to meet his unflinching eyes, and conscious of his magnetism and the uneven beat of her heart, she directed her gaze out of the window. How could she tell him how torn she was by what she felt for him and how strong she wanted to be, knowing she would have to leave him.

'Please, Kit,' she pleaded softly, emitting a tremulous sigh. 'Don't let us discuss this now.'

'Why? Does it trouble you?'

'Yes, if you must know, it does.'

'It needn't, if you didn't insist on keeping me at bay. Why do you?'

'You know why.'

'I may not have spoken about the moment I held you in

my arms at Addlington Hall—but it's a moment I shall always treasure in my memory. I respect your reasons for not wanting to become involved in something from which you know there will be no going back. But just remember that I am a man, Serena—flesh and blood, with a man's desires and needs. I apologise, if by allowing my ardour to get the better of me, it's made things difficult for you, but that's the way it is.'

'It certainly doesn't make it any easier,' Serena answered curtly. 'If I had stayed in your arms any longer that day, you would not have withheld your ardour and that would have been an end to my virtue.'

'It's the truth. My dearest wish is to make love to you— to ease the desire that plagues me day and night. It's only your plea that I control myself that keeps you safe from me and nothing else. But your response to my kiss was not exactly cool—in fact, I was both surprised and delighted to find you so yielding in my arms. It gave me reason to hope.'

'Oh, you beast,' Serena whispered. 'That's not fair. I do have feelings for you. I would be lying if I said otherwise— and with that irritating ability you seem to have of reading my every thought you would know it, too. I will not speak of this again, Kit—and neither will you.'

Kit's words tore through Serena more than any act of violence could have done. Determined not to give him the pleasure of seeing her moved by them, she turned away, her face set in determined lines as she tried her best to ignore him, while feeling smothered by his presence and the intentness of his gaze that never left her.

'Contrary to what you may think, it is not my desire to conquer you, to take from you what you do not want to give,' Kit said gently. 'What there is between us must be shared. I only ask that you grant me a little of your time, so that we may speak and discuss what the future may hold for us.'

'I know what the future holds for me—and you have a long struggle ahead of you to wipe away the accusation of being a traitor. I hoped you understood why there has to be this barrier between us. Nothing must hinder my resolve to go to my father.'

Kit's mood softened, his eyes dwelling on her as she continued wearing a hole in the carpet. In her ruby-coloured dress she really was a joy to look at. She was straining to adopt an attitude of self-assurance, but Kit was not deceived. He was aware that she was beset by a tumult of emotions, and that she was doing her best to fight them. He really would have to learn to curb his desires until she was ready to give herself freely. But the waiting would be hard indeed.

'Very well, Serena. I promise you will go unmolested by me until the day when you can no longer resist my ardour. So, where were we, before we became sidetracked by more delicate matters? As I recall, we were speaking of renewing your wardrobe. Don't you like dressing in borrowed clothes? Are Melissa's gowns not to your taste? Because, if so, I would not like to be the one to tell her.' He chuckled softly.

Serena paused in her pacing to glare at him, relieved he had changed the subject. 'Heaven forbid that I should be so rude. Melissa's clothes are lovely, but I would dearly like to go out and buy my own clothes. I am in dire need of new gowns, undergarments, footwear and a host of other things important to every female.'

Kit shrugged. 'That's not a problem. I know my mother would be happy to accompany you to the shops to purchase some. I may have had certain properties confiscated, but I am not a poor man. Just tell me how much money you will need and I will cover the expense.'

'Thank you,' Serena answered, her eyes keen and alert. 'But I do have the means with which to purchase my own clothes.'

'You do?'

'Yes. At least I will have when I sell the jewels I brought with me.'

Confounded, Kit's eyes opened wide with astonishment. 'Jewels! The devil you have! I didn't know you had any jewels with you.'

Serena ignored the shocked surprise on his face that made him suddenly sit up straight with interest. 'That's because I didn't tell you.'

He eyed her dubiously. 'They are yours?'

'Of course they're mine,' she retorted, affronted that he might think she'd stolen them. 'One of my reasons for going to Dunedin Hall the night you found me was to get them. They were hidden in a secret drawer in a chest. Fortunately they were overlooked by the searchers. I salvaged them in the hope that I could sell them to pay for my passage to Flanders. They were given to me by my father for my own personal use, but are of no great value, otherwise they would have been kept with the others that he gave to Uncle William for safekeeping.'

Kit chuckled, unable to disguise the admiration for her in his dancing eyes. 'You are a woman of many surprises, Serena. But don't you want to keep them—for sentimental reasons, if nothing else?'

'No,' Serena replied frankly. 'They're of no use to me and I don't want them. I would rather have the money instead.'

'You sound quite the little mercenary.'

'Do I?' she answered coolly, turning her hard green eyes on him. 'Perhaps that's because at this moment in my life— with my home confiscated, a Jesuit priest for a brother who will be hunted down and hanged if he dares to set foot on English soil, and a father who is a fugitive abroad—I have discovered that money is an extremely important commodity to help me get to Flanders. Without it I would be forced to ask you for a loan.'

'And I would be more than happy to oblige—be it for pretty gowns or a passage to Flanders.'

Serena looked at him a little petulantly. 'I thought you didn't want me to go.'

'I don't. But I will not stop you, Serena. Despite my own selfish reasons for wanting to keep you here with me, I do realise that you must go to your father. And, as you so bluntly pointed out earlier, I have the serious business of clearing my name of the crime for which I have been charged to attend to—which means I shall have to return to London. But it would be a shame to sell your jewels. I would be happy to give you the money you need.'

'No, Kit. Your offer is generous, but I cannot accept it. Forgive me if I seem ungrateful, but please understand that I would feel uncomfortable if you paid for my clothes. I am beholden to your mother enough as it is for letting me stay here. I have no wish to be beholden to you as well.'

'Beholden? What a strange woman you are, Serena. However, I have no wish for you to feel beholden to me either—for anything,' Kit said, clearly at pains to control his mirth.

'Good. And don't mock me,' Serena reproached, glaring at the wicked humour she saw dancing in his dark eyes. 'I am serious. Will you sell my jewels for me? You will know who will give me the best price for them. If you think it unwise to go yourself in case you are recognised, then perhaps someone else could go.' She frowned crossly when she saw Kit trying to stifle his amusement. 'Please, Kit. Do not hinder me in this. If you do, I shall be forced to take to the streets and sell my own jewels.'

Kit laughed, holding up his hands in mock surrender. Standing up, he moved towards her, hooking his thumbs into his belt and peering down at her. 'All right, Serena. I give in. I can see you will give me no peace until I agree to do as you ask. Go and fetch them and let me see.'

* * *

Kit obliged Serena by selling her jewels for a good price.
With the proceeds she was able to purchase some new
clothes and had a considerable amount of money left over.

Serena drafted a letter to her father, finding it a laborious
task having to explain why she'd felt she'd had no alternative but to leave Carberry Hall, telling him of Sir Thomas
Blackwell's assault on her person, and that because of his
own involvement in the Gunpowder Plot, it was likely she
would be arrested in its wake. She begged his understanding and asked him to give his permission for her to travel
to him in Flanders. Kit had the letter dispatched along with
his own with a sea captain at Leith, who was to sail for the
Low Countries any day.

Accompanied by Lady Mary, Serena went shopping, taking pleasure in indulging in something so light-hearted and
frivolous after weeks of anxiety. Not that her anxieties were
any less, but they were lightened by this simple pleasure.

Over the days they were together, and while they waited
for Melissa to return from Perth, Lady Mary showed Serena
some of the sights of Edinburgh, which held her enthralled.
It was a noble, rich and still-royal city, even after King
James had removed himself and his court to England two
years previously, on succeeding to the English throne on
the death of Queen Elizabeth.

Melissa, a dark-haired lively girl, with striking features
and a pleasant dispositon, eventually returned to Edinburgh
and was delighted to meet Serena. She was full of enthusiasm about her blossoming relationship with the young
gentleman who had been the cause of her extended visit to
Perth. Overshadowing the joy Melissa felt on being reu-
nited with Kit was the concern and distress she shared with
her mother about his assumed involvement in the Gunpowder Plot, which hung like a pall over them all and created
a tension felt by the whole household.

Not a man given to idleness, this time of inactivity

chafed against Kit's patience. With the utmost discretion he took to riding far afield to visit trusted friends in Perth and Stirling to the north, where he indulged in his favourite pastimes of hunting the red deer and fishing in the wide Highland rivers. The time he was away offered Serena and Kit some respite from each other, for it was becoming increasingly difficult for them both being together so much, each conscious of the other's tightly veiled feelings and passions.

News reached Edinburgh about the conspirators of the Gunpowder Plot being held in the Tower in London, of how they were being tortured to extract information out of them, but it was not until Sir Ludovick at last came to Scotland in March that they heard the full story. With Melissa and Lady Mary, Serena had been absent from the house for several hours, and on entering the hall Kit met them, his features grave.

'Ludovick has arrived in Edinburgh,' he told them. 'After coming here he returned to his lodgings, but he is to return later for supper. The good news is that Robin has been released from his captivity in the Tower and is here with him. He suffers no ill effects other than a loss of weight, owing to the poor diet.' Kit's gaze focused on his sister and Serena, whose eyes flew to his imploringly, desperate to know what news Sir Ludovick had brought—the news of Robin's release planting hope within her breast. 'I would like to speak to my mother alone for a few moments.'

'But I—'

'I'll speak to you in a short while, Serena. Go with Melissa and tidy yourself. I'll have one of the maids summon you presently.'

With that Serena had to be content, but as soon as the maid knocked on her door she went straight down, finding Kit alone in a small parlour. He was standing by the window, staring out unseeingly at the darkening garden beyond. His grim expression boded ill.

'Come in, Serena,' he said when she entered.

Closing the door behind her Serena hesitated, and after a moment Kit turned and went to the fire, hands behind his back and his eyes focused on the flames with concentrated deliberation. It struck Serena that the news Sir Ludovick had brought troubled him greatly. He looked up and beckoned her to the fire.

'Come and sit down. We have much to discuss.'

Serena went towards him but did not sit down, too apprehensive about what he was about to tell her to sit still. Wringing her fingers with an increasing disquiet she was attentive, watching him with worried eyes. His expression was neutral, but she was assailed by a sudden sense of dread and her stomach contracted with foreboding.

'What news is there from London, Kit?' she asked when she could stand it no longer. 'Have all the conspirators been captured?'

He nodded. 'Yes. And dealt with.'

Serena felt all the blood drain out of her face, imagining their awful suffering. 'How many were there?'

'Eight were condemned, but there were thirteen all told. Five died during capture. The executions took place on two consecutive days, the first on the thirtieth of January. The bodies of Catesby and Thomas Percy, killed during the raid on Holbeach House, have been exhumed from their Midland graves and their heads are being exhibited at the corners of Parliament House.'

'Which they planned to blow up,' whispered Serena. 'How ironical.'

'In addition to the plotters, several leading Catholic peers and the earl of Northumberland, who all had embarrassing connections to the abortive plot, have also been taken to the Tower—along with some Jesuit priests who, according to Robin, fare much worse. Without pity they have been put to the torture in order to gain information about the recusant safe houses where Catholic families harboured and protected them—houses which remain unknown to the authorities.'

'Then God help them,' Serena whispered. 'For them there will be no reprieve at the end either. And the others— the servants and relatives of the plotters who were connected, but had no part in its inner workings? What has happened to them?'

'For some the horrors are not over. When Ludovick left London at the end of February, people were still being taken into custody.'

'What will happen, do you think, to the Catholic peers who have been arrested—who were inadvertently drawn in?'

'To get back into the king's good graces they will no doubt have to pay enormous fines and undergo a spell of imprisonment.'

'Do you believe I did the right thing in leaving Carberry Hall, Kit?'

He sighed. 'As to that, you will have to make up your own mind. The English recusant community is suffering the relentless investigations by the authorities they have feared for so long. The authorities seek information regarding the conspirators, but there is a high degree of malice in the way they are going about it.

'Several people have also benefited out of the Gunpowder Plot. By implicating those they believe were connected to the plot to the earl of Salisbury, some have been rewarded with the properties of those they accused.' He looked purposefully and steadily at Serena, the expression in his eyes grave. 'Which could happen in Blackwell's case.'

A feeling of doom descended on Serena's already disquieted spirit. 'But surely Sir Thomas has achieved his aim by implicating you. What else has he gained from his malicious conniving and lying?'

'As yet nothing is certain, but he is hoping to acquire Dunedin Hall—at least, what is left of it, and the land that goes with it,' Kit said quietly.

Serena stared at him, unable to comprehend any of this. 'What is left of it? What are you saying?'

'Serena…on the night we left, Dunedin Hall caught fire and was almost gutted.' He sighed, taking her trembling hand in his own. 'I am truly sorry, believe me.'

Overcome by a deep sadness, this final tragedy affected Serena greatly. 'Fire? But—how did it happen?'

'Who knows? A candle left burning, a lantern. This has come as a blow to you, but it may help when I tell you that for some reason the king seems reluctant to bestow the property on Blackwell—who, it would seem, continues to suffer greatly from the wound I inflicted on him.'

'I should have known he would do this,' Serena said with deep bitterness. 'The boundaries of the Blackwell estate adjoin our own. Not being so well off and spending so much of his time breeding horses, some of my father's land became neglected. Sir Thomas's father tried persuading him to sell him some on numerous occasions, but my father always refused. If the king grants Sir Thomas his request, then he will have profited greatly. Has his marriage to Dorothea taken place?'

'Apparently so—before the new year.'

'And—and do you know if she is happy?'

'According to Ludovick she is.'

'I see. It would seem Sir Thomas's manners towards my cousin differ greatly from his manners towards myself.' Taking a deep breath, Serena looked up at Kit. So far she had been too afraid of what he would tell her to ask the question uppermost in her mind, but it could not be avoided. 'And what news of yourself, Kit? What had Sir Ludovick to tell you?'

Kit let go of her hand and combed his fingers through his hair, moving away from her. 'He was granted an audience with the king, who, it appears, was always uneasy about my arrest. But having taken swift and punitive action and ordering the arrest of anyone who carried the slightest suspicion of being involved with the conspirators, there was little he could do. However, nothing has been proved against me.

'Under interrogation Robin told them the absolute truth when he was questioned about my actions running up to the plot's discovery. He also told them about my association with Catesby and other conspirators. Mercifully he was not put to the torture. None of the plotters or priests tortured, confessed my name or incriminated me in any way—not even in the course of their conversations, which were secretly overheard.'

Serena's relief was enormous. 'But this is good news, Kit. If there is no evidence to substantiate the charge of treason it will be dropped.'

Kit nodded. 'Maybe. The king assured Ludovick that I will be given a fair trial when I return.'

'Does he know you are in Scotland?'

'Yes. When nothing was heard as to my whereabouts, he suspected all along that this was where I'd flown.'

'Are you likely to be arrested?'

'Not if I return to London of my own free will.'

'And will you?'

'Yes. I must.'

'And what of my father? Had Sir Ludovick anything to tell you?'

'Yes. He is one of several incriminated in the conspiracy who sought sanctuary abroad, and happily remain outside the long arm of the law. Salisbury would like to have them taken back to England for trial, but the archdukes are reluctant to extradite them.'

'Then I shall have to go to him. I am left with little

choice. If he has been branded a traitor, according to custom where traitors' families are concerned, I shall be pursued and humiliated. Anything my father left behind will be seized and confiscated to pay the enormous fines which will be imposed on him. Thankfully he did prepare himself for just such an event. In England he is not a rich man, but he has money and investments put away abroad for his relief.'

'Then he will not be entirely destitute. Naturally he is wanted for questioning—but the plotters refused to incriminate him. On being questioned, each one told their interrogators that Sir Henry was told the horses they purchased from him were to be used for the purpose of raising a troop of horse to send to the Spanish Netherlands, and nothing more.'

'And did the interrogators believe this?'

Kit shrugged. 'Whether they believed it or not, your father is still wanted for questioning.'

'Then I pray he stays in Flanders where he is safe. In any case, he has no home to come back to—and James will have need of him. Does Sir Ludovick know where he is?'

'Yes.'

'How did he find out?'

'By making a few discreet enquiries among his friends. The network of spies spread abroad also revealed his whereabouts.' Kit studied her closely. 'He is staying at the home of a close friend. Do you know who she is, Serena?'

Serena looked at him sharply and nodded, her throat constricting painfully. 'Yes. Mrs Davis.'

'A lady he has since married,' Kit told her quietly, moving to a table beside the door and picking up a sealed letter, one of two lying there unopened. Bringing it to where she stood, he handed it to her. 'This has just arrived. I have one, too. They're from Flanders—from your father. No doubt he has explained everything in his letter.'

The small room seemed to surge with the sensation of

the pronouncement. Serena had listened to Kit as though in a dream, a nightmare, scarcely able to grasp the reality of it. So her father had married Mrs Davis after all. This was just what she had feared. She stared down at the letter in shocked dismay, both saddened and disappointed by this unfortunate turn of events. Desperately she raised her eyes to Kit's, shaking her head and biting her trembling lip tearfully.

'But he can't have married her. It can't be true.'

'I'm afraid it is. According to the information Ludovick has managed to glean, your father has no intention of ever returning to England.' Watching her with a sombre gaze, Kit missed nothing. He realised by the pained look in her eyes just how much she was hurting inside, and he knew, at last, the reason why she had been hell-bent on going to her father. It was clear to him that this news of his marriage was most unwelcome and that she was displeased by it.

'Come—don't despair,' he said quietly, understanding her misery and longing to draw her into his arms to ease her pain. 'Why do you consider it such a bad thing that your father has married this Mrs Davis? Has she given you reason to dislike her?'

Serena shook her head in some confusion, her face white and stricken. 'No. I've never met her.'

'Then why do you think ill of her?' he asked gently, studying her face intently, seeing her eyes mist over with tears.

The tears Serena had been trying valiantly to suppress welled irresistibly and rolled out of the corners of her eyes and streaked unhindered down her cheeks.

'I confess to knowing very little about her, only that she is a wealthy widow who has been my father's mistress for some years—a woman who chose to make her home in Flanders where she is allowed to practice her religion with the freedom denied her in England. According to Andrew, she has been trying to coax Father into marriage for some time, but he always refused to live anywhere other than England. She also has children—two, I believe.'

'And does this offend you?'

'No. No—of course it doesn't—but—oh, how can I make you understand?' She wept unhappily. 'I can never accept this marriage. It can never be anything but a travesty.'

'Why? It is real enough—conducted before a priest in the proper manner. And if Mrs Davis has been your father's mistress for a number of years, then surely he has done the honourable thing by marrying her.'

'But I cannot forget how close my father and mother were,' Serena cried brokenly, trying to make Kit understand how bereft she felt. 'It hurts so much knowing another woman has taken her place.'

'Maybe in his life but not in his heart—not if he loved your mother as deeply as you say he did. Don't you think that perhaps you are being a little selfish and hard on him—that you are blinkered and unable to see anything but your own point of view? I would have thought you desired your father's happiness—especially at this difficult time in his life. Hasn't it occurred to you that you might even like his wife?'

In silent misery Serena hung her head. What Kit said was painfully true. She had never asked her father how he felt about Mrs Davis, what she was like, and she should have. 'You are right. I have always been wilful and selfish—always thinking of my own needs before those of others. It is wicked and sinful to want to keep him to myself.'

'Now you are being hard on yourself,' Kit said with mild reproach. 'Can't you try to be happy for him—for them both?'

Serena nodded dumbly, sniffing back her tears and wiping her face with the back of her hand, unconsciously taking the handkerchief Kit suddenly produced and drying her tears, handing it back to him with a tremulous smile when she saw it was the one he had taken from her the first time they met. 'I will try.'

'That's more like it. Now—go upstairs and make yourself presentable. Ludovick is coming to supper, and you know how taken he was with you when you met at Carberry Hall. I'm sure you don't want to disappoint him.'

'You told him I am here—in Scotland?'

'He already knew. In the hope of seeing you, he called at Carberry Hall on his way north. Lord Carberry—who is extremely vexed at your disappearance—told him that you had left in some haste. When your uncle recounted Blackwell's rendition of the events of the night you left and his encounter with us both at Dunedin Hall—how he tried to prevent you leaving, becoming injured in the affray which was all my doing—Ludovick knew you'd have come north with me.'

'Did he tell my uncle this?'

'No. Lord Carberry is under the assumption that we are both abroad.'

Still holding her father's letter, on a sigh Serena moved towards the door. 'I shall go to my room and read my father's letter before supper. No doubt you will do the same.'

Chapter Thirteen

The contents of her father's letter had Serena reeling and dashing out of her room in search of Kit, with a speed surprising for someone who had a few moments before been in the throes of misery and despair. Kit had just finished reading his own letter from Sir Henry and awaited the outburst he felt sure would come at any moment. He did not have long to wait. Knowing exactly what Serena's reaction would be when she read her father's letter, he was not disappointed. If he'd wanted anything to draw her out of her melancholia, this was it.

Whereas Serena had left him just a short time before in unhappy mood, she now burst into the room and faced him like a termagant, going to stand directly in front of him and waving the letter beneath his nose like a weapon of destruction. Kit saw rebellion in her eyes as she prepared to launch her attack—eyes which such a short time ago had been moist with tears. The mouth, which had been soft, sensitive and quivering, was now set in a hard line.

With a raised dark eyebrow and an amused light in his eyes, Kit looked at her hostile face. 'What the devil are you looking at me like that for? Dear Lord, Serena, must you glare at me like some infernal, threatening thundercloud?'

'Have you read what my father has written?'

'Of couse,' he replied calmly.

'Then would you be so kind as to tell me what you put in your letter to him that he should berate me so severely?'

Kit shrugged. 'Nothing untoward, I assure you.'

'My father has appointed *you* as my guardian, since I took it upon myself to run away from Uncle William. He is extremely angry by my behaviour and, according to him, in your letter you told him that, on the strength of your friendship, you are willing, along with Lady Mary, to undertake my welfare.'

'That is correct. But I did impress that it would only apply if, for some reason, he did not wish you to journey to him in Flanders.'

Serena glared at him incredulously. 'How dare you! You had no right.'

'Considering the circumstances, I had every right—and your father clearly agrees.'

'And did he tell you that he has strictly *forbidden* me to go to him?'

'He did. But, considering he has taken his bride on honeymoon to Rome on a visit to your brother, there hardly seems much point,' Kit murmured, his voice soft and deeply laced with humour, which provoked Serena to further anger.

'Then let me tell you that I shall go. I shall go to Italy myself, if necessary, and you will not stop me.'

'Calm down. You are beside yourself.'

She responded with derisive sarcasm, 'Aye, my lord, I'll calm myself. Just as soon as you relinquish your stance as my guardian.'

'I'm sorry, Serena, but I can't allow you to roam at will until your father returns from his honeymoon.'

Serena had great difficulty in refraining from stamping her foot in angry frustration. 'Don't taunt me with it, you—you churlish oaf. Isn't it enough knowing he has married his paramour without you thrusting his honeymoon down my throat, too? You can't keep me here in Scotland.'

Kit brought his face closer to hers. 'Believe me, Serena, if it were possible I would have you shipped to Flanders on the next available vessel and let your father deal with you. Little wonder he married—having suffered enough of your infernal carping and bleating over the years.'

'Oh!' Serena gasped, glaring with indignation at the hard light in Kit's eyes. 'You monster. You cannot force me to remain here.'

'Yes, I can.'

'I insist on leaving.'

Kit's black eyes seized hers in an unrelenting gaze. 'You may insist all you like, but I will not stir. For the time being, you will accept the hospitality of this house and be grateful.'

'Grateful? When you keep me here by force? Ha!' Serena exclaimed with heavy sarcasm. 'Your generosity overwhelms me.'

'I apologise if you think I am forcing you to stay here.'

'If you wish to make amends, you will allow me to leave.'

'I always knew you were a courageous wench, and that you would bravely sally forth and to hell with the consequences, but I have every reason to believe your wits have deserted you.' Kit stepped back, settling his gaze on her flaming cheeks and rapidly heaving bosom. 'Be reasonable, Serena,' he cajoled on a gentler note. 'Your father is in Italy.'

'Then that is where I shall go, or take lodgings close to James until he returns.'

'No.'

His blunt answer brought a scowl to her face. 'And what will you do with me when you go to London?'

'You will remain here with my mother and Melissa.'

'Then you would do well to remember that I ran away

from my uncle. I could just as easily run away from you, too.'

'At your peril, madam.'

'You cannot force me.'

'Can I not?' Kit looked at Serena with that faint amusement she had come to detest. It was the same amused but quelling look he would give a troublesome child. 'Try me. You may not like my form of persuasion, which might be construed as harsh, but while you reside in this house you will do as I say.'

'You beast. I have no wish to reside in this house—or any other house with you. I *shall* leave.'

'Do so. But you would not care for the humiliation of being brought back. Your father has placed you under my care—and my mother's. I advise you to remember that.' Seeing the dejection on her lovely face, Kit sighed. 'By my faith, Serena, please be sensible.'

'Faith!' she cried in frustration. 'What faith? You are naught but a heretic.'

Kit laughed infuriatingly. 'And you, my little pious one, are the peskiest wench it has ever been my misfortune to meet, with a tongue comparable to a nest of wasps.'

'Then take care you don't get stung,' Serena replied in spitting tones, turning from him, intending to leave, but he was behind her, placing his hand on her shoulder to halt her flight.

'What a proud, foolish woman you are,' he murmured softly. 'Stay a moment, Serena.'

'Why? So you can make a mockery of me, Lord Brodie?' she seethed, feeling the heat of his body and his hot breath on her cheek, becoming desperately afraid that he would succeed in breaking down the barrier she had so skilfully raised between them. Her knowledge of this man had taught her that however strong her will, he had the infuriating ability to shatter it beneath the onslaught of his fervour. 'Will you do me a great favour?'

'Of course. You only have to ask. What is it?'

'Go away—and stay away. Leave me alone.'

'I will do anything you ask,' Kit amended calmly, quietly, the fragrance of her silken tresses filling his mind, 'but that.'

Serena felt him move closer still and, despite her anger, there was nothing she could do to still the chaotic pounding of her heart. Her worries burgeoned when he gently drew her hair aside and dropped a warm kiss on her neck. She gasped at the feel of his lips on her flesh and the pleasurable sensations his kiss stirred.

'Your father may have appointed me your guardian, but we could discuss the terms of my appointment,' he murmured huskily.

'Never,' Serena answered, trying her utmost to retain her composure.

Kit smiled, recognising in her answer the same kind of hostility when he had tried to negotiate with men in unfortunate circumstances. Exactly like those men Serena felt powerless, and in her pride felt the need to retaliate by making things as difficult as possible for him. 'There's no reason why matters should not be amicable between us, Serena. I feel there is a way we could make life more endurable—and pleasant.'

Serena turned and looked at him warily. 'Really! How?'

'Like this,' he murmured, pulling her close, his arms slipping easily about her and crushing her to him. Bending his dark head, he captured her mouth in a soft, compelling kiss, warming and penetrating to the depths of her being. His mouth forced her lips apart, his tongue teasing.

Serena tried to turn her head, afraid that her will and her anger would crumble beneath his onslaught, but he held her in a gentle, but unyielding, grip, his hands boldly passing over her waist, her hips, possessively. For a moment her body responded eagerly, then mingled anger at his impertinence and horror at her own swift reaction caused her to stiffen in his arms.

Kit dragged his lips from hers and looked down at her, noting the telltale flush on her cheeks. Serena could only stare at him as she listened to the chaotic pounding of her heart.

'Please, don't,' she begged in a trembling voice, turning from him quickly, unable to look at him lest he saw the softening in her eyes. 'I—I don't think I like your terms.'

Arching a lazy black eyebrow and smiling crookedly, Kit reached out and placed his fingers gently beneath her chin, forcing her to look at him. 'You don't? You gave a fair imitation of it.'

The amusement in his voice made Serena's blood boil. 'How dare you kiss me in so casual, so cavalier a fashion— as if you own me. I would thank you not to repeat the offence,' she retorted angrily.

A wayward smile curved Kit's lips, as he knew perfectly well that she was on the point of losing her resolve. 'Very well. I realise I must take my new responsibilities seriously, so I shall try to restrain myself until a future date. But you will not always be hostile towards me, Serena. When I want something, I do not give up until I have it. The day will come when I will make you mine in every sense.'

Meeting his eyes Serena realised he meant every word he said and that he would have no pity on her. She could only wonder at his mood as she struggled to maintain her anger. 'And you, sir, are quite detestable and more conceited than I thought if you consider you have any claim on me.' She glared up at the sparkling black eyes, but the heated words she was ready to utter were silenced by the interruption of Melissa's feminine voice coming to them from the hall.

'Please excuse me,' Serena ground out. 'I have to change for supper.' With an imperious move she swept out of the room, her head held high.

Still smiling, Kit watched her go, feeling nothing but admiration for her. The idea of making this woman his wife settled comfortably on his mind. Serena was a rarity indeed. Light and dark, tender and bold, fire and water. What more could a man want? Life would never be dull married to her.

Serena tried to remove all traces of bad temper and smooth the lines of worry from her face for her meeting with Sir Ludovick. Moved to defy Kit, and by some feminine impulse to flirt with danger, she dressed in her finest gown, which set off her figure to perfection, and showed more of her décolletage than was seemly. She intended dealing Kit blow for blow for arrogantly assuming that he had every right to take charge of her life and order her about as he saw fit.

She went down to the dining parlour with Melissa, who was well acquainted with their guest. Kit and Sir Ludovick stood before the fireplace, with Lady Mary sitting close by on a sofa.

Serena swept into the room, looking regal in her deep rose-coloured gown, the sleeves slashed with ribbons of a paler hue, and the cuffs edged with fine lace. The firm stomacher displayed the slender curve of her waist, and the voluminous skirts had been drawn over a fathingale. She scorned the wearing of a ruff, having adorned her neck instead with a single strand of creamy pearls. Her hair was drawn from her face by a simple broad band of ribbon over the top of her head, and allowed to hang free in heavy waves down the length of her curving spine.

Kit's gaze studied her closely and he nodded ever so slightly, happy to see she had regained her composure. But then she was as fickle and changeable as a chameleon, which had the ability to change its colour at will. He really should not have expected anything else from the minx. It didn't take him long to realise that she was going out of her way to avoid looking at him, and a small, lazy smile crept across his handsome face.

Ludovick, splendidly garbed in sapphire blue doublet and puffed trunk hose, stepped forward to greet them—Melissa first, who bobbed a little curtsy and told him how delighted she was to see him again.

'My dear Melissa,' he declared. 'You grow fairer each time I see you. It's difficult to believe you are sister to this reprobate,' he said in light-hearted reference to Kit. 'I hear from Lady Mary that a certain event might be taking place in the near future,' he murmured with a conspiratorial lowering of an eyelid, 'that a certain gentleman from Perth has become quite smitten by you.'

'And you, sir,' Melissa accused with a smile and a twinkle in her dark eyes, 'are as big a tease as you ever were. You ply your tongue with the skill of an accomplished flatterer—but I have no mind to become one of your conquests. No doubt you will bestow similar prose on Serena,' she laughed, taking Serena's hand and drawing her forward.

Ludovick grinned broadly, turning his full attention on Serena. 'My dear, Mistress Carberry—Serena, if I may be so bold,' he enthused, placing a hand to his chest and making a gallant bow. 'I can't tell you how astounded I was to learn you had taken flight with Kit. You must have been quite desperate.'

'I was,' she laughed, watching Kit out of the corner of her eye.

'He has been taking care of you, I hope?'

'Of course,' she replied pleasantly, admiring Sir Ludovick's fine attire and going out of her way to ignore Kit. 'But let me assure you that I am quite capable of taking care of myself.'

'Aye, I'm sure you are. And I see you are just as lovely as I remember,' Ludovick complimented, making small effort to subdue the delight that shone in his eyes as he appraised her.

'And Melissa was right when she told you you are an

accomplished flatterer,' Serena laughed. 'Are you to stay long in Edinburgh?'

'Long enough to become better acquainted with you, Serena. I'm in no hurry to leave for Argyllshire. I could not believe my good fortune when I realised I would have the pleasure of seeing you in Edinburgh. Do you like Scotland?'

'Well enough—at least what I've seen of it. I would fare better if I understood the dialect. Not all Scots are as easy to understand as yourself.'

'Since the Scots are renowned for their cursing, most of it would be unrepeatable if you could,' he laughed jovially. 'Whilst I am in Edinburgh I shall act as your translator, allowing only what I think is suitable to pass your delicate ears.'

Serena smiled, casting a surreptitious glance at Kit, a glance which told him she would give him neither rest nor respite in the desire for revenge which had taken hold of her. He was observing her gracious greeting of his friend with narrowed eyes, always wary where she was concerned, never knowing what she would do next, but she had worn so many different guises this day that he could be forgiven for thinking they had a changeling in their midst.

Sensing Kit was a little put out by Sir Ludovick's close attention pierced Serena's pleasure. Tweaking his nose a little further, she slid her gaze away from his and curved her lips in her prettiest smile.

'You honour me, Sir Ludovick.'

Supper was announced and Serena placed her hand on Ludovick's proffered arm, allowing him to escort her the short distance to the table. Following with his mother and Melissa, Kit felt a strong thud of discomfort as he admired the gentle sway of Serena's hips as she walked ahead of him, certain there was added movement because she knew he was watching her and wished to goad him further. With narrowed eyes he watched Ludovick's familiarity towards her, observing how his hands brushed the incredibly narrow curve of her waist as he pulled out her chair. Kit's frown deepened when Serena tilted her head to smile her thanks, testing Kit's restraint beyond the limits of endurance.

Supper passed pleasantly enough, with Serena languishing in the attention of her admirer, and frequently meeting the dark, challenging eyes of her tormentor, who watched her from across the table with unswerving tenacity. She feigned a smile that would have torn asunder any man's defences who was off his guard, but Kit was not deceived by her mellowing mood.

Serena flattered Ludovick, listening to him with rapt attention, and she was joined by Melissa in encouraging him to speak of life at court. Throughout supper Serena's smile remained beguiling, and her soft, sweet perfume teased Kit's senses—along with the creamy, tantalising swell of her breasts, which he was uncomfortably aware of each time she leaned his way. Afterwards they gathered round the fire, Lady Mary sitting a little away from them as she engaged her time embroidering a small sampler, the candles on the table illuminating her work.

Kit's irritation mounted and he scowled as he watched Ludovick playing the doting swain to the woman he had claimed for himself. It was clear to him that his friend had singled Serena out as the supreme target of the hunt and, reading the maid's response to Ludovick's flattery—how she seemed to hang with breathless expectancy on his every word and laugh at all the right moments—the tournament would be easily won.

During a moment when they found themselves out of earshot of the others, Kit was about to caution Serena, to rebuke her, but decided against it, not wishing to add tinder to any mischievous intent that lurked behind those brilliant green eyes staring innocently into his.

Over the days that followed Ludovick was frequently at the house. Kit's restlessness became a torment when he saw

Serena being wooed by another man—a right he felt a desperate urge to reserve for himself alone. His thoughts wandered like a homeless bird that could find no place to roost. Every time his friend approached her, jealousy would raise its ugly head and go searing through him. It was a dilemma. And yet how could he put himself forward as a suitor when she saw him as a villain and her tormentor, with nothing to offer her at the moment but himself?

Lady Mary watched what was happening with a keen, quizzical eye. Highly sensitive to her son's moods, and after observing Kit and Serena closely since the arrival of Ludovick and Sir Henry's letters, it was evident that things were very wrong between them. On a day when Kit and Ludovick had taken themselves off for a day's hunting, she spoke to Serena as they strolled around the garden.

'Forgive me if I speak out of turn, Serena, and it is certainly not my intent to embarrass you but, since the arrival of your father's letter, I have noticed that matters are strained between you and Kit. Is it because you resent his interference in your affairs?'

Serena was a little taken aback by the question, and also ashamed that Lady Mary felt she had the need to broach so delicate a subject. 'He—he does tend to take a great deal upon himself where I am concerned, Lady Mary,' she replied hesitantly.

'That's because he's concerned for your welfare, not because he harbours any cruel intent. Faults he has, but cruelty is not one of them.' Lady Mary smiled. 'Kit is hasty sometimes, and as obstinate and stubborn as all the mules in Spain put together, but he has a soft heart beneath that fearsome manner of his. Don't be too hard on him. I know your heart was set on going to your father but, all things considered, it is best that you remain with us here in Scotland—for the time being, at least.'

'I'm beginning to realise that now. I'm sorry if I've

seemed ungrateful. You have been so gracious and kind and I have no wish to cause offence. But you are right, of course. My father's letter came as a shock to me. Not only because of his refusal to let me go to him, but also when I learned of his marriage—without a word to me.'

'Kit told me about that, and I can understand your disappointment. But your father must be allowed to live his own life, Serena. And if he has found happiness, then be happy for him.'

'Yes. I am coming round to it.'

'Good.' Lady Mary smiled, linking her arm companionably through hers. 'And please go easy on my son. You may not have noticed in your preoccupation with dear Ludovick, but of late Kit has been going around with a face like a thundercloud.' Her eyes were soft when she looked at Serena's troubled features, having some inkling of this young woman's secret feelings. 'Don't you think you've punished him enough? End his misery, Serena.'

Overcome with mortification, Serena halted and looked at Lady Mary. 'Oh, Lady Mary—I hope you don't think—'

'What?' She laughed. 'That you're trying to make Kit jealous with Ludovick? My dear Serena, when a woman goes out of her way to make a man jealous by playing him off against another, it can only be because she cares for him. And it is a rarity for a man to be immune from jealousy when he cares deeply for a woman.'

To cover Serena's confusion they carried on walking a little way in silence, but then Lady Mary said at length, choosing her words with care in an effort not to seem as though she was prying, 'You do seem to get on well with Ludovick—but do you really prefer him above Kit?'

The conversation was becoming difficult for Serena, and she carefully fudged the question, feeling unable to answer it. It was an inquiry tactfully phrased by Lady Mary, but still a request for an explanation. 'Sir Ludovick is a friend,

Lady Mary. Our relationship will never be anything more than that,' she told her in complete honesty.

'Then don't you think—in the light of Ludovick's growing affection for you—that you should dissuade him from any further involvement?' Lady Mary said gently.

Guilt suddenly assailed Serena, for Lady Mary had voiced what she intended to do. Although she was reluctant to admit how deeply she had come to care for Kit, she did realise that she had allowed her friendship with Sir Ludovick to go too far. The situation worried her and she felt regret at having encouraged Kit's friend, her sole reason for playing on his attention being to tweak Kit's nose a little. She now realised she had been foolish and must step back, to allow Sir Ludovick's ardour to cool before it all got out of hand and he declared himself.

She had searched for a way to sever any romantic ideas that might be forming in Sir Ludovick's mind, but it was difficult finding the right words to say that would let him down gently without spoiling their friendship. Having encouraged his attentions, the dilemma she now faced was of her making entirely.

'No matter how it looks, it was never my intention to become romantically involved with Sir Ludovick. He has been very kind.'

'So has Kit.'

Serena flushed, averting her eyes, unable to meet that probing, gentle gaze. 'I know,' she murmured quietly, suddenly ashamed that Lady Mary was aware of her ploy to repay Kit for trying to assert his authority over her by giving Sir Ludovick her undivided attention whenever he called. She now realised how very childish and silly it all was.

'I know I shouldn't be discussing this, Serena, that it's a private matter between you and Kit, but you must understand my concern in the light of that awful conspiracy and not knowing what will happen to him when he returns to London to stand trial. What if those trying him don't believe him? I am so afraid.'

Serena was unprepared for the agony that tore through her when Lady Mary quietly uttered those words. Until now she had deliberately shied away from the thought. Lady Mary's voice was so distressed that, thoroughly alarmed, Serena halted and looked at her, not fully realising until just then how much this gracious woman was silently suffering for her son. The smile had faded from her face, which suddenly looked drawn. There were lines of worry on her forehead and her eyes were deeply troubled. Reaching out, Serena took her hand in an effort to comfort her.

'But they must believe him. They have to. They have not the least shadow of proof that Kit was involved in the conspiracy. All they have is mere slander uttered by Thomas Blackwell, a man so cruel and so wretched that he should be beneath contempt. The king has promised Kit a fair trial. He will be pardoned.' Serena swallowed, trying to believe the conviction of her own words. 'He has to be,' she whispered fiercely.

'Pilot could find no basis for the charges against Christ— but he still crucified him,' said Lady Mary quietly. She sighed deeply, discerning Serena's own anguish and looked with deep concern into her pain-filled eyes. 'You do care for Kit, don't you, Serena?'

'Yes,' Serena admitted softly, unable to speak anything but the truth. 'I have come to care for him a great deal. Looking back, I had every reason in the world to hate him for forcing me to abandon my decision to go to my father in Flanders, and in my anger I could not see that he was offering me a measure of security I would lack on my own. I cannot deny that wars have been waged between us during the time we have been alone together, and complaints aired with so much aggression that I did not pause for one moment to question my emotions—not until we reached Addlington Hall and idleness forced me to search my heart.'

'If you love him enough to accept everything that's happened, and live only for the moment, then you must be by
his side when he goes to London. I intend accompanying
him myself. He's going to need all the support he can get
if he's to survive this.'

Serena made a point of speaking to Sir Ludovick the
following day when they were returning from one of their
rides through Holyrood Park. They were discussing Kit and
his forthcoming journey to London, and Ludovick had just
expressed his regret that he would not be returning with
him to add his support.

'With his property confiscated and title stripped from
him, there's little wonder Kit is so concerned about his
future. At present no one has been named to replace him
and Thurlow remains empty. I believe that may have something to do with the king himself. Because of Kit's loyalty
and the bond of friendship that existed between them before
the abortive plot, I feel King James is reluctant to have him
hounded to Scotland.'

'What was the king's reaction when he was told of Kit's
suspected involvment?'

'He was deeply shocked when it was brought to his attention by Salisbury that Kit might have colluded with the
conspirators—that he might even have been one of them
himself. Because of the severity of the crime, the king had
no alternative but to agree to his arrest.'

'Thank goodness he escaped.'

'Aye. Being a man with a skill learned on the battlefields
on the continent—and knowing he was innocent—Kit did
not care to sustain the attentions of His Majesty's torturers
and the hangman's rope. But one thing I am certain of is
that his allegiance to King James has never wavered. The
loss of his honour, his estates and title he will find hard to
bear, but that the king should believe him guilty of betraying his trust is the greatest. It has injured him deeply. He

burns with vengeance and will not rest until his name has been cleared.'

'What do you think his chances are?'

Sharing Serena's fears for Kit with equal pain, Ludovick's face became set in worried lines. 'If Kit can prove that for malicious reasons of his own Blackwell set out to discredit him, then I see no reason why the king will not show clemency. Besides, he earned considerable merit in his duties towards His Majesty when he was in Scotland.'

Serena glanced across at him, seeing the weak sunlight playing on his flaxen hair, hating herself for what she was about to tell him. 'When Kit leaves for London, Ludovick, it is my intention to go with him.'

His astonishment obvious, Ludovick stared at her, fingering his beard thoughtfully, his blue eyes suddenly wary. 'Has Kit asked you?'

'No. He's no notion of what I intend.'

'But, Serena—I had hoped to speak to you, to—'

'No, Ludovick,' she interrupted quickly, sensing what he was about to say and wanting to save him from any embarrassment. 'Please don't go on. I know what you want to say, but I must tell you that—'

'You have decided against me,' Ludovick stated bluntly.

He looked at her with an expression of such mortification and incredulity that Serena had to look away, moved by a terrible feeling of remorse. 'No, not at all. I am flattered by your attention and admire and value your friendship greatly—but my interest lies elsewhere,' she told him quietly.

'You are in love with Kit,' he stated.

She nodded. 'Yes.'

Utterly deflated, a long, heavy sigh escaped Ludovick's lips and he seemed to slouch in the saddle. 'I should have seen it. It was foolish of me to pretend, or to try to believe the impossible. I should have known that the many days you spent alone together could not fail to draw you close.

I have never underestimated Kit's magnetism for gaining the attentions of the opposite sex, or his own attraction where they are concerned, so I should not be surprised that this has happened.'

'I am only sorry for my delay in telling you. I should have spoken before, I know—but I wanted to avoid causing you pain.'

'And you and Kit have not exactly been seeing eye to eye since my arrival in Edinburgh, have you, Serena?' he said, voicing his musings softly, meaningfully.

'You are very perceptive, Ludovick,' she smiled.

'I would have to be blind not to notice.'

'In case you are wondering, that has more to do with the contents of my father's letter making Kit my guardian than any grouch where you are concerned.'

'Then what is there left for me to say?' said Ludovick, deeply wounded by Serena's declaration, but he had no intention of letting it affect his much-valued friendship with Kit—or Serena, for that matter, a woman he held in such high regard that he had considered asking her to be his wife.

'I wish you both every happiness—and I'm glad you're to go with him to London. With so much beauty set before him, the king will be dazzled and charmed into offering Kit clemency,' he smiled, the familiar roguish gleam back in his eyes, which gladdened Serena's heart and brought a light-heartedness back to the conversation.

'Now there I shall have to disagree with you,' she laughed. 'The only response His Majesty will have to my appearance in London will be to have me clapped in irons for my father's involvement in the plot. I fear I am the one who will be in need of saving, not Kit. So what now, Ludovick? Will you stay in Edinburgh?'

'No. My mission is done. I'm away home to Argyll. Besides…' he grinned, his eyes twinkling merrily, '…if I steal any more of your time, Kit will have me dangling on the end of his dirk like so much raw meat.'

Alone, Serena quietly reviewed the past weeks she had come to know Kit, dissecting each moment they had shared with meticulous deliberation in an attempt to put some semblance of order to her emotions. It was no use hiding from the fact that they had been violently attracted to each other from the beginning, despite her show of outrage at his persistence to chafe and vex her at every turn.

Kit had the infuriating ability to pluck at the worst of her nature, to see what no man had ever seen before, to exasperate her beyond words and drive her to passionate fury. But, she thought, on a warm tide of feelings, he also had the ability to tease, to cajole, to delight her senses in a way no other man had succeeded in doing before. He had created yearnings inside her she was a stranger to, yearnings she wanted to satisfy, and only Kit could do that.

He had a mastery over her and he knew it, and he had made it plain that he wanted her as a man wants a woman. But she had refused to yield, crushing the yearnings felt by them both, and now, in this weakening of her will, her longings would not be still and she wanted to discover the mystery of this man who had succeeded in bringing her to a state of submission. How could she even think of breaking away from him and leaving him forever?

Chapter Fourteen

Retiring for the night, Serena was almost startled out of her wits on entering her chamber. Kit was waiting for her, sitting calmly in a chair beside her bed, his black hair and masterful face set in taut, unreadable lines. Closing the door, she slowly moved towards him, looking down into his dark eyes which held no warmth to soften the moment. A trickle of fear trailed down her spine. Never had she seen his eyes so cold or so angry before.

Serena wanted nothing more than to throw herself into his arms, to declare her love and be done with all the shilly-shallying between them, but her ire was pricked on finding he had entered her room without being invited in. Lifting her head, she stared at him haughtily.

'So! Not only do you appoint yourself my guardian, but you also invade the privacy of my bedchamber. I can only hope you do not extend your newfound authority to my person. Where is my maid?'

'I dismissed her,' Kit growled, his voice, like his expression, noticeably lacking in warmth.

With a flippant air Serena moved away from his glowering regard, Kit's eyes following her, watching the natural sway of her hips and how the firelight turned her hair to a living flame. She was so beautiful, so bravely, defiantly beautiful, and when he thought of her deliberate, provocative behaviour over recent days, he felt anger pound against his temple.

'Well, Kit? What do you mean by this impropriety?'

The menace in Kit's eyes holding hers with a terrifying glitter was visible and deadly. Rising out of the chair, he approached her with the quiet stealth of a cobra about to strike. A deep crease had formed between his eyebrows, and in his eyes was a simmering anger, a violence fighting its way up to the surface.

Fear began to take its grip on Serena when he remained silent. 'I don't know the reason for your dark mood, but please leave, Kit. You—you look awful.'

When she tried to pass him, his arm shot out and he pushed her brutally against the wood panelling beside the fireplace, glowering down at her. Averting her gaze from his angry face, her eyes were drawn to the dark hairs exposed beneath his rolled-up shirtsleeves on his forearm. There was something so masculine in the strength of that arm preventing her escape that her heartbeat quickened.

'Don't play games with me,' Kit growled, his eyebrows drawn together with brittle anger. 'You tempt and entice me like a woman tempted by desires of her own. I warn you to take care because you push me to my limits.'

'Kindly release me,' Serena demanded bravely. With his jaw set and his nostrils white with anger, she realised he was in a tyrannical mood from which no human power could move him. 'I think you forget yourself.'

'Nay, lady,' he growled, his fingers tightening on her shoulders, gritting his teeth against violence as her heady scent invaded every pore of his being. 'It's you who forget yourself. It's you who plays the strumpet with my closest friend.'

Serena threw him a taunting smile. 'Are you jealous, my lord?'

Kit's eyes narrowed dangerously, the black orbs burning

ruthlessly down into her own, his anger surmounted by growing passion. 'I'm not a man inclined to jealousy, but this time—with you— Goddamn it, Serena, I'm not a eunuch. I warn you to have a care, especially where Ludovick is concerned. I worry about the manner in which you are leading him by the nose like a poodle down a path to nowhere—how you show romantic interest without having serious intentions. Are you so simple that you cannot see he's taken the bait and means to have you?'

'As his mistress or his wife?' Serena goaded through her fear. Kit's taut face was close to hers, his hot breath fanning her face.

'Ludovick will be content with either. But he hasn't spent weeks alone with you like I have. I know you in a way he never could.'

'And how is it that you have such knowledge about my emotions when I have not expressed them?'

'Because I do not imagine what your eyes say to me. They are far too eloquent, Serena. Nor did I imagine what your lips said to me.' Kit's eyelids drooped as his eyes fastened themselves on her lips, as if he meant to sample their sweetness once more, but they returned to her eyes.

'I congratulate you. You play your part to perfection. Your talents as a temptress are not lacking. No sooner did Ludovick arrive than you began your enticement, and if you don't care for him you should tell him so. I am heartily tired of your game. I will not watch you parade and flaunt yourself brazenly before Ludovick any longer, as though it pleases you to make a fool of me.'

'Game! I play no game.'

'No? You shamelessly exhibit your charms with such expert ease that I ask myself—how many other unsuspecting swains have you lured into your net?' He spoke sarcastically, with cold contempt.

Ire brought a fiery sparkle to Serena's eyes. She struggled against his hands still clasped like a vice over her shoulders, his fingers bruising her soft flesh until the pain brought tears to her eyes, but he refused to relinquish his hold or to take his merciless eyes off her.

'Was Blackwell one of them?' Kit hissed cruelly. 'Did you harbour a romantic fancy and play the temptress to entice him—only to find your naïve, unsuspecting female heart was faced with a rampaging beast with no thought other than to violate you?'

'How dare you say that to me—after what he did to me, after what he's done to us both,' Serena flung back at him. Her face changed from crimson to white, and she fought with all her strength to hold back the tears that swamped her.

'Aye, the man has maimed us in different ways,' Kit rasped, 'but at least you can be sure of surviving with your neck intact.' Suddenly his fingers relaxed their terrible hold and he dropped his arms, taking a step back from her. His face was as if carved from granite, and there was a saturnine twist to his mouth which made Serena want to hit him. 'When Ludovick calls on you tomorrow, you will send word with one of the servants that you are indisposed. You will not see him. Is that understood? I will witness no more flaunting of yourself beneath this roof.'

Defiance showed through Serena's fear. 'And you think that because you give me shelter you can dictate my every move?'

'Have a care,' he snarled, fury blazing in his eyes, noting a pulse beating in the long curve of her throat that almost drove him crazy. 'Whilst you reside in this house and remain in my charge, you will do exactly as you are told.'

'And you, sir, will allow me some privacy by removing your odious presence from my eyes and my room this instant before I raise the whole house. How will you explain that to your mother, pray?'

Incensed by her tenacity, Kit's hands clamped down hard on her shoulders once more, bringing a moan to Serena's lips when she felt the renewed pain. 'If you so much as open your mouth to create such havoc, I will give you cause to regret it,' he growled, his face close to hers. Illuminated in the dim light from the candles, his face was contorted with fury and desire, the line of his mouth cruel.

Hiding her fear, Serena tossed back her head and glared at him defiantly. 'How dare you? Whatever you hope to gain by remaining in my room when you clearly have so low an opinion of me baffles me.'

Kit thrust his face close. 'Then I think it's time I showed you.'

She stood still, her face flushing with indignation as his eyes boldly raked her, from her face to the gentle swell of her partially exposed bosom. When his eyes came back to her lips she spoke, trying to move back, but his hands held on to her shoulders and she found her back still pressed against the wooden panel of the wall. 'Don't you dare kiss me,' she said as his face came closer. 'I'll scream.'

His fingers slid through and gripped the hair on either side of her face. 'With my lips on yours I would say that's a physical impossibility.'

Letting his anger and need dictate his actions, Kit ground his lips savagely against hers so that she could hardly breath. There was nothing tender in that kiss. It was punishing and bruising. Often Serena had dreamed of him kissing her in the same tender manner as when he had kissed her before, not like this, in anger and contempt. It took the breath from her body and for a moment she swayed against him, hating him, and hating her own body for the treacherous ease with which it betrayed her.

Recollecting herself she fought him, intent on inflicting pain and careless of receiving it. Suddenly he released his grip. No longer supported, Serena lost her balance and crumpled to the floor, but that kiss had laid bare the pitiless, hopeless love she felt for him. For an instant Kit remained motionless, looking down at her, listening to the chaotic pounding of his heart as desperation died and it slowly returned to normal. He was aware of the woman huddled at his feet—of her stricken face, her hair a wild tangle about her shoulders, her soft lips bruised and trembling.

The shock of the last few minutes had eaten into the deepest cavities of Serena's being and she remained where she had fallen. With eyes alive with fear, vivid and awash with tears, she raised them to Kit's, and Kit despised himself for what he had just done. The sight of her tears and, God forgive him, the fear in her eyes when she looked at him drained away the last of his anger and almost unmanned him.

Unable to see her so distraught, he groaned wretchedly, wanting to hold her, to beg her forgiveness. Swiftly he fell down on one knee beside her, gathering up her unresisting body and drawing her gently into his arms, burying his face in her tumbling, sweet-scented hair and feeling a deep surge of compassion and grieving for the hurt he had caused her.

Unable to pull away from his all-enveloping arms, Serena placed her face on his chest and huddled against him like a child. She tried to speak, but couldn't find the words because of the scalding tears rolling down her cheeks and filling her throat. The pain was so great she was unable to utter a word. Kit felt her body convulse against him and his arms tightened.

'Don't cry, Serena,' Kit entreated, his voice hoarse and strained. 'Please, my love, don't cry. Forgive me. I'm a brute—I know it. Please, love—don't cry. You are the last person in the whole world I would hurt.'

Raising her head, she gazed at him, meeting his eyes on a level with her own, wondering if she had heard that small word of endearment. His eyes were disarmingly tender as they gazed into hers, which made her heart beat wildly and a soft glow spread over her features. His fingers gently brushed away her hair clinging to her wet cheeks and, bending his head he began to cover her tearstained face with feather-light kisses.

'I do forgive you,' Serena whispered, glorying in his closeness. 'But what did you call me?'

'My love,' he breathed, looking deep into her eyes. 'There, you have it, Serena. I love you, which is why I cannot bear to see another man touch you. Not even Ludovick, my closest friend.'

'You—you jest.'

'I would not jest on so serious a matter. Do you love me?'

Serena gazed at him. 'Deeply. Mock if you will, but I do love you.'

'I will not mock—Serena—my love. My darling girl, I have loved you from the start.'

To be told he loved her, that he had loved her from the first, even when they had fought and been at odds with each other, touched the deepest and most sensitive chord within Serena. Savouring the exquisite happiness, the only thing she was aware of was Kit holding her, his hand gently stroking her hair and the comforting, masculine smell of him.

He placed his lips softly against her head, his arms tightening around her. 'What is between us is too strong to deny, Serena. Can you tell me you don't feel what I feel, that you don't tremble when I hold you and kiss you—that you don't want what I want?'

She tilted her head and looked at him, drowning in his dark-eyed stare. 'That is exactly how I feel, Kit. But I had to fight it. I was so afraid that I would be unable to leave you when the time came.'

'And now?'

She sighed against him. 'I was right. I cannot leave you,' she murmured, raising her lips and placing them tenderly on the warm flesh of his neck. 'I believe I have loved you from the start without knowing it, but I fought it—and you.

I told myself that I wanted nothing from you—that I desperately wanted the journey to Scotland to end so that I could go to my father and put some semblance of order back into my life. But I could not escape the fact that my heart rejoiced every moment I was with you.'

Kit's arms tightened and he planted a kiss lightly on her hair. 'Bless you for that, my love. Poor Ludovick,' he said after a moment, suddenly remembering his friend and how disappointed he was going to be. 'We must tell him.'

'I already have. I realised I couldn't fight what I feel for you any longer, and I realised I was being silly trying to make you jealous with your friend.'

'So—you admit it?'

'Yes. Absolutely.'

'Then why didn't you tell me you'd already told him, instead of letting me bluster on?'

Serena's cheeks dimpled in a smile. 'Perhaps that's because I enjoy your blusterings, my lord. They've certainly given added spice to my life of late. Why didn't you tell me you loved me?'

'I had to consider very carefully what it would entail before I made any commitment to you. After being the recipient of your tongue on frequent occasions, I realised there was need for caution. I was fearful in case a lifetime with you by my side reduced my life span by a decade or more. And besides,' he murmured, a hint of gravity entering his voice, 'I knew you had set your heart on going to your father. I didn't want to stand in your way—and I knew I could not give you the life you deserved—not until my name has been cleared of the foul accusations against me and my honour restored.'

Serena looked at him with loving eyes. 'You're wrong, Kit. Honour! You still have honour. It is something no king can give. It's something you give yourself. That, no man can take away from you.'

Kit met her gaze, his dark eyes probing hers deeply.

'You're a strange woman, Serena Carberry. In all truth I cannot make you out.'

'Then don't try. Do you know how fine you are to me, Kit Brodie?'

'No—but you can always show me,' he breathed, his lips hovering enticingly over hers. 'I'm not the kind of man who wears his heart on his sleeve—but suddenly the treacherous thing just fell there and there it remains, my love.'

'And that is where I insist you keep it.'

'That is music to my ears. Will you be my wife, Serena? Will you marry me now—here in Edinburgh, before I leave for London?'

'There is nothing I want more. But not only do I want to be your wife, but your lover and your friend—and as such I will go with you to London to be by your side throughout your trial.'

'I'm reluctant to allow you to put yourself at risk on my account. There's every possibility that you will be arrested when it's discovered who you are. But it will be difficult leaving you behind. Being alone with you for so long transported me to heights beyond all endurance. No man should be made to suffer so.'

Serena listened to him while her heart beat in chaotic rhythm. 'I didn't mean for you to suffer so, Kit. Had I known, I would have—'

'What?' he murmured, touching her responsive lips with his own. 'Relieved my suffering?'

'Only by removing myself from such close proximity,' she teased.

'Never do that. You drove me hard, Serena. You were always so close—yet so elusive that it became torture for me just to look at you. I was soundly caught in a trap, my love.'

Unable to resist her a moment longer, he lowered his lips and covered her mouth, snatching her breath into his own, teasing her lips when they opened to his. Pulling her down on to the carpet beside him, he slipped his hand about her waist as she stretched out her body against his, touching full length while he kissed her in a passionate frenzy, amazed and intrigued by the mixture of innocence and boldness which fired this woman with whom he would spend the rest of his days. Raising his head, he looked down at her, unable to get enough of her.

'Here, let me look at you,' he murmured, pushing back the hair which had fallen over her face. 'You're so adorable.'

Serena sighed, allowing him to look his fill. He had never looked at her like this and she found it oddly disturbing. 'Kit,' she whispered.'

'Hush,' he breathed, leaning over her, his mouth teasing hers, her lips warm, eager and sweet as sweet could be opening under his own. Kit felt her whole body quiver with desire. She was so appealing he felt his heart turn over. 'Don't talk. I don't want to waste time talking. I've waited too long for this moment. We may have so little time to be together.'

Serena stiffened against him. 'Kit! Why do you say that?'

'I have no illusions about my trial—what may happen. There is every possibility that I shall be found guilty and condemned.'

In alarm Serena sat up, her glorious flame-coloured hair tumbling over them both like a silken sheet. 'No. It can't happen—can it, Kit?'

'It's not unlikely.'

Fearfully Serena looked down at him, his achingly handsome face languid and his dark eyes heavy with passion as his fingers gently traced the line of her throat. 'Please tell me all is not lost,' she begged.

'I can't,' he answered, pulling her down, wishing he'd never mentioned the trial.

Kit's heart was beating so hard Serena could feel it

against her own. His mouth consumed hers with a hunger that demanded more, rousing her sensations and persuading her heart to beat in a frantic rhythm. Her fervour mounted by the second, and she caught her breath as suddenly she was overcome with a sense of panic. Feeling there might be few times for them to be together like this, she was lifted high by a love stronger than fear or reason.

'Kit—love me,' she said in a shaken whisper, his passion having ignited a flame within her that would not be easily quenched. 'If that is what you fear love me now—before it's too late for either of us.'

He raised his head and gazed at her, her words spiralling through him dizzily as he battled with his desire. Hot blood flowed into his loins, heightening his tormented, hungering need, and he knew he must leave her now, otherwise there would be no stopping him. 'No, my love. Your kisses set my body ablaze for want of more, but difficult as it will be we must wait until we are man and wife.'

Deliberately Serena disengaged herself from his arms and got to her feet, taking it upon herself for what would happen next. Not taking her eyes from Kit, who remained lying sideways on the carpet, his head propped up on one arm and his gaze fastened intently on her, silently she began removing her clothes, one by one, dropping each article on to the floor as he watched in fascination, making no attempt to stop her as she fired his appetite a degree more with each garment she discarded.

She was wanton, bold, and she performed without modesty, like a consummate artist, who knew the secrets of kindling a man's desire. In the golden glow of the firelight her exposed, proffered beauty stole Kit's breath away, and the harsh intake of his breath was the sweetest accolade of all to Serena.

Proud and unashamed, she went to the bed and turned back the covers, slipping between the cool sheets, knowing as she waited, her body trembling and burning with anticipation, that he would follow. She was not disappointed. Kit rose from the carpet and advanced towards the bed, magnificent and masterful, his eyes boring into hers. He moved a candle closer to see her better, and after removing his clothes he bent over her.

'You wanton. You witch. You she-devil. You are my undoing,' he murmured, a husky tone having invaded his voice. He felt the sudden quickening of his desire as he lay and drew her into his arms, feeling her womanliness and the hard peeks of her rounded breasts pressed to his chest as he prepared to hold dear the fullness of her response.

'Love me, Kit,' Serena begged with her lips against his cheek, her eyes dark and sultry, 'and show me how to love you—how to please you.'

'Have no fear, madam. I have a thing or two to teach you as regards pleasing me. I trust you will be an avid pupil. But it's a hard thing for me to restrain myself and be tender, when I'm a man starved for so long of feminine pleasure.'

'Remember that I am not as fragile as you consider me to be. I will remind you that you must please me, too, my lord,' Serena sighed, her lips finding his as his hands boldly explored and caressed every inch of her.

'And so I shall, my sweet,' Kit murmured, looking deep into her eyes. 'And by all that is holy, I shall love you until I die.'

His mouth became like a living flame as it skimmed over her flesh, his passion gathering in intensity until she was quivering from the pleasure his lips evoked. Serena was enslaved by him, and the heat of his mouth laid bare all her senses as her sanity fled and he covered her naked form with his own, crushing his lips over her proffered mouth, fired by a hungry urgency that would not be denied.

In that dimly lit bedchamber, Serena gave herself will-ingly to the man with whom she wanted to spend the rest of her life, matching his rhythm with her own, clasping him to her as something wild and primitive built inside her and went racing through her veins, her soft moans of pleasure smothered by lips both masterful and tender. For a time that seemed endless they made love with a savage passion which exploded and made her gasp and cry out and, giving her no respite, Kit would begin again, driven on by unparellelled agonies of desire, and they became forgetful and oblivious of everything but each other and their incomparable joy.

Afterwards, there were no regrets for what they had done. Their pleasures had been willingly shared, but until they were man and wife there would be no more such stolen, exquisite interludes in a house in which family and servants would be scandalised by such behaviour.

It soon became clear to everyone that something important had happened between Kit and Serena. There was a distinct softening in their attitudes towards each other. Serena positively sparkled, and Kit no longer went around with a face like an angry bear. Lady Mary was highly delighted when they told her they were to be married, yet she was not surprised.

'I cannot marry Kit until my father has been approached for his permission,' Serena told her.

'There's no need for that,' Kit said.

Both ladies turned and looked at him. Where he lounged indolently in his chair he quirked a casual eyebrow.

'Oh?' they said simultaneously.

'Your father gave his consent in his letter to me,' he told Serena casually. 'Well—words to that effect. In fact, I would even stretch my neck out and say it was bordering on an order that I marry you.'

Serena went to him, looking down into his face in stupefaction. 'Kit!' she chided, cross that he had kept this information from her. 'What are you saying? Will you kindly explain?'

'Of course, my pet,' he grinned up at her. 'In my letter to your father I told him of the circumstances of our being thrust together. He expressed his relief that you are safe, but accused me of compromising you by bringing you to Edinburgh alone with me. He wrote insisting that I have a care for your reputation and, since I am the one who carried you off, I must defend your good name until I either make you my wife or return you to his care.'

Serena stared at him in incredulity, not having seen the letter and having no idea that her father had given her over to Kit's care so completely. She frowned, distrustful of this wily future husband of hers. 'I would very much like to see this letter, my lord.'

'I wouldn't mind seeing it myself,' retorted Lady Mary. 'Before any wedding plans are set in motion, I want to make quite certain it will be with Sir Henry's approval.'

After reading her father's letter confirming what Kit had told her, Serena wondered what Kit had really put in his letter to her father—thinking it better for her peace of mind not to ask.

'I could not endure the wait,' Kit told her when they were alone. 'It could have been months before a reply arrived from your father—when I could make you truly mine and join my starving body with yours. I could not have borne it and would have been forced to break my vow not to touch you and find my way to your chamber for release.'

Serena tipped her head and gazed at him with a coyly flirtatious smile. 'And I would have welcomed you most willingly. In fact—' her radiant smile widened, '—speaking of release—'

'No, minx,' Kit returned on a laugh, reading her mind perfectly and pretending to be shocked by what she was about to suggest, while secretly pleased at her boldness. 'Have you no shame?'

'None at all where you are concerned.'

Kit smiled lazily, his eyes glittering. 'Then I thank God

for that. But I intend observing all the betrothal formalities—so don't tempt me.'

'I thought you enjoyed my tempting you, my lord.'

'You are all I ever dreamed of and more, my darling, but I mean what I say.'

'And when you are my husband,' she said on a more serious note, 'will I be able to practise my religion? To go to Mass when possible—and on holy days for the official festivals of the church?'

Kit smiled down at her softly, knowing how important her faith was to her. She had welcomed and taken comfort in the opportunity to celebrate Mass with his mother whilst in Edinburgh. 'I may be your husband, my love, but our marriage will not be torn asunder by religious differences. I shall have no authority over your soul.' He gathered her into his arms, gently touching her proffered lips with his own. 'It will be a hardship waiting to make you mine, but I shall endure it as best I can.'

Which he did, and it was the longest three weeks of his life.

The wedding party was small that collected in St Giles' High Kirk of Edinburgh one April afternoon to see them married, Ludovick having left for Argyll two weeks earlier.

Melissa didn't accompany Lady Mary, Kit and Serena, with two maids and Robin, to London when they left Edinburgh the day following the wedding. She went to Perth instead to stay with friends and to become better acquainted with her suitor.

The journey south was long and tedious, although it offered more comforts for Serena than when she had travelled north. Her one regret on leaving Edinburgh was that she had to leave Polly, her faithful mare, but Melissa had promised to take good care of her until she returned.

On reaching London they went to Chelsea, where Ludovick had put his house at their disposal. They were all content to do little for the first few days, Kit and Serena, knowing their time together might be limited, wanting to savour every moment. But their anxieties were building up as the time drew near when Kit would go to Whitehall to see the king.

Lying in bed, Kit breathed deeply of the perfumed heat of Serena's body, satiated after the deep fulfilment of their lovemaking. He kissed the silken top of her head where she lay in the fold of his arm and snuggled against him, her arm thrown across his waist, her body still glowing and throbbing from his caressing hands. At first he was almost afraid of the pure perfection of her naked body, but his love and his need for her overcame his fear. He was amazed and delighted that she returned his passion with equal fervour.

Their lovemaking had an intensity neither of them understood. It was as if each time might be the last. Serena was aware of how much pleasure her body was capable of giving, and how much pleasure Kit was capable of giving her, and they spent many long hours throughout the nights discovering each other—unashamed, greedy and besotted.

Serena tilted her head upwards and looked at Kit, and she could see that his mind had wandered down a different path. For the moment he was not thinking of her. She often found him like this, his expression guarded and unreadable. While his features were in repose she studied the terse lines of his face, seeing shadows round his eyes and the uncompromising lines at the side of his mouth. Wriggling onto her stomach, she looked at him on a sigh, tenderly placing a kiss on his chest.

'Won't you share your troubled thoughts with me, Kit? You are concerned about going into the city today, I know.'

'Aye,' he murmured, knowing he would be going to the Palace of Whitehall to seek an audience with the king on the pain of death. 'It's worrying but it must be faced if I'm to shed this cloud that is smothering our lives. I wish to

God this whole damned business was behind us. I rue the day I heard the name of Robert Catesby and became embroiled in this wretched business.'

'It was a shameful and savage work,' Serena whispered. 'The work of Satan and no less.'

'Satan in the guise of Salisbury. Of late I am not alone in thinking that the Gunpowder Plot has its roots elsewhere, that certain members of the king's council have spun a web to embroil the Catholics.'

'And you believe Salisbury to be behind it?'

'It's highly probable.'

'But it was a Catholic conspiracy spurred on by resentment of the king's broken promises, surely. Why would Salisbury devise such a wicked plot?'

'A number of reasons that I can think of. His own advancement, for one, to deliberately damn the Catholics for ever is another—or to demonstrate his service to the king by first contriving a plot and then uncovering it. The more odious the plot, the greater the service and the more the king would depend on him in the future—just one of his subtle ways of manipulating His Majesty.'

Serena sighed, resting her cheek on her husband's broad chest. 'You speak in riddles, Kit. I'm baffled. What you say is all so strange.'

'Before Queen Elizabeth's death, when she was reluctant to name her successor, Salisbury, knowing King James was the prime candidate for the English throne, set up a correspondence with him. One thing I learned about the king during the time I spent at his court in Scotland was that he had an inability to resist love when it was offered—be it in the female form or his own gender.

'Deprived of both his parents during childhood—his father murdered and his mother Mary, the queen, imprisoned and then executed—he was starved of affection, so it is easy to see why, with his sights set on the English throne, he allowed himself to be influenced by Salisbury—which was the beginning of Salisbury's rise to power.'

'But don't you think it all sounds too far-fetched, Kit?'

'Not at all. The evidence against me—that I kept the company of some of the leading conspirators—could also be applied to Salisbury. Thomas Percy was frequently seen coming out of Salisbury's house in the early hours.'

'Percy! But wasn't he killed along with Catesby at Holbeach House?'

'He was,' Kit replied drily. 'Their deaths were convenient—maybe deliberately brought about, to stop their mouths. It would not have suited Salisbury for them to have been taken alive and put to the torture. It's possible he was afraid they might incriminate him. If Salisbury did instigate the plot, using Catesby and his cohorts as his agents, he has covered his tracks well. It is no secret that Salisbury, with his wide intelligence service, had foreknowledge of an impending stir. He even showed the king a mysterious letter warning of the plot, which had been delivered to him several days prior to the explosives being discovered beneath Parliament House.'

'But all this is conjecture, isn't it, Kit?'

He sighed, absently curling a long silken tress of her hair round his finger. 'Perhaps it is only a theory and we will never know the truth of it. There are many varied intricacies going far back to Queen Elizabeth—and other plots which have been hatched against King James which, I believe, are all connected to the Gunpowder Plot. They are so chequered with agents and counter-agents that the truth of them is almost impossible to unravel. But whatever the truth behind the plot—which was without doubt cleverly contrived and may remain hidden forever—I must go to the king without Salisbury's knowledge.'

'But he is not your enemy, Kit.'

'Not openly. But according to Ludovick, it was not the king who ordered my arrest when the conspiracy was uncovered, but Salisbury. He will thwart me before I speak to the king if he can. When he discovers I am in London, in secret he will have me arrested and thrown into the Tower and swiftly disposed of before word can reach the king.'

'How will you reach the king? Because of his constant fear of assassination he is closely guarded, and Salisbury is never far away.'

'I do have friends at Court I can trust—one who is a Gentleman of the King's Bedchamber. My mother is also seeking an audience with the queen. She frequently attended services at the chapel in Scotland when the queen converted to Catholicism, and for this Her Majesty bore her a great personal fondness. I may manage to slip into White-hall when some entertainment is being held and find my way into the king's presence.'

'Do you think he will grant you an audience?'

'I believe so. The king has a canny reserve and an ability to keep his own counsel and form his own judgement. In the past I was fortunate to be called his friend, and when he lacked money to rule and govern his realm in Scotland, both myself and my father before that dug deep into our coffers to fund the Royal Treasury of Scotland. Loans were given and remain unpaid to this day. My father's family down the ages have paid dearly both in coin and blood in their steadfast loyalty to the monarchy.'

'And will you remind him of this?'

'I hope I am too much of a gentleman to do anything so base. But I know the king has not forgotten. As for the rest—never fear, my love,' he murmured when he saw the anxiety in her lovely eyes.

'But I do fear, Kit. How I wish I could go with you.'

'Thank you, my love,' he said, lightly kissing the tip of her nose. 'I appreciate your concern for me. But you are forgetting the danger to yourself. When I leave I must know that you are safe, at least.'

'And what of Thomas Blackwell? Will you see him?' Serena asked. It had come to their ears that he was in London with Dorothea.

'No. I doubt anything can be accomplished, only further strife, which I wish to avoid.'

'But it can't be concealed how Sir Thomas has maliciously tried to connect you to the Gunpowder Plot.'

A smile lifted Kit's mouth when he looked down at his wife's angry little face upturned to his. 'Try not to worry, my love. Ludovick informed me that since Blackwell encountered the point of my sword, his health has been considerably weakened.'

'All the more reason for him to want to cause you further harm.' Serena scowled. 'I have a good mind to visit Dorothea.'

Kit's face hardened and his voice lost its warmth. 'It would be most unwise to go anywhere near your cousin until this business is done with. I absolutely forbid it.' There was an imperious edge to her husband's voice which warned Serena that he would not tolerate any disobedience.

'But as his wife she may—'

'No, Serena,' Kit said sharply, gripping her shoulders and forcing her to meet his hard gaze. When she continued to scowl at him, he struggled to control his exasperation. 'For once in your life you will do exactly as you are told. You will go nowhere near your cousin whilst my mother and I are away from the house. And don't give me that injured look. You are far too stubborn for your own good, and I can see I'm going to have to take a firm stance with you. It's time you learned submission to your husband and master,' he said, softening a little, aware of her closeness.

Serena felt her indignation rising. 'Why, you impudent oaf! Master, indeed! Why, you—' but she broke off when she saw the glitter in her husband's eyes, recognising the signs of his awakening desire.

Chapter Fifteen

Ludovick had taken the house in Chelsea close to the river for its sweet air and amenities, but also for quick access by boat to the Palace of Whitehall, which was the method Kit and Lady Mary, accompanied by Robin, used in an attempt not to draw undue attention to themselves. They entered the palace by the water gate, unaware as they did so of the still figure watching them from one of the windows over-looking the river.

Confidently Kit and Lady Mary moved through the col-ourful, jostling throng of courtiers. Some of the ladies stared in open admiration at Kit's handsome, tall physique, whilst others who recognised him failed to conceal their disbelief that he dare be so bold or so reckless as to appear at Whitehall, where he was certain to be arrested by the king's guard.

As soon as Kit gleaned the information that Salisbury was at Parliament House, he did not hesitate in going to-wards the king's apartments. Lady Mary left him to reac-quaint herself with Queen Anne, urging her son to be guarded and ready to flee if need be.

King James had always liked Kit Brodie, even though Salisbury did not. In the beginning James had listened to accusations against Kit, who was one of his most trusted and loyal courtiers, in disbelief, feeling betrayed and angered beyond words that Kit might have been involved in the evil conspiracy against him. But his anger had been brief, mostly due to Ludovick Lamont having come to plead his cause.

Granting him an audience, James stared at Kit when he entered, at the resplendent man whom Salisbury had insisted had plotted against him.

'Ah, Kit,' he said thickly.

'None other, sire,' said Kit, bowing deeply. The king, hardly an arbiter of elegance, was an ungainly, shambling man, with slack features and a head that seemed too large for his body, which nodded and lolled as he walked up and down the room in agitation.

'So—you have the courage to show your face at Whitehall,' said James, with a tongue too large for his mouth so that he had difficulty speaking clearly. But there was nothing wrong with his eyes, which were shrewd and expressive, settling on Kit with something akin to admiration. The suppliant was as splendid as he remembered, dressed in a dark blue satin doublet slashed with gold, its high-standing collar edged with small black pearls, his spun silk hose sculpturing the long, masculine legs. 'You have returned of your own volition?'

'Aye, Your Majesty. I've come to you to throw myself on your mercy. If you can show me none, then I must abide by the consequences,' Kit said humbly.

James looked at him hard, wanting so very much to believe in the innocence of this man who had shown him so much loyalty in the past. 'Did you behave treasonably against me, Kit?'

'No, sire—only in the opinion of others. Nothing could draw me away from my loyal allegiance to you. But I hoped, after my own and my family's long service and loyalty to Your Majesty, that it would count for something. I have willingly risked my life many times in service to you, sire, both in Scotland and in the Low Countries, so does that not attest to my devotion to you—and to the love and honour in which I hold you?'

'Aye, Kit. You were always loyal. But it grieved and pained me deeply when it was brought to my notice that you were suspected of being one of those men who plotted against me—a treason most foul—and I thank God for my deliverance. How did it come about?'

'Because of the prejudice of one Sir Thomas Blackwell.'

The king's long tongue licked his slack lips. He ambled towards the window and stood looking out. The name of Blackwell had always perturbed him. He had the reputation of being a crackbrained hothead, and there was something about the man and the manner in which he fawned up to Salisbury that tweaked his annoyance. He neither liked nor trusted the man who had been too ready to accuse Kit of treason in a way that made him suspicious.

'I was told you kept close company with the plotters, Kit, that you were one who plotted against me.'

'Never, sire. The plotting was none of my doing. On reflection, I realise Catesby played me for a fool.'

James wagged his head and arched a satirical eyebrow. 'Really! You surprise me, Kit. I always thought you were too clever to be taken advantage of.'

'So did I, sire.' Kit grinned roguishly. 'But I now realise that Catesby sought my friendship—rather than I his—to serve his own ends and to cloak his infamous intentions. When I was arrested and managed to escape my captors, finding myself at a serious disadvantage I fled the realm, intending to return to try and clear my name—and to re-affirm my devotion to you, which has never wavered—when the stir died down.'

'Nothing is that simple,' the king declared. 'When you were arrested you shouldn't have flouted the guard. You should have come to London to take your place with the others to stand trial.'

'And had my neck stretched in the process?' growled Kit. 'Forgive me, sire, for blunt speaking, but I had a great deal to lose.'

'So had the others.'

'They were guilty men. Your Majesty knows I am not of their faith and had no reason to conspire against you. You must believe that.'

James nodded slowly. 'In my heart I always did.'

'I swear to you, sire, I was not let into the secret and deny any complicity. Indeed, like Your Majesty, I, too, was the recipient of a plot. Most men pursue some quarry. With some it's power, others wealth, some position. Blackwell pursues me. Our paths have crossed on several bitter and savage occasions during our time in the Low Countries, when circumstances set us firmly against each other.

'Blackwell sought to avenge himself when he discovered I was the one responsible for registering complaints against his outrageous behaviour towards prisoners and his own men, and ultimately for having him recalled from his duties. When the Gunpowder Plot came to light it offered him the perfect opportunity to bring me down.'

James's ungainly body shuddered suddenly, and his eyes clouded over. 'I'm in awe of plots, Kit,' he mumbled, stumbling over his words, saliva wetting his loose lips which he licked away uneasily, 'of blood and cold steel. Monarchs are subject to more storms than ordinary mortals—and as you know, I've been subjected to more storms than other monarchs. No one knows it more than those who were with me through some of my darkest times in Scotland—you and Ludovick.'

Kit knew this to be true. All his life James had been possessed of a horror of violence and a fear of assassination, believed to have been born in him when his mother's secretary had met a savage death in her presence shortly before she was delivered of James. He had been kidnapped on one occasion, wretchedly humiliated, terrorised and threatened throughout his adolescence by those who wished him ill.

'Blackwell is not generally trusted at court—and with good reason when one remembers his record for violence and his atrocities abroad,' said the king. 'He has gone to considerable pains to insinuate himself with Salisbury, carefully weaving his tale while Salisbury lent him an ear to accusation. Why he should believe such a renegade escapes me.'

Kit was cautious not to be drawn on Salisbury. Whatever his own opinions and suspicions regarding the king's chief adviser, Kit was aware of Salisbury's dislike for himself, and that he resented the fact that he was a much-valued part of James's past. Little wonder he had lent an ear to Blackwell in an attempt to discredit him in the king's eyes.

However, Kit had no intention of airing his opinions to His Majesty. But James was no fool and knew Salisbury for what he was. James also knew Salisbury to be a man of integrity and tireless industry, and would continue to keep him in office as his chief adviser.

'I may look like a bumbling fool, Kit, but when the trials and executions were over and Blackwell persisted in pestering to have you hounded and brought back to stand trial, when I realised it was a personal vendetta, and that your life depended on the word of that slanderous rogue, I saw there was some skulduggery at play.

'Perhaps I am too forgiving,' James went on, suddenly thoughtful. 'I will not pursue the charge of treason—but you do realise that if our friendship was not of long standing this would not be allowed to pass?'

'I do, sire. I am in your debt.'

The king's expression softened. 'Nay, Kit. Let us speak plain. It is I who am in your debt, and we both know it. The devoted service and generous loans and funding of the royal coffers by your family over the years is not forgotten. I thank you for not referring to the debt—which cannot be said of others. I am not unaware that you could sue the Crown in the Scottish courts for repayment.'

'I wouldn't, sire. It was money gladly given,' said Kit, having been tempted in the past to do this, but always shrinking from it. On his inheritance of Thurlow, he had decided to write off the debt, knowing there was little chance of the full amount being repaid if he sued the Crown and took the matter to the Scottish courts.

'I shall begin by returning to you all your properties and titles that were confiscated. You will find Thurlow as you left it. I could not find it in me to put anyone else in there.'

Kit was overwhelmed by the king's generosity. 'Thank you, sire.'

'Will you return to Thurlow, Kit? Or have you a hankering to live on your mother's estates in the north?'

'No, sire. I shall live at Thurlow—with my wife.'

An interested gleam lit up the king's eye and his rubbery lips broke into a smile. 'Who is the lady? Do I know her?'

Kit braced himself, ready for a tirade of anger. 'Her name is Serena Carberry, sire, Sir Henry Carberry's daughter, of Dunedin Hall in Warwickshire.'

'Carberry! Blackwell has done his best to malign him also, which, I think, may have something to do with him coveting Sir Henry's property. I know the house suffered badly when a fire broke out there—after Sir Henry had escaped to the continent rather than stay and face arrest.'

'I—had heard something to that effect myself, sire.'

The king eyed him shrewdly. 'All sins do not go unpunished, Kit. By all accounts Blackwell is in ill health— which, I hear, you have something to answer for. But whatever occurred is between the two of you and I have no desire to be made privy to it. Lord knows I have enough to contend with without adding to my troubles. You may tell your wife that nothing has been proved against her father other than his selling of the horses to the conspirators. His estate was not forfeit since he has not been condemned for treason—and nor was anything disclosed by the main conspirators to incriminate him.

'I realise it does not follow that all English Catholics are guilty of the same as Catesby and the others. Sir Henry Carberry, despite his record for being a malcontent during Queen Elizabeth's time, was as seduced by Catesby as many more who were fooled by him. But should Sir Henry return to England he must stand trial.' James's eyes narrowed when something else was brought to mind. 'The same applies to his son, who is a Jesuit priest currently serving at the Vatican in Rome, I believe.'

Kit glanced at him sharply. 'You know that?'

James chuckled. 'Nothing escapes Salisbury's intelligence network. So, Kit, your wife is a Catholic.'

'Like your own, sire,' Kit answered pointedly.

'A quiet one, I hope.'

Kit grinned. 'So do I, sire.'

'Tell me, Kit. Do you have good hunting at Thurlow?'

'The best,' he replied, aware of the king's obsessive love of hunting, a sport in which he tried to elude the cares of state, while the wild deer tried to elude him. 'It would honour me greatly if Your Majesty would partake of it some time.' He bowed deeply, kissing the king's hand when he indicated that the interview was at an end. 'Thank you, sire.'

James sighed. 'Go with my blessing, Kit.'

Serena was astonished when Dorothea drifted into the house in Chelsea, taking note of her cousin's slightly thickening waistline. The two kissed each other fondly, and at any other time Serena would have been happy to see Dorothea, but she was too eaten up with worry about Kit to be overjoyed by her cousin's untimely and unexpected visit.

'Forgive me if I seem surprised, Dorothea. For obvious

reasons Lord Brodie and I hoped to keep our presence secret for the time being.'

'Thomas saw Lord Brodie alighting from a boat at the water gate at the Palace and asked the boatman where he had come from.'

Serena paled. 'And the boatman told him?'

'But of course,' smiled Dorothea, having no knowledge of the large bribe her husband had passed to the boatman for that information.

'I see. I—it is good to see you, Dorothea. You are well, I hope?'

'Perfectly. It is good to see you again, too, Serena. But I really ought to be cross with you—running off with Lord Brodie of all people.'

'Whom I have since married.'

Dorothea was both surprised and shocked to hear this. 'No, Serena! But then…I don't suppose you could have done anything else, under the circumstances—being alone with him for such a long time.'

'Precisely,' Serena replied stiffly.

'Do—do you love him?' Dorothea enquired tentatively.

'Yes—deeply. He is the finest man I know.'

Dorothea studied her cousin calmly. 'It's good that he married you and not me. You are alike you two—the same fiery, wilful spirits. I think my father may have done you both a favour when he rejected his suit. He was furious when he discovered you had run away like that to Flanders.'

'I didn't go to Flanders. Kit and I went to Scotland, where his mother has land and properties.'

Dorothea was clearly surprised. 'You were there all the time—when everyone thought you had gone to your father?'

'Yes. We were married in Edinburgh.'

'You—you know Dunedin Hall was almost destroyed by

fire on the night you left—when Kit wounded Thomas in a fight?'

'Yes—and despite what your husband may have told you, Dorothea, the fight was fair and of his instigation.'

'But—but Thomas told me—'

'What, Dorothea?' asked Serena coolly. 'What did he tell you about that night? Did he tell you that Kit attacked him?'

'Why—yes. Thomas told me a light attracted him to the house, and when he went to investigate he encountered you. He said he was trying to persuade you to stay when Kit arrived, having followed him there, and attacked him. Apparently he'd escaped his captors and sought Thomas out because he believed he was the one responsible for his arrest.'

'And naturally you believed him,' retorted Serena drily. 'Kit was unjustly accused by your husband for no other reason than to settle old scores. The accusations against Kit were based on Thomas's testimony. He put evidence forward to incriminate Kit falsely. It was an act of personal revenge and nothing more. Your husband meant to ruin Kit—and if it meant seeing him hang for a crime he was innocent of, then so be it.'

Dorothea whitened significantly. 'No, Serena. This cannot be true.'

'On the night I left, when I went to Dunedin Hall to collect a few personal items, your husband arrived and viciously attacked me. If Kit had not arrived, I shudder to think what he would have done to me.' Dorothea shook her head in disbelief. Serena looked at her levelly. 'Have you ever known me to lie, Dorothea?'

Tears welled in her cousin's eyes and she shook her head. 'No. But why did he attack you? For what reason?'

'He bore my father a grudge because he refused to sell land to his own father. I know he hopes to acquire Dunedin Hall now it has been confiscated by the Crown. He also attacked me because I am a Catholic. You must know he has an obsessive hatred for anyone of my faith.'

Dorothea nodded dumbly. 'That I do know. Please forgive me, Serena—I didn't know. You should have told me.'

'I did try. But would it have made any difference?'

Dorothea shook her head. 'No. I would still have married him. I—I love him, you see.'

Looking deep into her cousin's eyes, Serena could see she had changed, and she had no doubt that marriage to Thomas Blackwell was responsible for that. Despite her avowed love for the man, there was a brittle hardness in her eyes and a steely set to her jaw. The innocence and vulnerability had been wiped clean away.

'Why does he hate Kit so much—enough to want to ruin him?'

'It goes back to when they were in the Low Countries,' Serena answered, and went on to tell her cousin about Sir Thomas's crimes and the part Kit had played in having his regiment recalled in disgrace. 'It is something your husband will never forgive.'

Dorothea was clearly deeply ashamed of this part of her husband's life which she knew nothing about. 'When Sir Ludovick called at Carberry Hall to see you, I knew by what he said that Thomas may have had something to do with Kit's downfall. I tried telling myself it was all in my imagination, but deep down the suspicion gnawed at me. I told Thomas of my unease, but he laughed and freely admitted that he was no saint. But he has never been cruel to me. In fact, he has always treated me with tenderness. Since the night he was wounded he has been very ill. The sword pierced his lung, you see.'

'But knowing of his cruelty to others, how can you still love him?'

'I don't know. But I do. No matter what manner of man or devil I am married to, it will always be so.'

'Then he does not deserve you, Dorothea.'

'As you will have observed, I am to bear his child. Thomas needs and depends on me. He is often in great pain.'

'Which is no better than he deserves,' retorted Serena coldly, unable to feel any sympathy for the man who had tried so viciously to ruin both herself and Kit.

'If you were to see him, you would see he is much changed.'

Serena withdrew from her as if she had been stung. 'Never. Because of your husband's thirst for revenge, at this very minute Kit is seeking an audience with the king to plead for his life—simply because he did what any self-respecting, honourable man would have done on seeing a monster persecuting innocent people. As far as I am concerned, your husband is beneath contempt and I never want to set eyes on him again.'

'I am sorry to hear that,' rasped a voice behind her.

For one heart-stopping moment Serena froze, but then, on a gasp, she spun round to see Thomas Blackwell standing in the open doorway. Hardened as she was towards him, she could not repress a feeling of horror. He was thin, his face gaunt, with a pinched and hollow look, but there was a brooding, moody look about him. That same arrogance which had led him through life was not diminished by his obvious ill health.

Quickly Serena looked at Dorothea accusingly, who was uneasy about her husband's sudden appearance. 'Dorothea! You should have told me he was here.'

'Forgive me. I came alone and had no idea Thomas would follow.'

Thomas moved into the centre of the room with the aid of a walking cane. 'Don't you recognise me, Serena?' he rasped.

His mocking tone reawakened all Serena's anger and hatred. 'I recognise a villain when I see one. Will you kindly leave?' she demanded, trying to still her trembling limbs.

'You were not invited into this house—and you would not be here were my husband at home.'

'Husband, eh! So—the blackguard married you. Congratulations, Serena—although your marriage will be short-lived. No doubt he has already been arrested and is being escorted to the Tower as we speak.'

'Then I must disappoint you,' came a voice from the doorway.

A gasp of indescribable joy escaped Serena's lips when Kit entered. Their eyes met and locked for a moment, each conveying a message of love and hope to the other, but then Kit's gaze became focused on the man in the centre of the room, who swayed as if he had just been dealt a resounding blow. Kit's eyes never wavered as he approached the most malignant of his enemies, his tread measured with a sinister steadiness.

'Nothing can shake you, can it, Blackwell?' he said with deadly calm, a feral gleam in his dark eyes. 'My good friend Ludovick Lamont tells me you are ill—that it's I who am responsible. After what you are guilty of, it's no better than you deserve. You made a serious error when you chose to focus all your hatred on me, not to mention your personal crusade to see every Catholic eliminated— especially my wife, but not until you had defiled her.'

'And all this time my attempts have been thwarted.'

Kit smiled wryly. 'And you are clearly in no fit condition to fight on. Good God, man, you're as sickly as an aborted calf. All your conniving to incriminate me in that foul plot and slander my name has come to nothing. I return from His Majesty who can find no charge for me to answer to. All that was confiscated from me has been returned—which is also the case with Sir Henry Carberry. Until such time as he is able to return to England, his estate will be in the care of my wife.'

This was a blow to Thomas. His look was venomous, for he had indeed hoped to secure all Sir Henry Carberry's property. If Kit had raised his voice or a fist he might have borne it better. Instead, Kit kept his tone ice cold, only the black eyes showing his loathing for the other man.

'The king is more of a fool than I took him for,' hissed Thomas, beads of perspiration breaking out on his forehead when his face became convulsed by a spasm of violent rage.

'It's you who would be the fool if you weren't so dangerous. You'd collude with the devil if it gave you a means to an end. Why are you here, Blackwell? Did you intend trying to persecute my wife yet again?'

'I would destroy anyone with Popish ideals. When I saw you at Whitehall I was certain I had gotten rid of you at last.'

'Then you were mistaken. But one look at you makes me doubt you will be allowed to escape what is clearly going to be an unenviable fate. You have plied your skills dispassionately and without mercy in the past. It's time to lay down your sword, Blackwell, and cease hounding me.'

'Never,' Thomas snarled.

'Don't risk what time you have left by trying to settle old scores. You are successful, a wealthy landowner in your own right, with a wife and soon a child,' he said, having taken note of Dorothea's delicate condition when she had risen from her seat. 'Don't let pride make you risk losing all that, in this last ruse to condemn me further. What you have chosen to disregard is that the plotters themselves have proved I am innocent of the charges you made against me.'

'Perhaps. But I shall wish you harm with every breath I draw.'

'Then you are a fool. Your hatred and resentment of me has festered inside you and crippled you spiritually. You will destroy yourself with hatred and fanaticism to what you believe to be a holy cause against Catholics—and your undying malice towards myself.'

Dorothea, who had stood patiently listening to what Kit was saying, now went to stand by her husband, looking him straight in the eye, her stance and her tone imperious when she spoke. In fact, she displayed a dignified authority more defiant and more proud than either Serena or Kit had given her credit for. Was it possible for a woman with so gentle a spirit as Dorothea to rule a despot like Thomas Blackwell?

'I am disappointed in you, Thomas. Isn't it enough to get beaten without becoming a backstabber? Do you want your child to grow up knowing its father brought dishonour to his name? I have stood by and tried to ignore what you are beneath your air of respectability—but I can do so no longer. Come. It is obvious to me that you offend Kit and Serena by coming here, so we will take our leave.'

Thomas suddenly seemed to shrink before her accusing glare. He moved awkwardly towards the door where he paused and looked back at Kit. The pain and humiliation of this meeting had cut deep, and he was under no illusion that he was too ill to pursue it further.

'As you see, Brodie, I am in no condition to challenge you. You would slay me as quickly as a helpless lamb.' On that note Thomas straightened himself up, his eyes staring straight into Kit's. All the hatred and malice surrounding him was concentrated in that one pair of eyes.

When her husband had disappeared and only the tapping of his cane could be heard, Dorothea hesitated and looked at Kit. 'I beg of you to forgive our coming here today. When Thomas saw you arrive at Whitehall by the water gate, the boatman told him where you had come from and that a flame-haired woman had stood and watched you leave from the jetty. My instinct told me it might be Serena, and my desire to see her again was so great that I came to Chelsea immediately by the river. I left Thomas at Whitehall but, as you see, he followed me. It was not my intention to upset either of you.'

Perhaps because he pitied Dorothea her embarrassment and her husband, the severity of Kit's face relaxed. 'It's no fault of yours that your husband is a dangerous rogue, Dorothea. And it was not my intention to make you feel unwelcome in this house. Knowing of the closeness that exists between you and Serena, you must feel free to visit her whenever you wish at Thurlow—but you must understand that, for reasons you have now become aware of, the invitation does not extend to your husband. I wish for no more encounters between us.'

'I understand. Enough harm has been done. As you have seen, Thomas is very weak and ill. The physician does not hold out much hope that he will live beyond two years at the most. I—I can only hope that he will live long enough to see the birth of his child.'

In silence Kit put an arm about his wife, and together they went to the door to watch them depart. But they gasped on seeing Dorothea lose her footing on the slippery slope down to the river and stumble and fall. Quickly they ran towards her, but before they could reach her, with a cry of anguish Thomas had thrown down his cane and stooped to assist his wife, the concern written on his still-handsome face there for all to see.

'Dorothea,' he cried, helping her to her feet. 'Are you hurt?'

With immense relief Serena and Kit watched Dorothea regain her footing and brush the dirt from her skirts, turning to wave to them, indicating that she was unhurt. After Thomas had rescued his cane, seeming to be generally distraught over his wife's fall, he put his arm about her waist to prevent her falling again.

'Well, well,' murmured Kit as they watched the pair climb into the boat at the jetty and Thomas take his place beside his wife, taking her hand in his own. 'It seems strange to me that Blackwell should be so concerned about his wife—which makes me wonder if I am seeing a small redeeming quality in this man who suddenly seems so vulnerable and to possess the same cares and anxieties that trouble others.'

Together Kit and Serena turned and went back inside, and only when they were alone did Kit take his wife in his arms, feeling her tremble against him.

'Thank God he's gone,' Serena whispered. 'As long as I live I pray I never have to look at that man again.' Raising her head, she looked at her husband. 'What did the king say to you, Kit? Does he accept you had nothing to do with the Gunpowder Plot—you will not face a trial?'

'That is true. My title and Thurlow have been restored to me—and we can leave London just as soon as you are ready.'

'And my father? Is he absolved, too?'

Kit shook his head. 'No. Not entirely. His Majesty made it quite plain that if he returns he must stand trial for his part in selling horses to aid the conspirators. However, because of the lack of evidence against him—and the conspirators' failure to incriminate him—he accepts that, like myself, it is possible that he was fooled by Catesby and is not guilty of any treasonable offence.'

'Oh, Kit. You have no idea how relieved I am to hear that.'

He smiled. 'So until the time when your father sees fit to return—if he wants to, or unless the archdukes extradite him from the Spanish Netherlands along with others who are suspected of having a hand in the plot—his estate is in your hands, my love. All things considered,' Kit murmured, gazing down into his wife's upturned face and planting a kiss on her brow, 'I would say that we've both come out of it very well.'

Tears of joy and relief sprang to Serena's eyes. Kit saw them shimmering on her lashes before one of them traced unheeded down the smooth curve of her cheek.

'I cannot believe it, Kit. I cannot believe that it's over at last.'

Seeing that she was tortured by her tears, on a sigh Kit produced the handkerchief he had won the right to keep when they had ridden together at Dunedin Hall and she had challenged him to a race. She took it and looked up at him in wonder, smiling through her tears.

'Why, Kit Brodie! Despite the tough and formidable man you profess to be, you are nothing but a sentimental romantic at heart,' she teased, mopping up her tears. 'Here,' she murmured, giving it back to him. 'You'd best keep it—in case I should need it again.'

'Nay, my love. The time for tears is past.' He grinned down at her crookedly, taking it from her. 'But I'll keep it all the same.'

Epilogue

Thurlow was a prosperous emblem of the Brodie family, an establishment which symbolised the rewards of the family's loyal service in both England and Scotland. Nothing had prepared Serena for its magnificence—an enormous Tudor edifice with turrets and tall chimneys, its front a mass of leaded windows, the glass lit up like a wall of flame in the setting sun. It stood on a rise, looking out upon an endless stretch of parkland, surpassing anything Serena had ever seen.

Kit smiled, seeing that her eyes were warm in their admiration. 'Well?' he enquired softly. 'What do you think of your new home, Serena?'

'Kit—it's—it's quite the most beautiful house I have ever seen.'

'I hope the house will be as appreciative of its new mistress—the new marchioness of Thurlow. There hasn't been a marchioness in residence for some twenty years or more.'

Serena laughed with delight, finding it difficult coming to terms with such a grand title. 'Then it's a formidable task that faces me. I can only hope I do it credit.'

In the weeks and months that followed, Serena grew to love Thurlow, and to her pleasure she conceived their first child almost immediately. When their son was three years old—a child who, it soon became evident, had inherited his father's charm as well as his looks—they went on a visit to Serena's father in Flanders, where his enforced exile was far from miserable.

To most people exile was like a malicious humour rotting away inside a man, taking away his hope and self-respect. But most humours are granted succour, and it immediately became clear to Serena and Kit that Sir Henry, who had begun breeding horses once more, was blissfully happy with his wife and had no intention of ever returning to England.

And why should he? Sir Henry had laughed jovially, when he had everything he could possibly want right here in Flanders. And Kit could see what held him in thrall. His wife, whom Serena had been loath to meet, and who now regretted her hasty determination to dislike everything about her because she feared losing her father, was so charming and loving Kit might have been tempted himself, had he not been married to a woman who outshone all others.

Andrew journeyed from Italy to see his sister and her husband, and his eighteen-year-old brother James. James, a tall, serious young man whose studies would soon be complete, was impatient to return to England and begin rebuilding the estate. Much heartened, Serena returned to England to bear Kit his second child, a daughter they named Anne, after Serena's mother.

Kit was amazed how quickly Serena regained her figure after the birth of each of their children. She was quite remarkable. Her eyes were bright, her full lips smiling one day when she swept into the room from the garden, and Kit's breath caught in his throat, thinking she was too exquisite to be flesh and blood.

His eyes gleamed appreciatively at the sight of her. The mellow softness of the afternoon light played about her white throat, throwing deep shadows down into the hollow between her rounded breasts. She was beautiful in a gown of scarlet velvet, the heavy auburn swathe of her hair falling from beneath her matching bonnet. But never would she look as fetching to him as she had once looked in her breeches when they had ridden to Edinburgh.

'Come here, my love, I must talk to you.'

She moved towards him like moonlight walks on water, and there was no denying the look of melting love in her eyes when they lit upon her husband. Going to stand behind his chair, she slid her arms lovingly down his chest, placing a kiss on the top of his dark head, loving the smell of him, of pine and leather.

'What can be so important, Kit, that it makes you look so grave?'

'I think it's time we visited Ripley, Serena. James will soon have finished his education and you know how impatient he is to return to take over the running of the estate.'

And so it was that Serena went back to Dunedin Hall, visiting Dorothea and her son at Ashcombe Manor and making her peace with Uncle William. She remembered how she had been unable to repress the relief she had felt on learning of the demise of Thomas Blackwell just six months ago. God had granted him slightly longer that the physician had predicted.

She visited Eliza, their old housekeeper who lived with her sister and her husband in Ripley, and John, who vowed to return to work at Dunedin Hall just as soon as Master James came home. James would take up residence in a new house that was already being built close to the old, burned-out shell of the one in which he had been born.

An eerie, haunting silence reigned among the ruins of Dunedin Hall. There was an unearthly quiet about this place that had been Serena's home, that she had loved with all the intensity of a child seeking a safe haven at its mother's breast. It struck deep into her heart as she tried to recall what it had been like on that terrible night when she had left it.

Most of the building had escaped the flames. Some walls stood with big, gaping holes in them, and the giant chimney stacks rose into the sky like giant sentinels. A lump rose in Serena's throat when she looked into the empty stables, buildings which had once pulsated with the lives of men and horses alike.

She stood in silence, gazing at the ruins of the once-noble house. It made her think of something beautiful after it had been through the throes of death, and she was weighted down by a terrible sadness. The old place was crumbling, taking with it all the memories of the past. Sunset blazed red over the empty shell, decay and rot running riot over the smoke-blackened walls.

She listened to the sound of the wind as it went sighing and whispering, searching the holes and crevices that had been given over to a past long since gone, and she watched a bird fly out of the ruins and go soaring and searching in a silent sky. In some strange way it reminded her of herself—flying free at last.

Turning, she walked away from the ruins, seeing Kit holding their young daughter in his arms just a short distance away, and their five-year-old son scampering about the grass. Moving towards them, she stooped to pluck a solitary white rose from a briar that clung to the wall, courageously defying the decay all around it. Holding it to her nose, she could smell its soft, sweet perfume. It was such a gentle, fragile thing.

Holding it in her hand, she walked towards her husband, a little smile playing on her lips, and Kit sighed with relief and put his free arm tenderly about her shoulders, drawing her close. He'd had deep reservations about them making this journey back into the past, not knowing what to expect. But now he had no regrets. At last all their ghosts could be laid to rest.

*   *   *   *   *

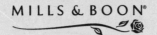

MILLS & BOON®

Makes any time special

Enjoy a romantic novel from
Mills & Boon®

Presents...™   *Enchanted™*   TEMPTATION®

Historical Romance™   ⅃MEDICAL ROMANCE®

FREE

2 BOOKS
AND A SURPRISE GIFT!

We would like to take this opportunity to thank you for reading this Mills & Boon® book by offering you the chance to take TWO more specially selected titles from the Historical Romance™ series absolutely FREE! We're also making this offer to introduce you to the benefits of the Reader Service™—

★ FREE home delivery   ★ FREE gifts and competitions
★ FREE monthly Newsletter   ★ Exclusive Reader Service discounts
                ★ Books available before they're in the shops

Accepting these FREE books and gift places you under no obligation to buy; you may cancel at any time, even after receiving your free shipment. Simply complete your details below and return the entire page to the address below. *You don't even need a stamp!*

YES! Please send me 2 free Historical Romance books and a surprise gift. I understand that unless you hear from me, I will receive 4 superb new titles every month for just £2.99 each, postage and packing free. I am under no obligation to purchase any books and may cancel my subscription at any time. The free books and gift will be mine to keep in any case.

HOEC

Ms/Mrs/Miss/Mr ....Initials ....
                                                                    BLOCK CAPITALS PLEASE
Surname ....

Address ....

....

....Postcode ....

Send this whole page to:
UK: FREEPOST CN81, Croydon, CR9 3WZ
EIRE: PO Box 4546, Kilcock, County Kildare (stamp required)

Offer valid in UK and Eire only and not available to current Reader Service subscribers to this series. We reserve the right to refuse an application and applicants must be aged 18 years or over. Only one application per household. Terms and prices subject to change without notice. Offer expires 31st December 2000. As a result of this application, you may receive further offers from Harlequin Mills & Boon Limited and other carefully selected companies. If you would prefer not to share in this opportunity please write to The Data Manager at the address above.

Mills & Boon® is a registered trademark owned by Harlequin Mills & Boon Limited.
Historical Romance™ is being used as a trademark.